MAZE RUNNER:
THE
SCORCH
TRIALS™

OFFICIAL GRAPHIC NOVEL PRELUDE

MAZE RUNNER: THE SCORCH TRIALS OFFICIAL GRAPHIC NOVEL PRELUDE, June 2015. Published by BOOM! Studios, a division of Boom Entertainment, Inc. Maze Runner: The Scorch Trials is © 2015 Twentieth Century Fox Film Corporation. All rights reserved. BOOM! Studios™ and the BOOM! Studios logo are trademarks of Boom Entertainment, Inc., registered in various countries and categories. All characters, events, and institutions depicted herein are fictional. Any similarity between any of the names, characters, persons, events, and/or institutions in this publication to actual names, characters, and persons, whether living or dead, events, and/or institutions is unintended and purely coincidental. BOOM! does not read or accept unsolicited submissions of ideas, stories, or artwork.

A catalog record of this book is available from OCLC and from the BOOM! website, www.boom-studios.com, on the Librarians Page.

BOOM! Studios, 5670 Wilshire Boulevard, Suite 450, Los Angeles, CA 90036-5679. Printed in USA. First Printing.

ISBN: 978-1-60886-750-9, eISBN: 978161398-421-5

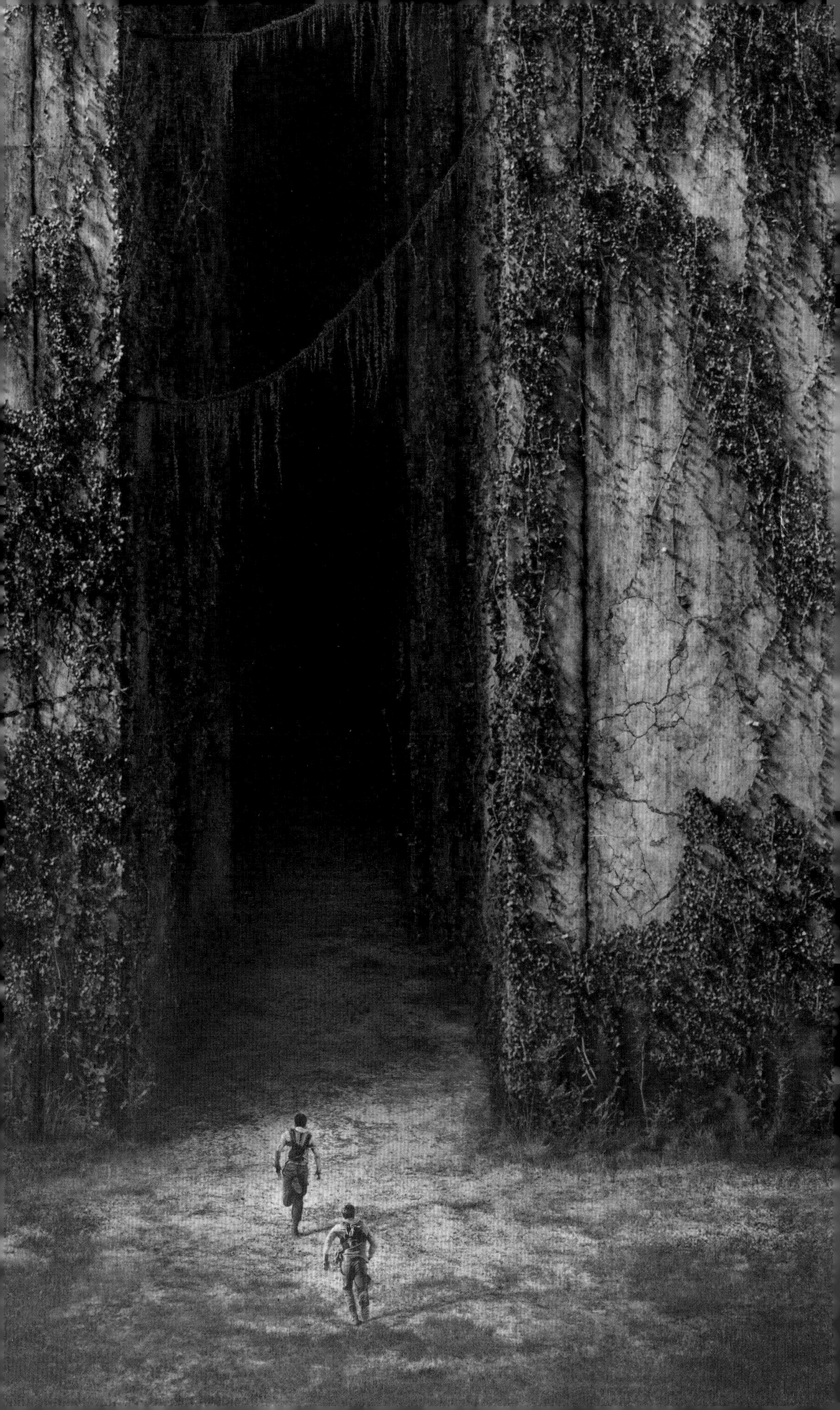

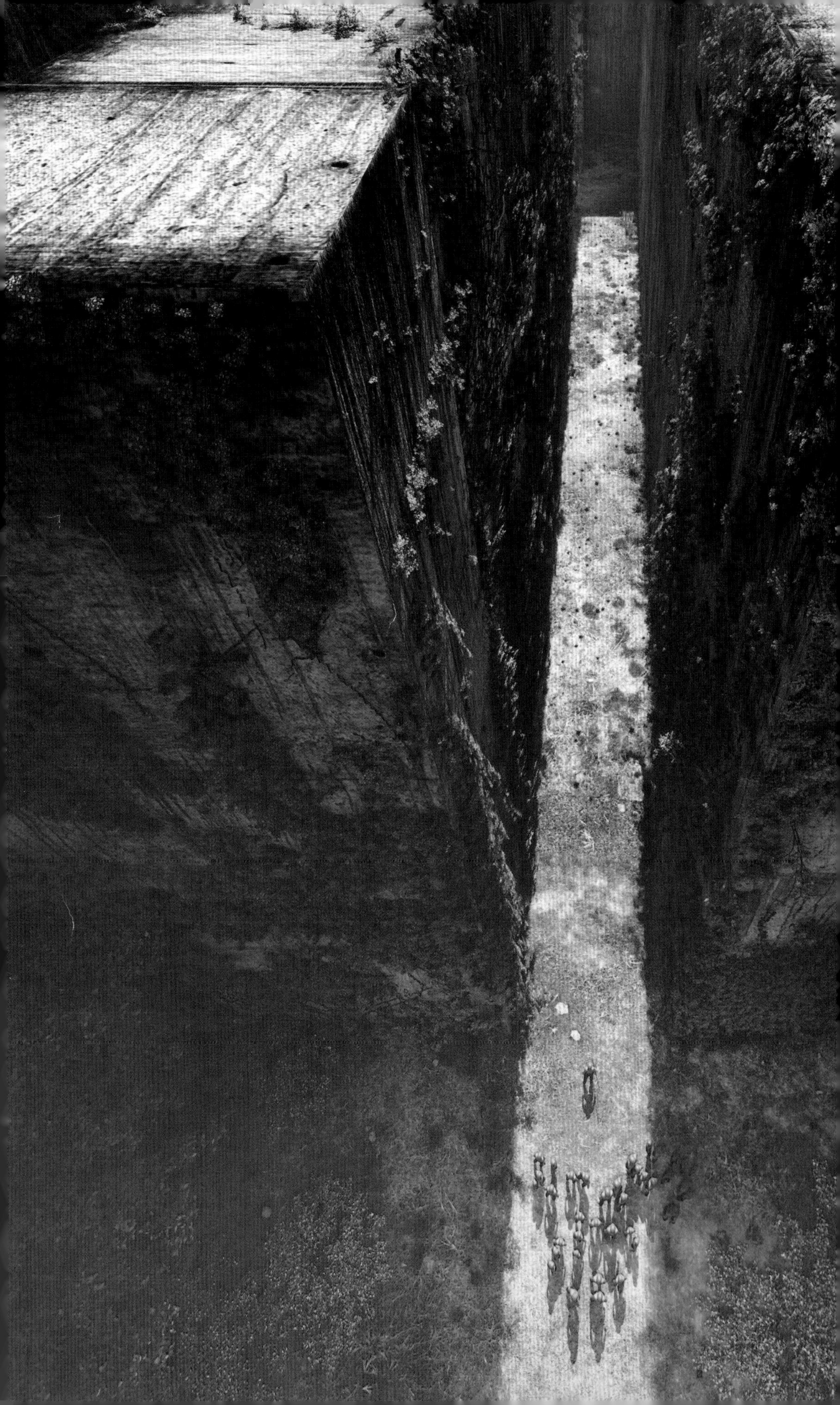

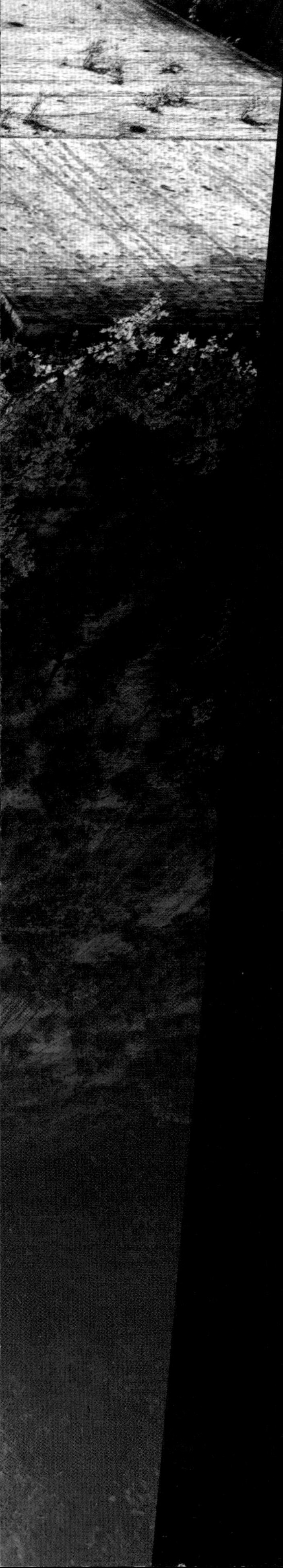

"RUN ALONE"

Story by Wes Ball & T.S. Nowlin
Script by Jackson Lanzing & Collin Kelly
Pencils by Marcus To
Inks by Richard Zajac & Marcus To
Colors by Josan Gonzalez
Letters by Deron Bennett

"MY FRIEND GEORGE"

Written by Wes Ball & T.S. Nowlin
Art by Marcus To
Colors by Josan Gonzalez
Letters by Deron Bennett

"TRUE MAZE"

Written by Jackson Lanzing & Collin Kelly
Art by Nick Robles
Colors by Josan Gonzalez
Letters by Jim Campbell

"SCORCHED"

Written by Jackson Lanzing & Collin Kelly
Art by Andrea Mutti
Colors by Vladimir Popov
Letters by Jim Campbell

"WORLD GONE WICKED"

Written by Jackson Lanzing & Collin Kelly
Art by Tom Derenick
Colors by Whitney Cogar
Letters by Jim Campbell

Designer: Kelsey Dieterich
Associate Editor: Whitney Leopard
Editor: Dafna Pleban

From the world of the 20th Century Fox Feature Film
MAZE RUNNER: THE SCORCH TRIALS

Written by T.S. Nowlin

Based on the novel by James Dashner

Produced by Wyck Godfrey, Marty Bowen,
Ellen Goldsmith-Vein, Lee Stollman, and Joe Hartwick Jr.

Directed by Wes Ball

Special thanks to Wes Ball, T.S. Nowlin, Wyck Godfrey, Cristina Mancini, Jason Young, Ryan Jones, Joshua Izzo, Nicole Spiegel, and Stephen Christy.

INTRODUCTION *BY JAMES DASHNER*

I had a life-defining moment when I was about ten years old. Miraculously, my mom let me spend the night at a friend's house. Who knew what sort of shenanigans might ensue? Well, my friend John pulled this huge box out of his closet, and it was bursting at the seams, full of comic books. Everything from *Spider-Man* to *Casper the Friendly Ghost*. So, instead of roaming the neighborhood that night like little demons, we stayed up all night reading those comics, devouring them until the sun came up.

It made me realize—traditional book nerd that I was—that there were other, just-as-cool ways to escape to another world for a time.

Storytelling. It's my favorite thing in the universe.

Books, comics, movies, music, theater—whatever form it may take. The escape of it, the journey, the heartbreak and laughs, the sheer entertainment of it all. I love when someone creates a world that becomes real to me in every way, whether it be an alternate version of this one, a far-off planet named Arrakis, a magical elfin land, or something I'd never be able to dream up myself. Like a playground, I love to go play in that world, release my imagination into its wonders for awhile.

The biggest accomplishment of my writing career has been creating a world in which millions of *others* have willingly found themselves lost. (It's still so hard to believe!) This has been the world of *The Maze Runner*—a future version of our own world that's bleak and harsh but still full of things like friendship, loyalty, and a fierce will to live. And characters that have become so real to so many. Seeing it all come to life on film—on the big screen—has been indescribably thrilling for me. Yes, I'm an author, but I could never find the right words.

Are there differences between the *Maze Runner* movies and the books? Of course. Having been involved from the beginning of the process, I supported

those changes from novel to film. It's a simple fact: some things that work on the page don't work in a movie, and vice versa. That's just the way it is. And it's okay! That's the great news! No one is more familiar with the novels than I am, and yet the films let me live that world and the characters in a way I never have before.

This is how I see the movies, side-stories, art, fan fiction, and the WCKD websites developed by the creative team behind the films. It's also how I see this new series of graphic novels depicting the events leading up to Thomas entering the Maze. Again, are there differences between "book canon" and "movie canon"? Certainly. But that's okay. Look at it as a means to experience parts of the story, or characters that you love, in a whole new way all over again. A way to enter the world and have it still feel fresh and new and exciting. (And, of course, terrifying.)

Like me, I hope you'll set aside any concerns over differences between these two versions of the same world. The characters you love are there, the spirit and tone and world structure are there. The differences are subtle enough to keep you on your toes and allow you to experience the roller coaster as if it's the first time you had the guts to step into the Maze, all over again. The books will always be there. Thomas, Alby, Teresa, Minho, Newt, Chuck, Gally—all of them live, and sometimes die, within those pages. Nothing ever *will* change within those volumes. Keep them on your shelves and open them up when you want those original, familiar moments.

Now, I invite you to step inside our playground for new adventures, new angles, new interpretations, new twists and turns. Familiar and different all at once. Come on in, and enjoy the ride.

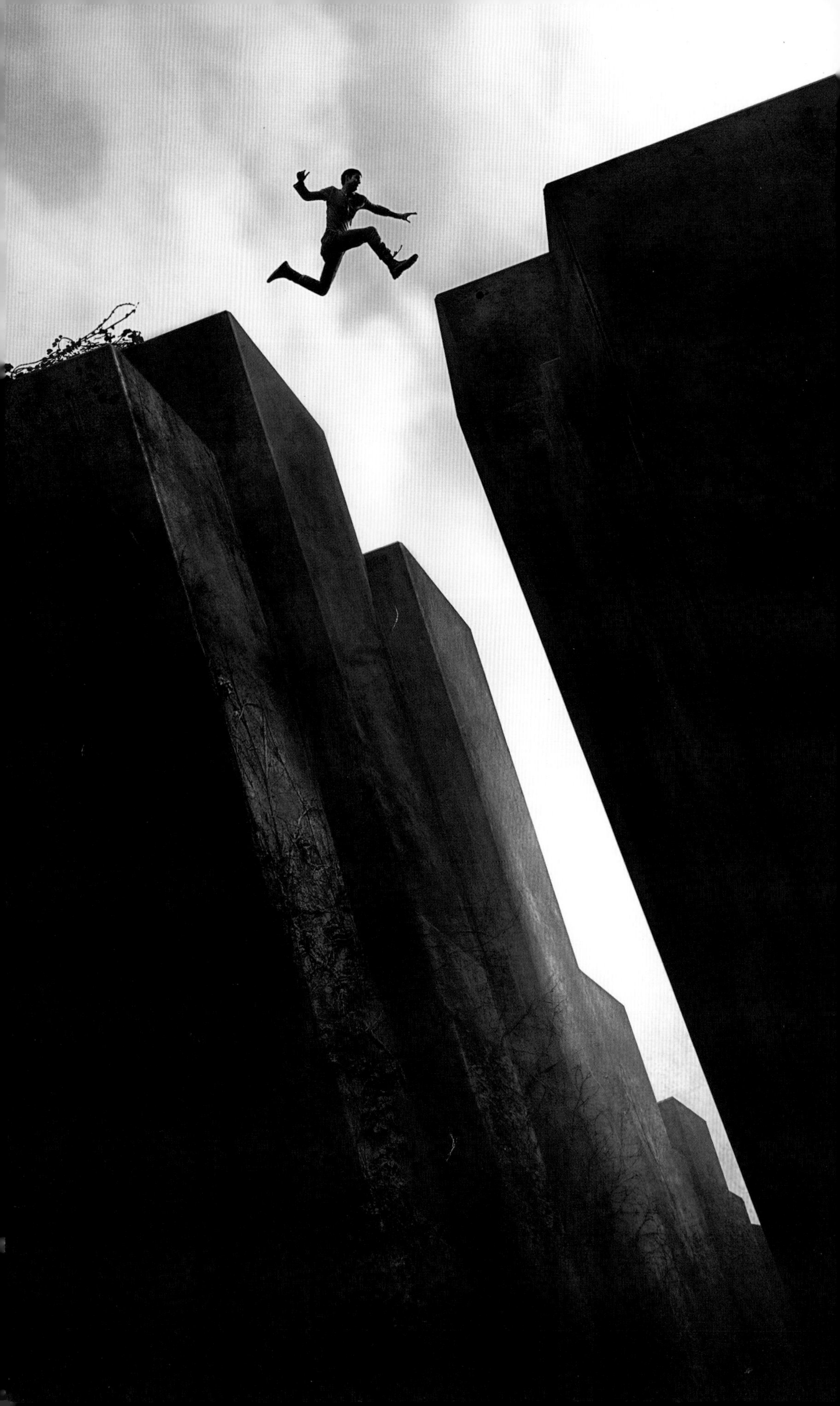

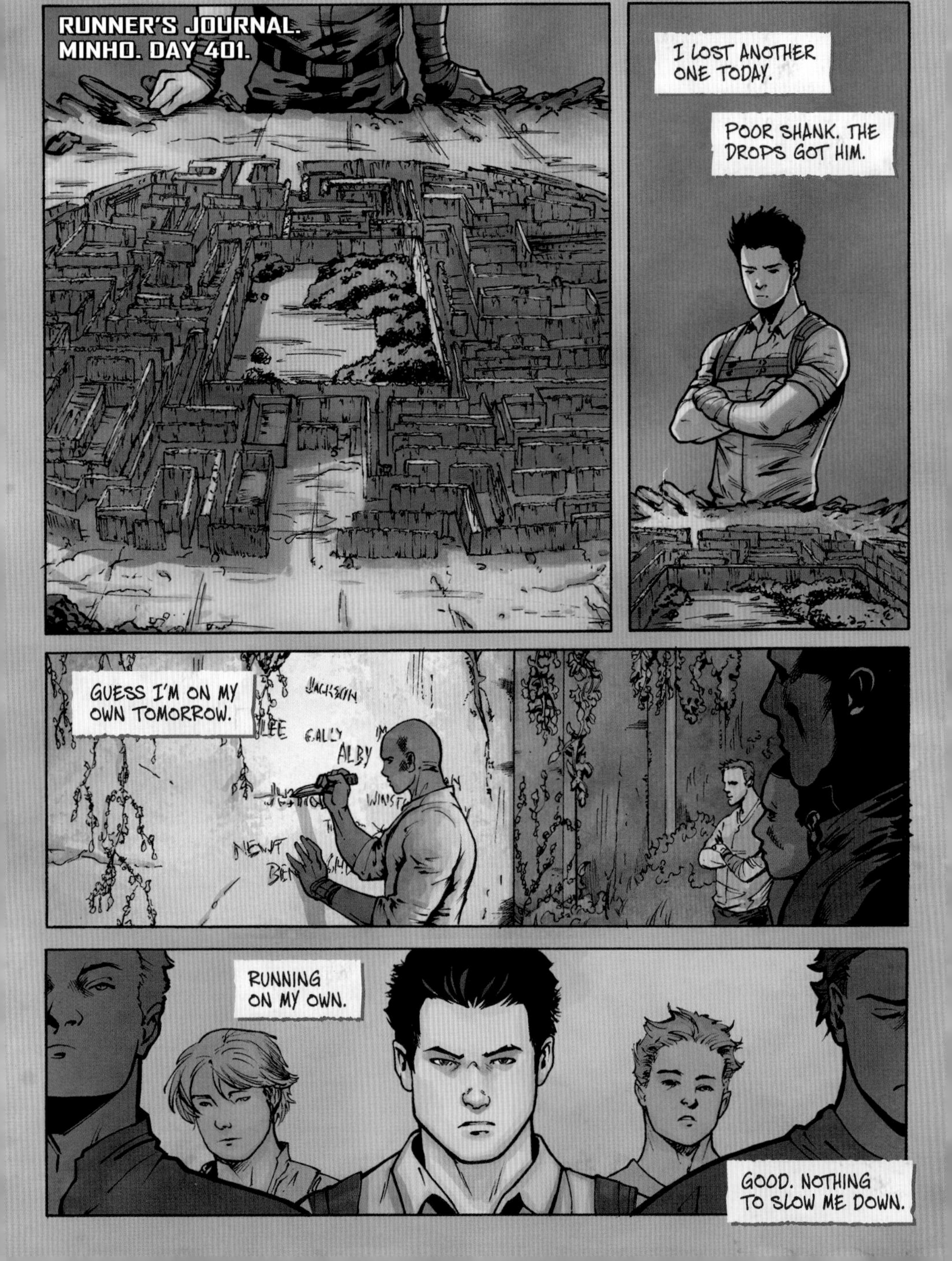
RUNNER'S JOURNAL.
MINHO. DAY 401.
I LOST ANOTHER ONE TODAY.
POOR SHANK. THE DROPS GOT HIM.
GUESS I'M ON MY OWN TOMORROW.
GALLY
ALBY
NEWT
RUNNING ON MY OWN.
GOOD. NOTHING TO SLOW ME DOWN.

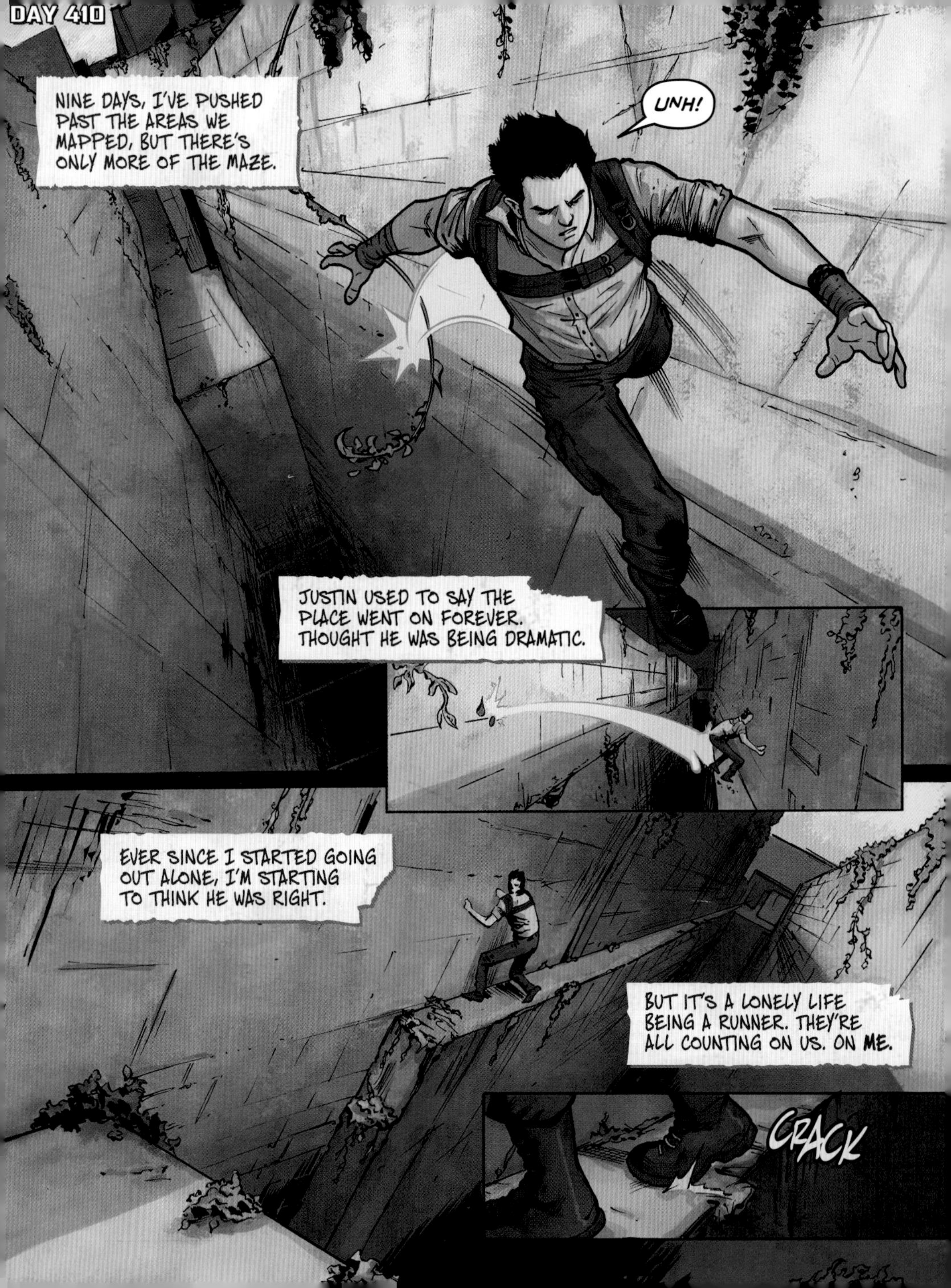
DAY 410
NINE DAYS, I'VE PUSHED PAST THE AREAS WE MAPPED, BUT THERE'S ONLY MORE OF THE MAZE.
UNH!
JUSTIN USED TO SAY THE PLACE WENT ON FOREVER. THOUGHT HE WAS BEING DRAMATIC.
EVER SINCE I STARTED GOING OUT ALONE, I'M STARTING TO THINK HE WAS RIGHT.
BUT IT'S A LONELY LIFE BEING A RUNNER. THEY'RE ALL COUNTING ON US. ON ME.
CRACK

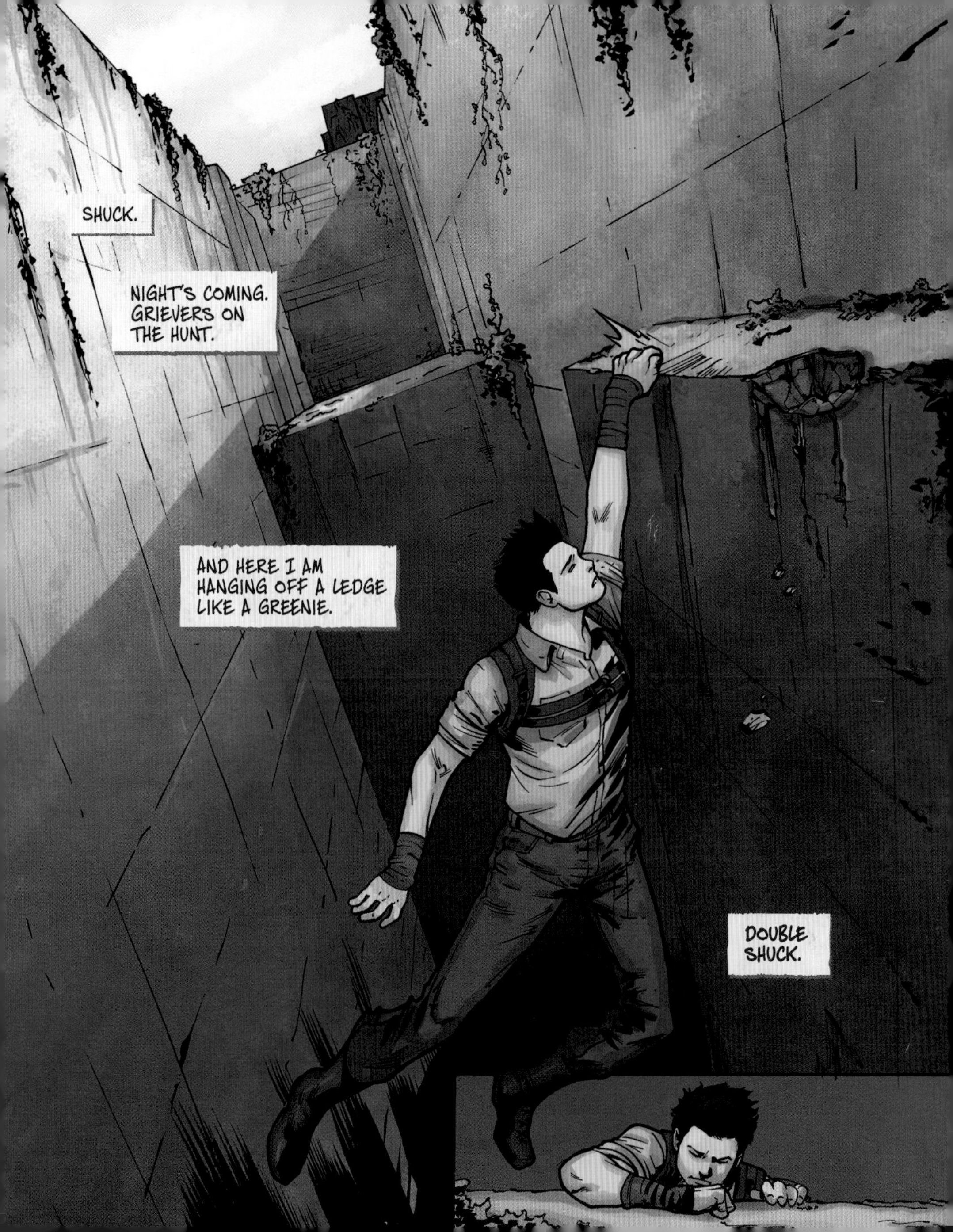
SHUCK.
NIGHT'S COMING. GRIEVERS ON THE HUNT.
AND HERE I AM HANGING OFF A LEDGE LIKE A GREENIE.
DOUBLE SHUCK.

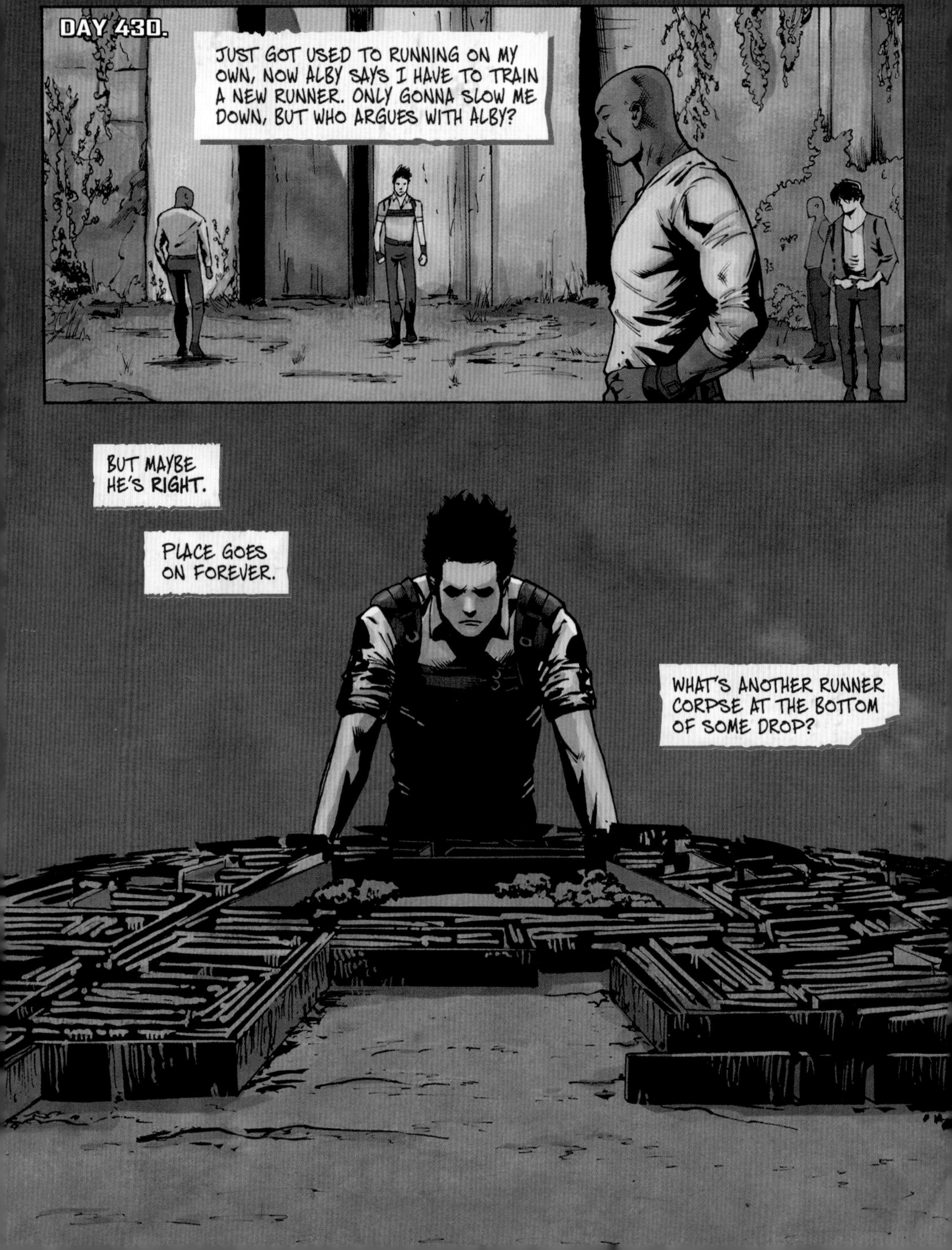
DAY 430.
JUST GOT USED TO RUNNING ON MY OWN, NOW ALBY SAYS I HAVE TO TRAIN A NEW RUNNER. ONLY GONNA SLOW ME DOWN, BUT WHO ARGUES WITH ALBY?
BUT MAYBE HE'S RIGHT.
PLACE GOES ON FOREVER.
WHAT'S ANOTHER RUNNER CORPSE AT THE BOTTOM OF SOME DROP?

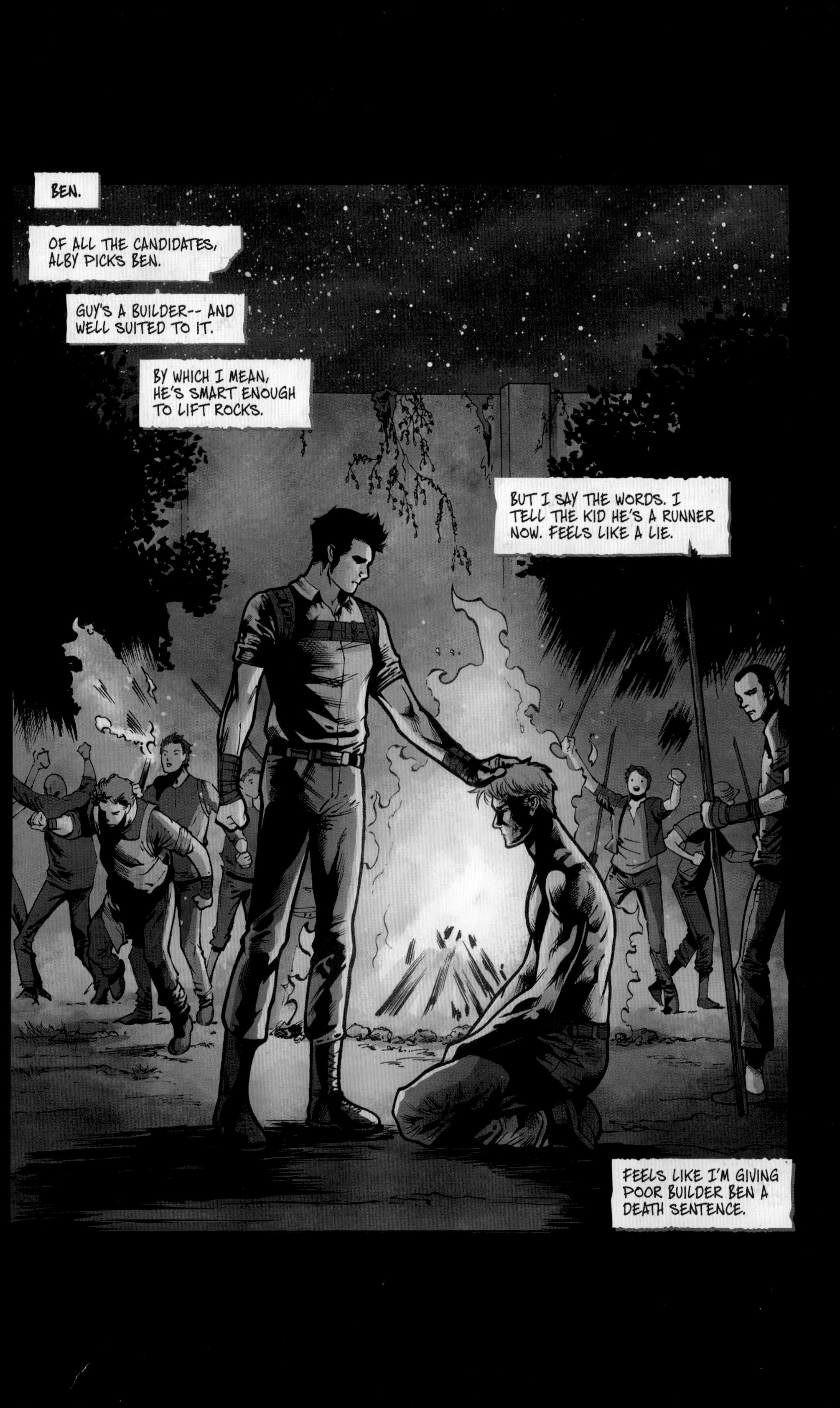

BEN.
OF ALL THE CANDIDATES, ALBY PICKS BEN.
GUY'S A BUILDER-- AND WELL SUITED TO IT.
BY WHICH I MEAN, HE'S SMART ENOUGH TO LIFT ROCKS.
BUT I SAY THE WORDS. I TELL THE KID HE'S A RUNNER NOW. FEELS LIKE A LIE.
FEELS LIKE I'M GIVING POOR BUILDER BEN A DEATH SENTENCE.

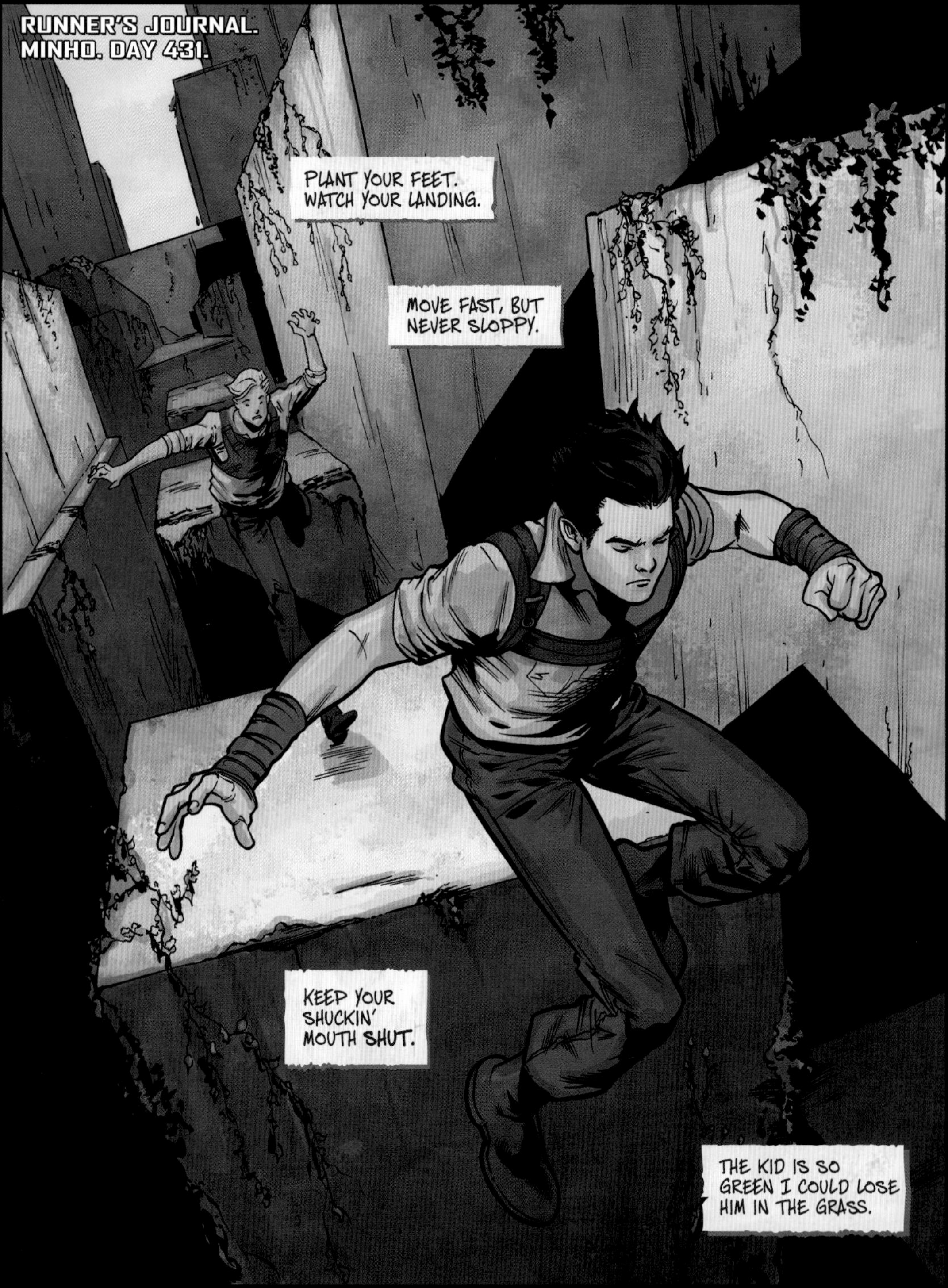
RUNNER'S JOURNAL.
MINHO. DAY 431.
PLANT YOUR FEET. WATCH YOUR LANDING.
MOVE FAST, BUT NEVER SLOPPY.
KEEP YOUR SHUCKIN' MOUTH SHUT.
THE KID IS SO GREEN I COULD LOSE HIM IN THE GRASS.

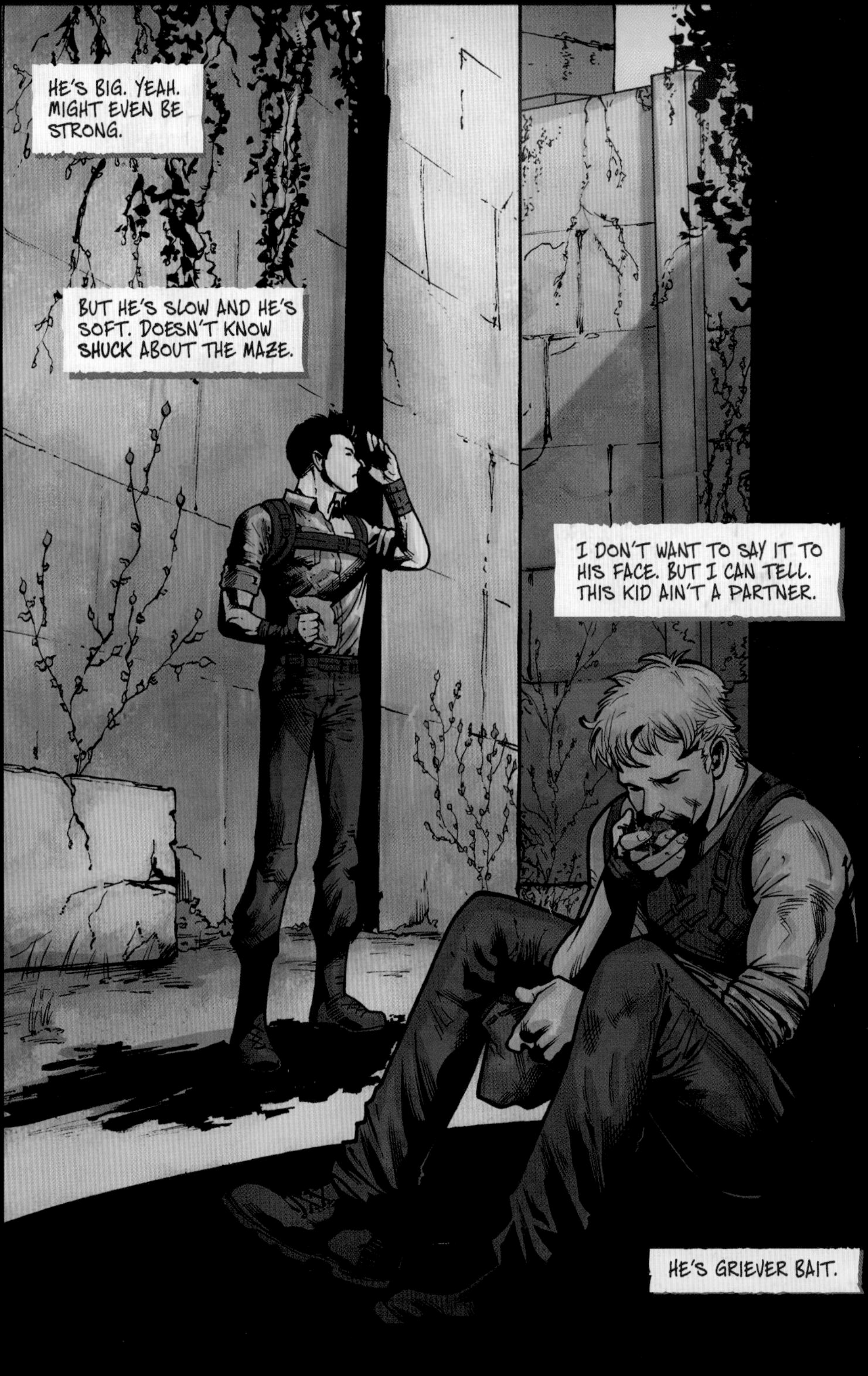
HE'S BIG. YEAH. MIGHT EVEN BE STRONG.
BUT HE'S SLOW AND HE'S SOFT. DOESN'T KNOW SHUCK ABOUT THE MAZE.
I DON'T WANT TO SAY IT TO HIS FACE. BUT I CAN TELL. THIS KID AIN'T A PARTNER.
HE'S GRIEVER BAIT.

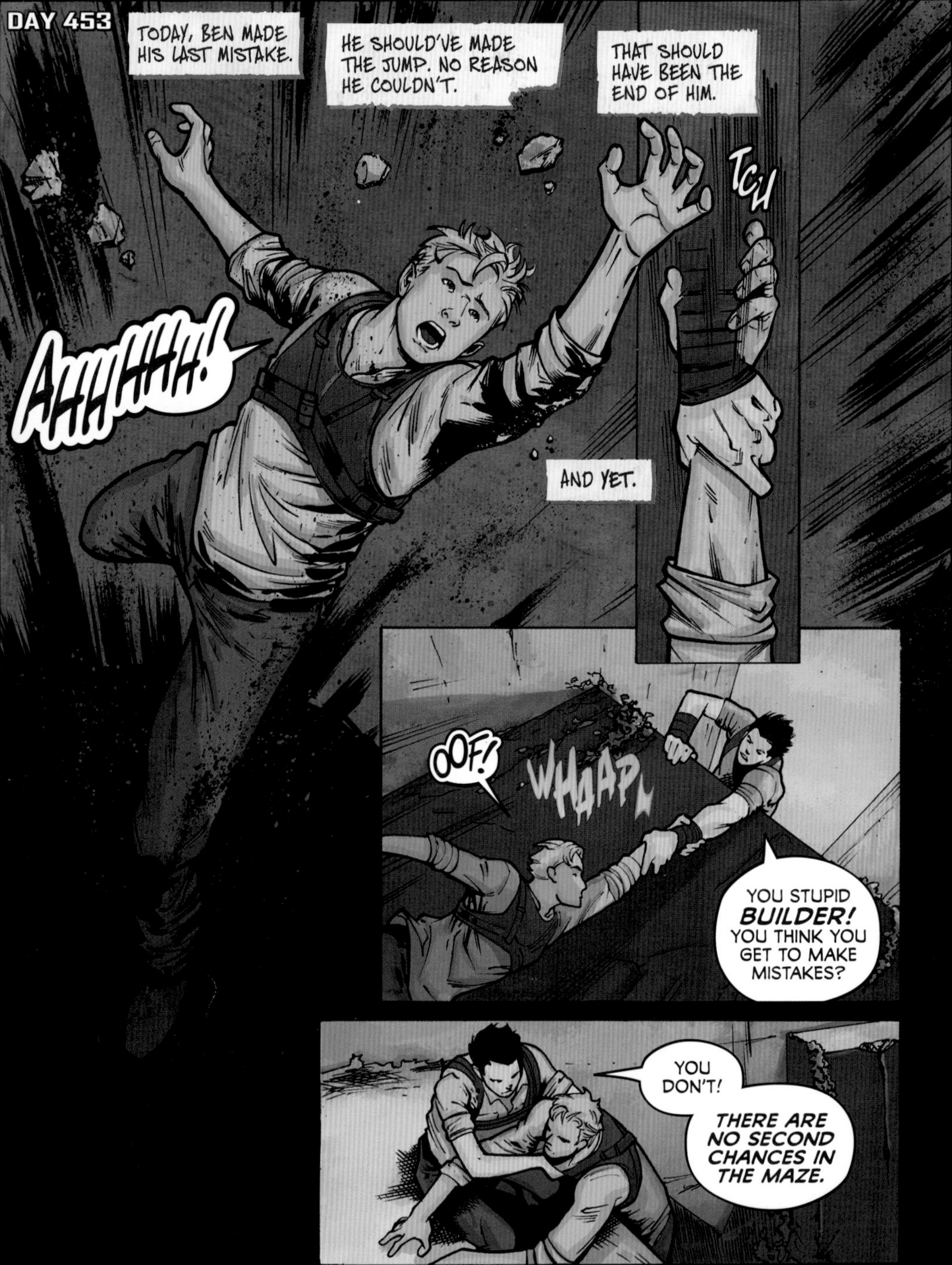
DAY 453
TODAY, BEN MADE HIS LAST MISTAKE.
HE SHOULD'VE MADE THE JUMP. NO REASON HE COULDN'T.
THAT SHOULD HAVE BEEN THE END OF HIM.
AHHHHH!
TCH
AND YET.
OOF!
WHAAP
YOU STUPID BUILDER! YOU THINK YOU GET TO MAKE MISTAKES?
YOU DON'T!
THERE ARE NO SECOND CHANCES IN THE MAZE.

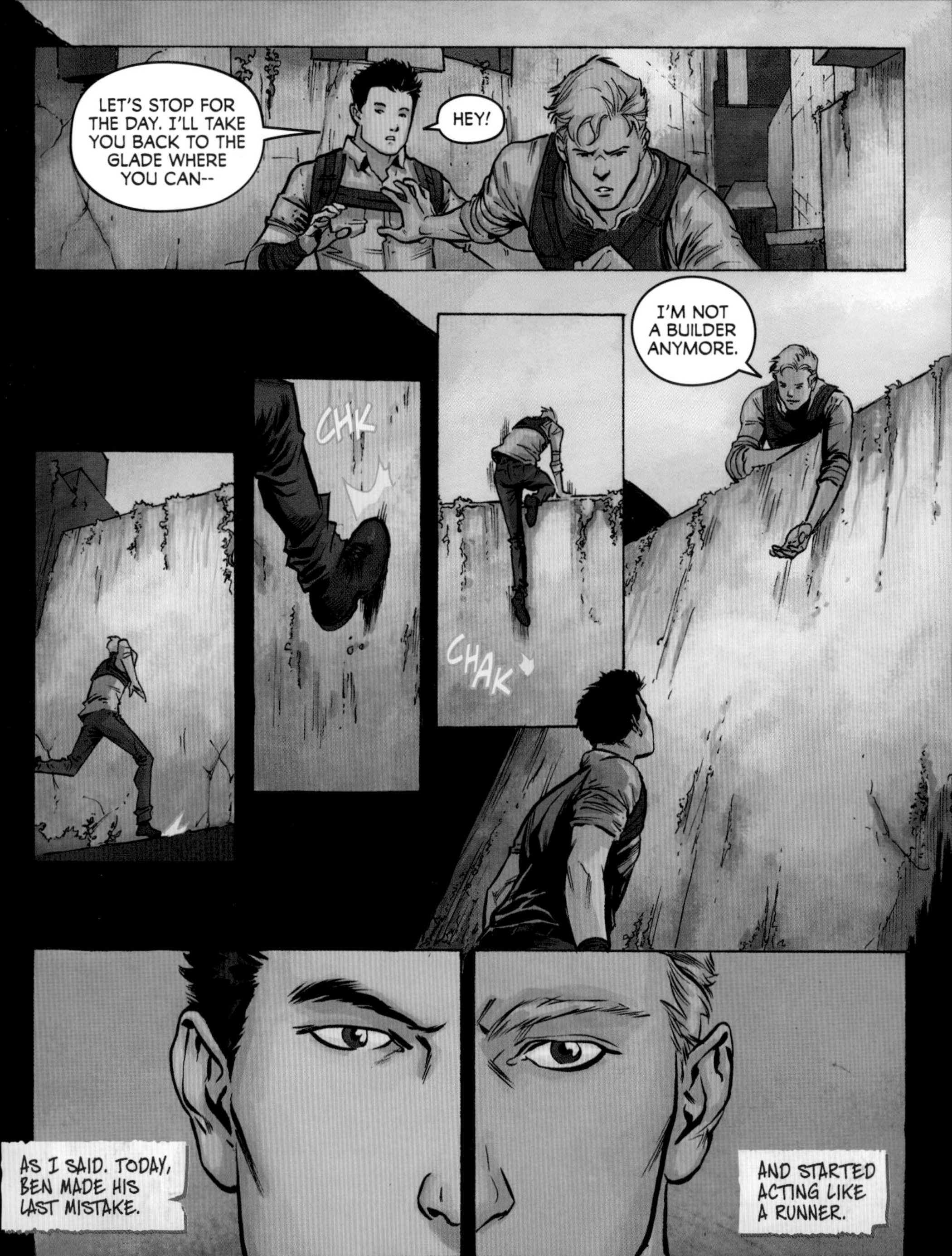
LET'S STOP FOR THE DAY. I'LL TAKE YOU BACK TO THE GLADE WHERE YOU CAN--
HEY!
CHK
CHAK
I'M NOT A BUILDER ANYMORE.
AS I SAID. TODAY, BEN MADE HIS LAST MISTAKE.
AND STARTED ACTING LIKE A RUNNER.

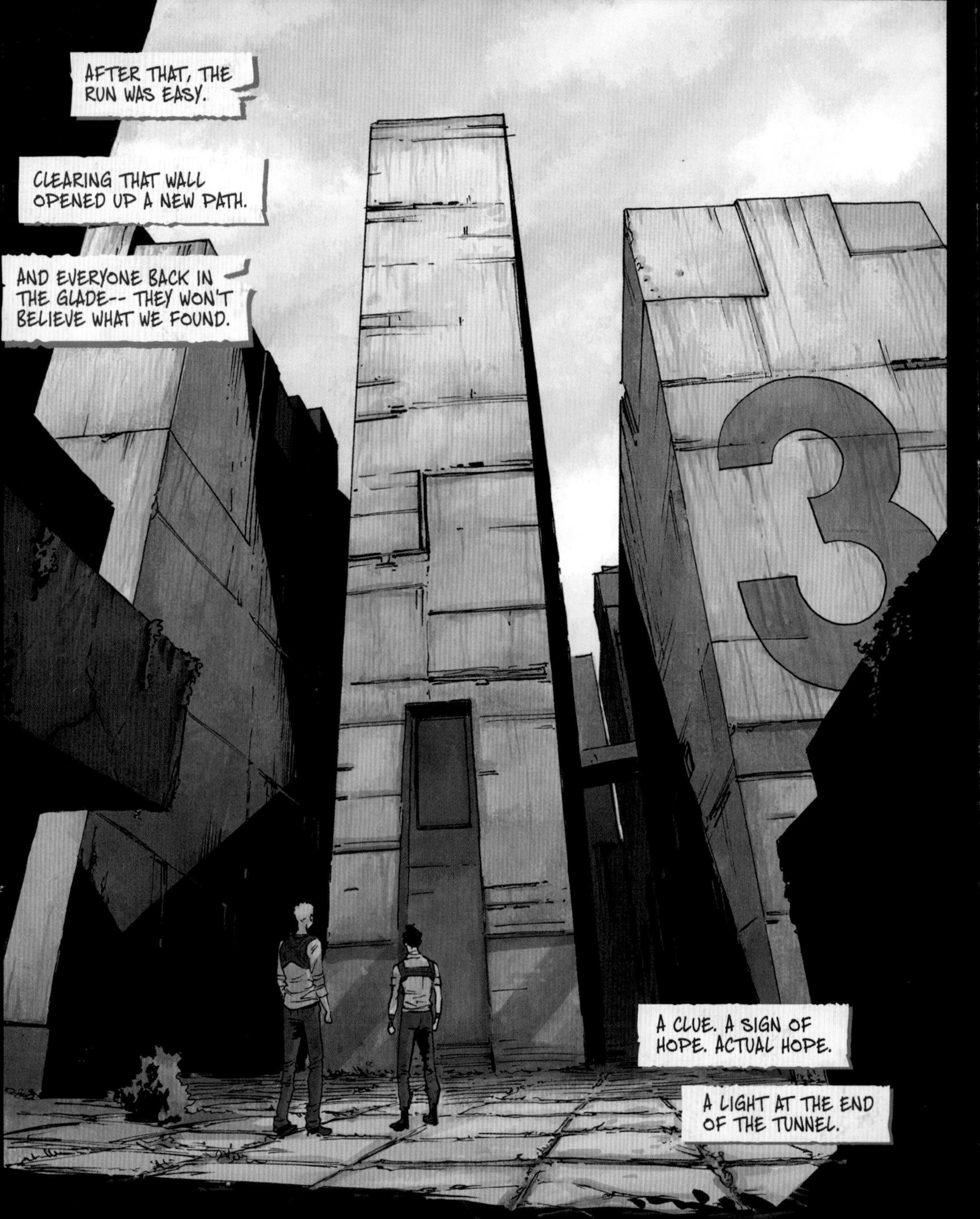
AFTER THAT, THE RUN WAS EASY.
CLEARING THAT WALL OPENED UP A NEW PATH.
AND EVERYONE BACK IN THE GLADE-- THEY WON'T BELIEVE WHAT WE FOUND.
3
A CLUE. A SIGN OF HOPE. ACTUAL HOPE.
A LIGHT AT THE END OF THE TUNNEL.

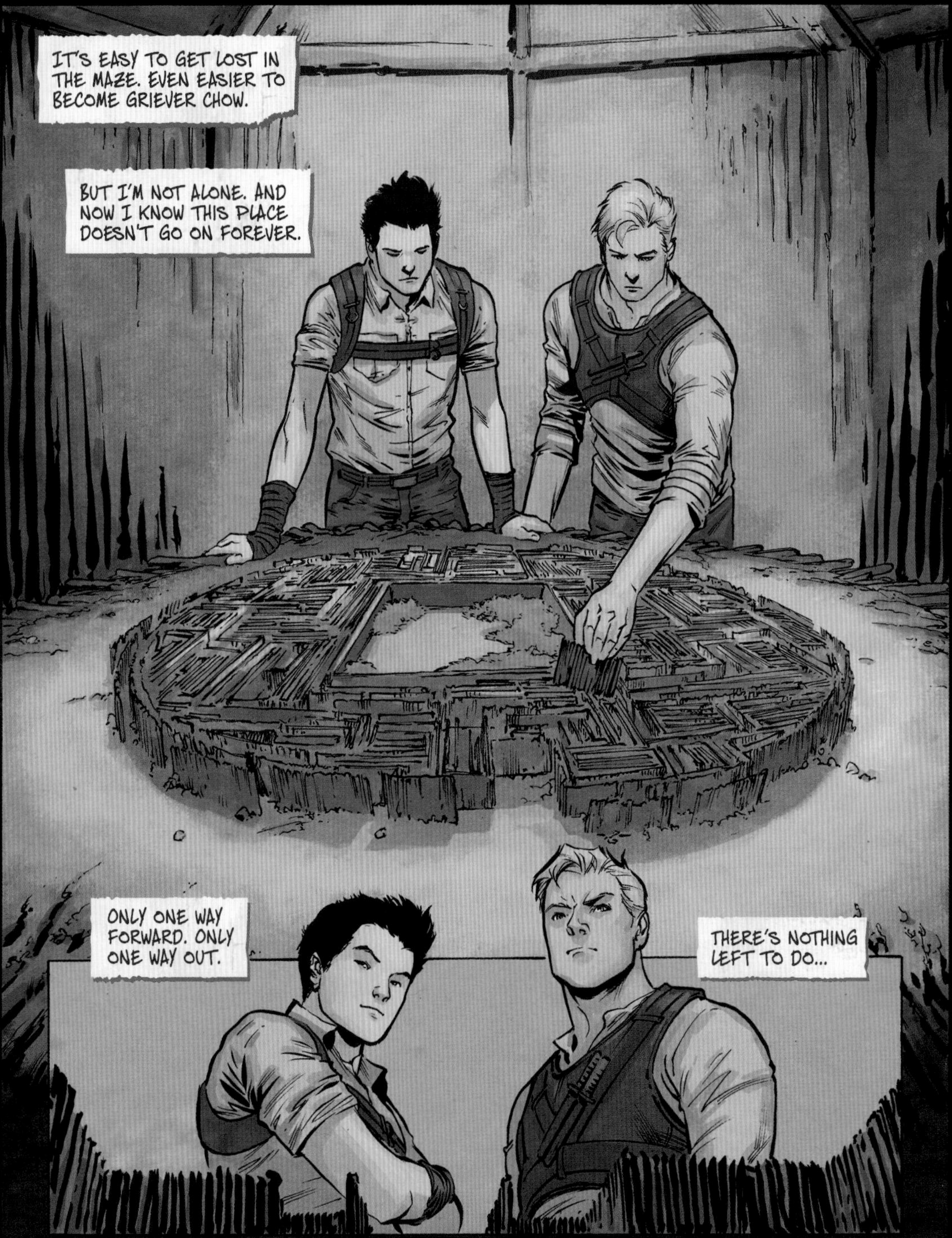
IT'S EASY TO GET LOST IN THE MAZE. EVEN EASIER TO BECOME GRIEVER CHOW.
BUT I'M NOT ALONE. AND NOW I KNOW THIS PLACE DOESN'T GO ON FOREVER.
ONLY ONE WAY FORWARD. ONLY ONE WAY OUT.
THERE'S NOTHING LEFT TO DO...

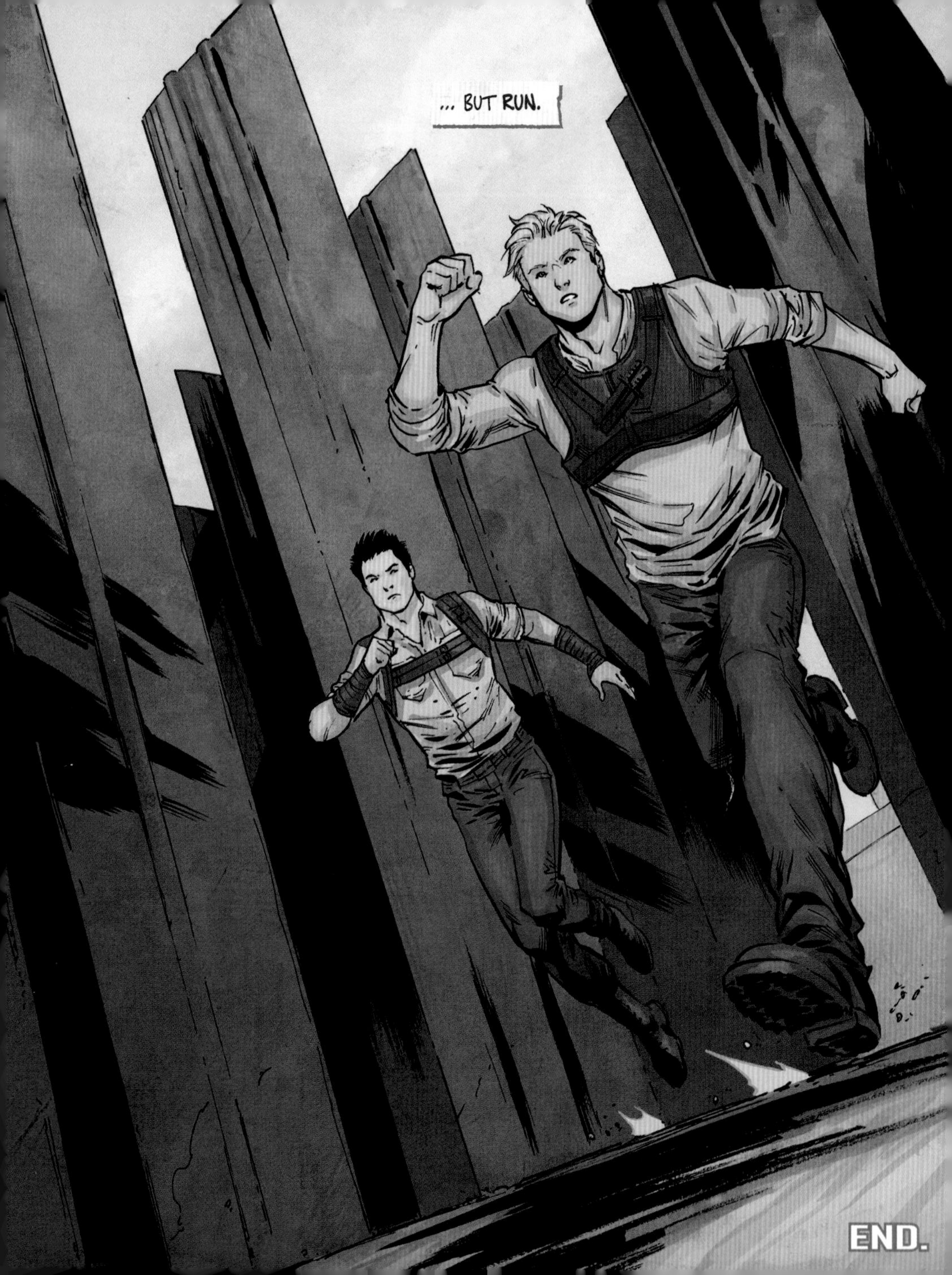
... BUT RUN.
END.

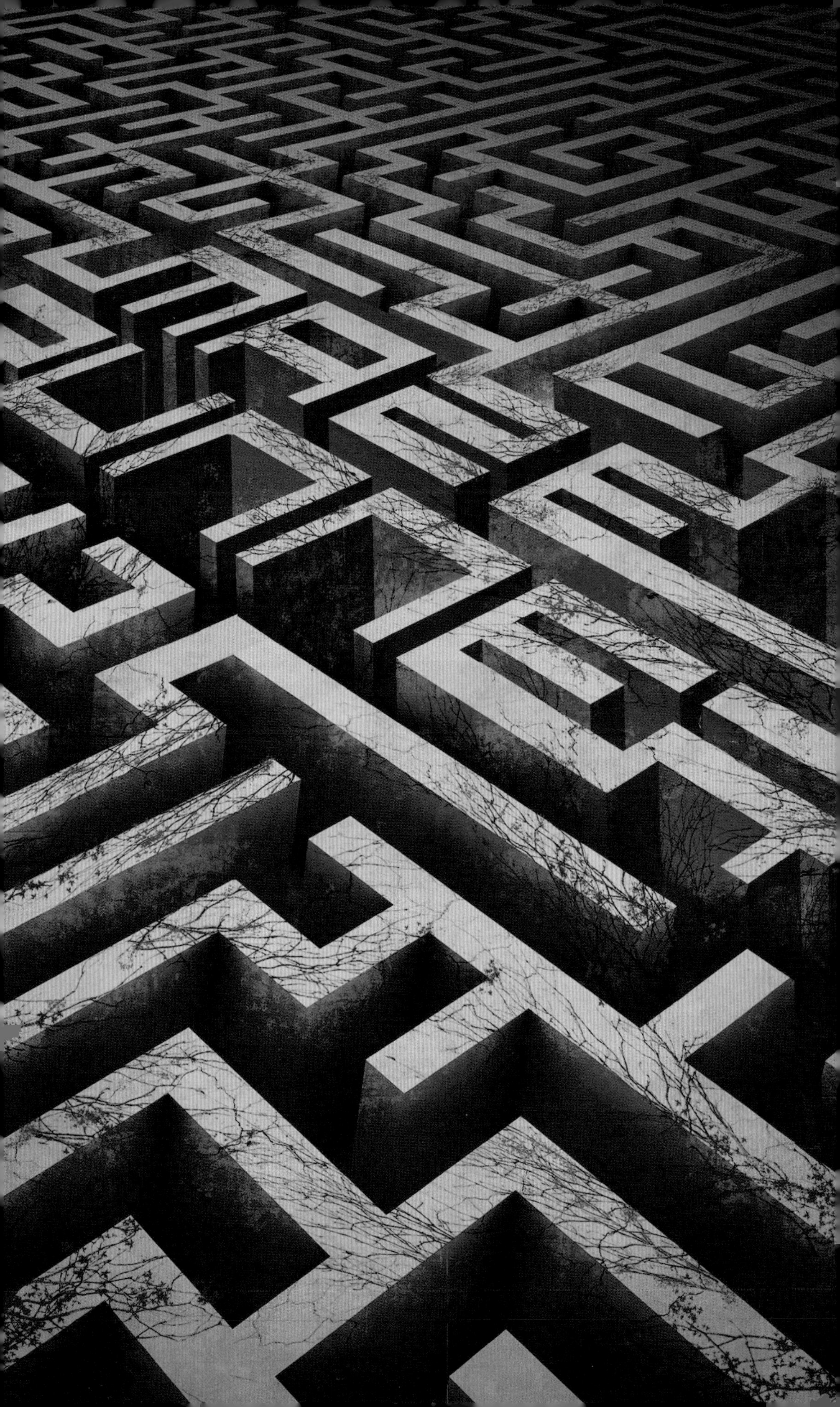

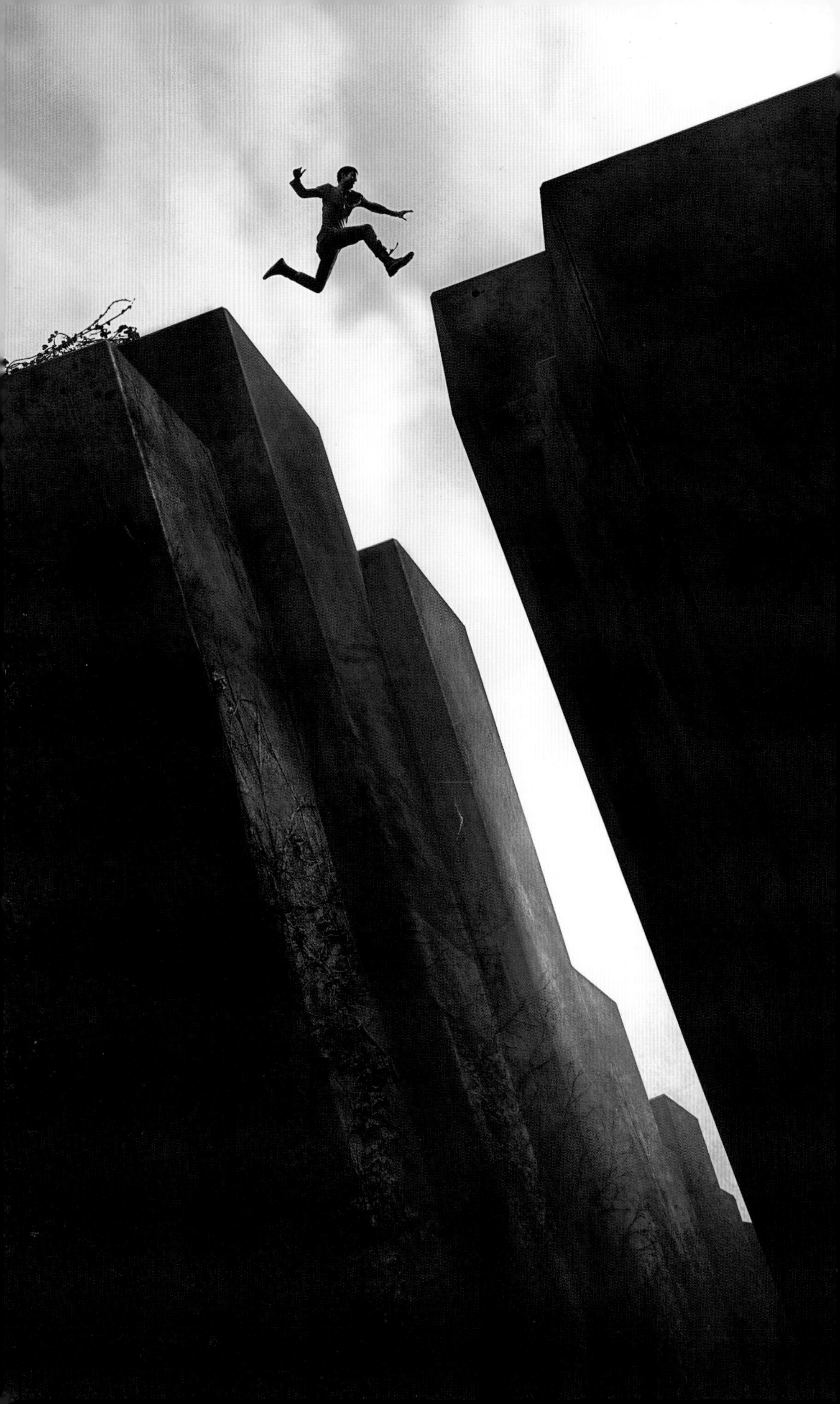

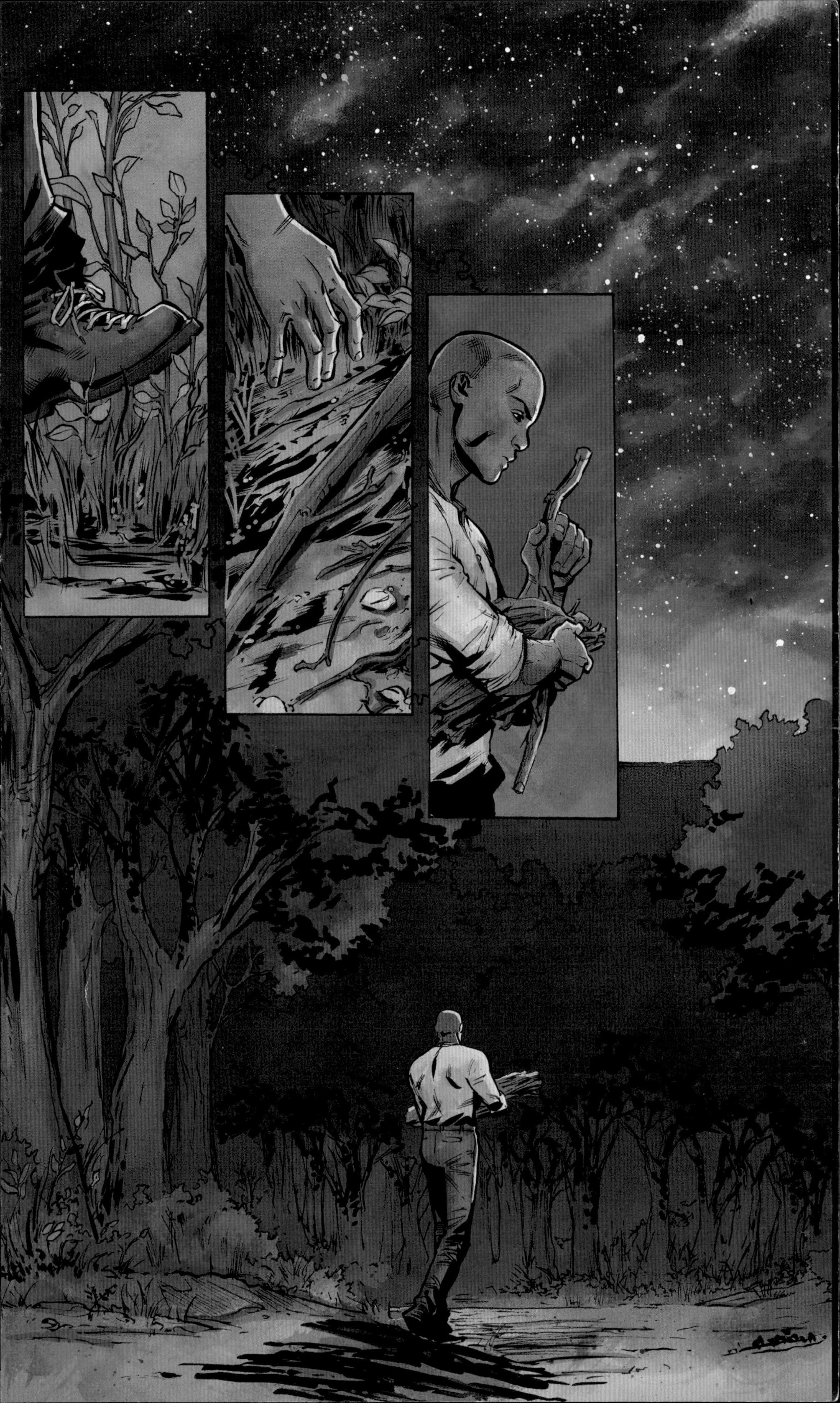

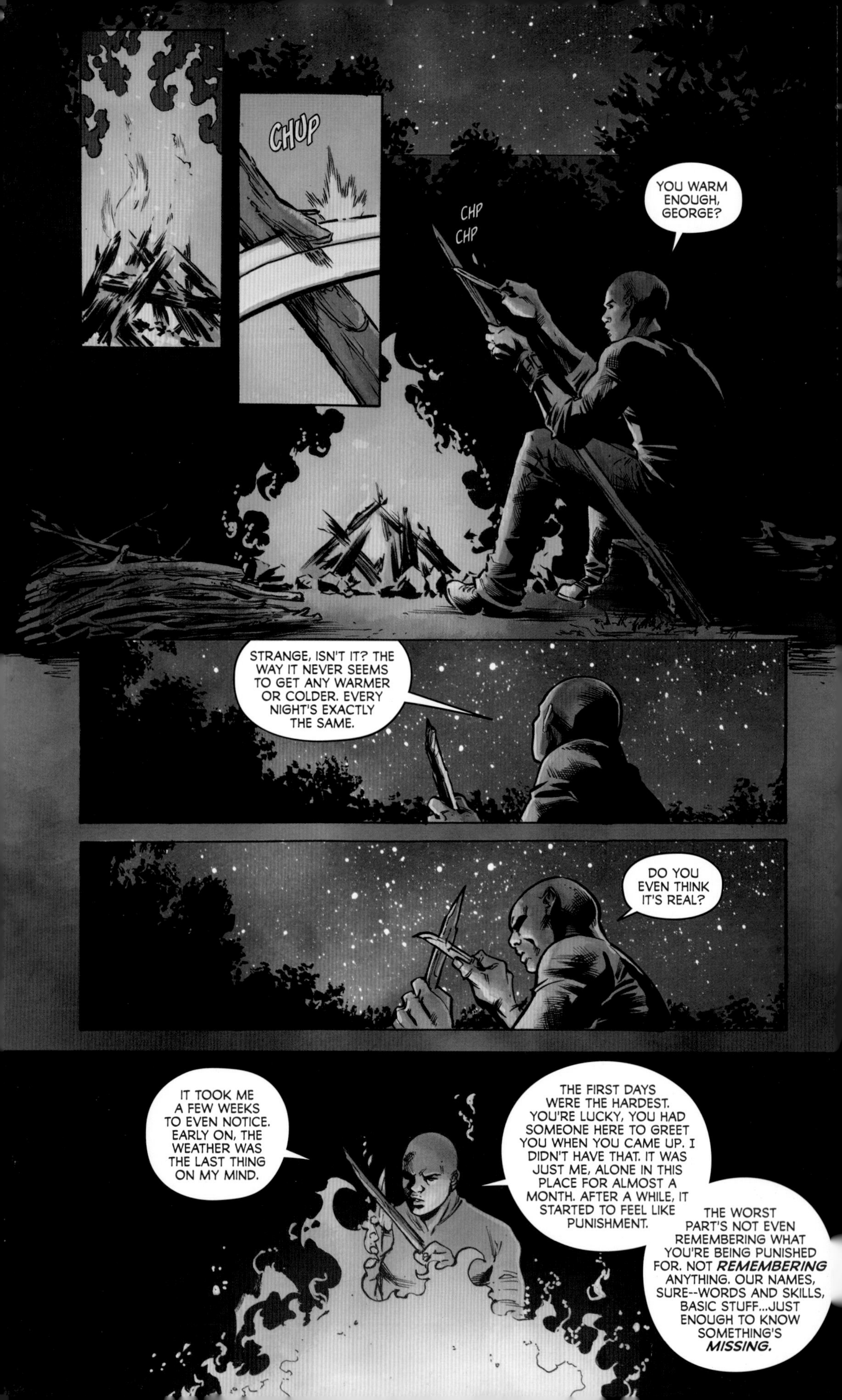
CHUP
CHP CHP
YOU WARM ENOUGH, GEORGE?
STRANGE, ISN'T IT? THE WAY IT NEVER SEEMS TO GET ANY WARMER OR COLDER. EVERY NIGHT'S EXACTLY THE SAME.
DO YOU EVEN THINK IT'S REAL?
IT TOOK ME A FEW WEEKS TO EVEN NOTICE. EARLY ON, THE WEATHER WAS THE LAST THING ON MY MIND.
THE FIRST DAYS WERE THE HARDEST. YOU'RE LUCKY, YOU HAD SOMEONE HERE TO GREET YOU WHEN YOU CAME UP. I DIDN'T HAVE THAT. IT WAS JUST ME, ALONE IN THIS PLACE FOR ALMOST A MONTH. AFTER A WHILE, IT STARTED TO FEEL LIKE PUNISHMENT.
THE WORST PART'S NOT EVEN REMEMBERING WHAT YOU'RE BEING PUNISHED FOR. NOT ***REMEMBERING*** ANYTHING. OUR NAMES, SURE--WORDS AND SKILLS, BASIC STUFF...JUST ENOUGH TO KNOW SOMETHING'S ***MISSING.***

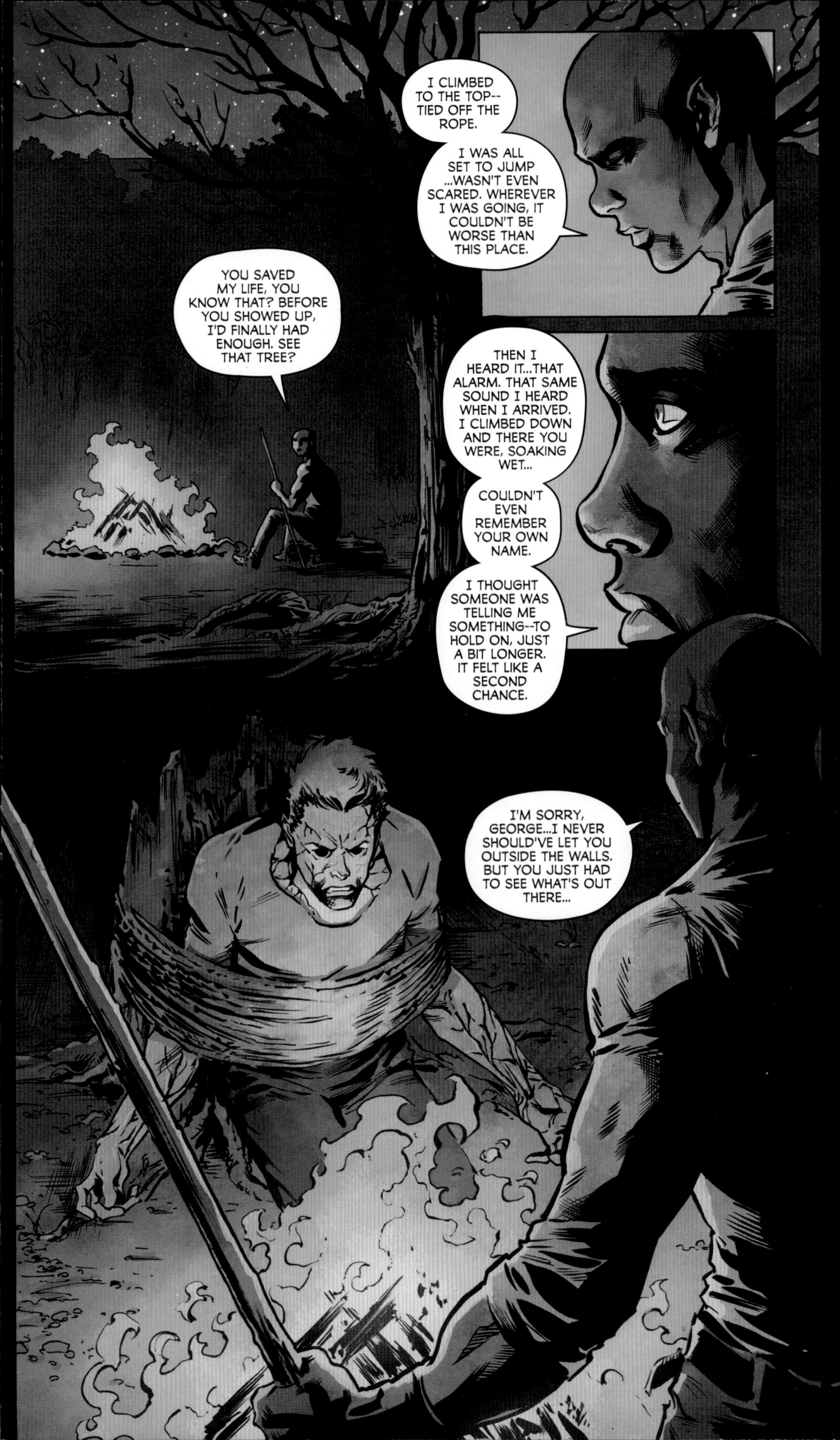

YOU SAVED MY LIFE, YOU KNOW THAT? BEFORE YOU SHOWED UP, I'D FINALLY HAD ENOUGH. SEE THAT TREE?
I CLIMBED TO THE TOP-- TIED OFF THE ROPE.
I WAS ALL SET TO JUMP ...WASN'T EVEN SCARED. WHEREVER I WAS GOING, IT COULDN'T BE WORSE THAN THIS PLACE.
THEN I HEARD IT...THAT ALARM. THAT SAME SOUND I HEARD WHEN I ARRIVED. I CLIMBED DOWN AND THERE YOU WERE, SOAKING WET...
COULDN'T EVEN REMEMBER YOUR OWN NAME.
I THOUGHT SOMEONE WAS TELLING ME SOMETHING--TO HOLD ON, JUST A BIT LONGER. IT FELT LIKE A SECOND CHANCE.
I'M SORRY, GEORGE...I NEVER SHOULD'VE LET YOU OUTSIDE THE WALLS. BUT YOU JUST HAD TO SEE WHAT'S OUT THERE...

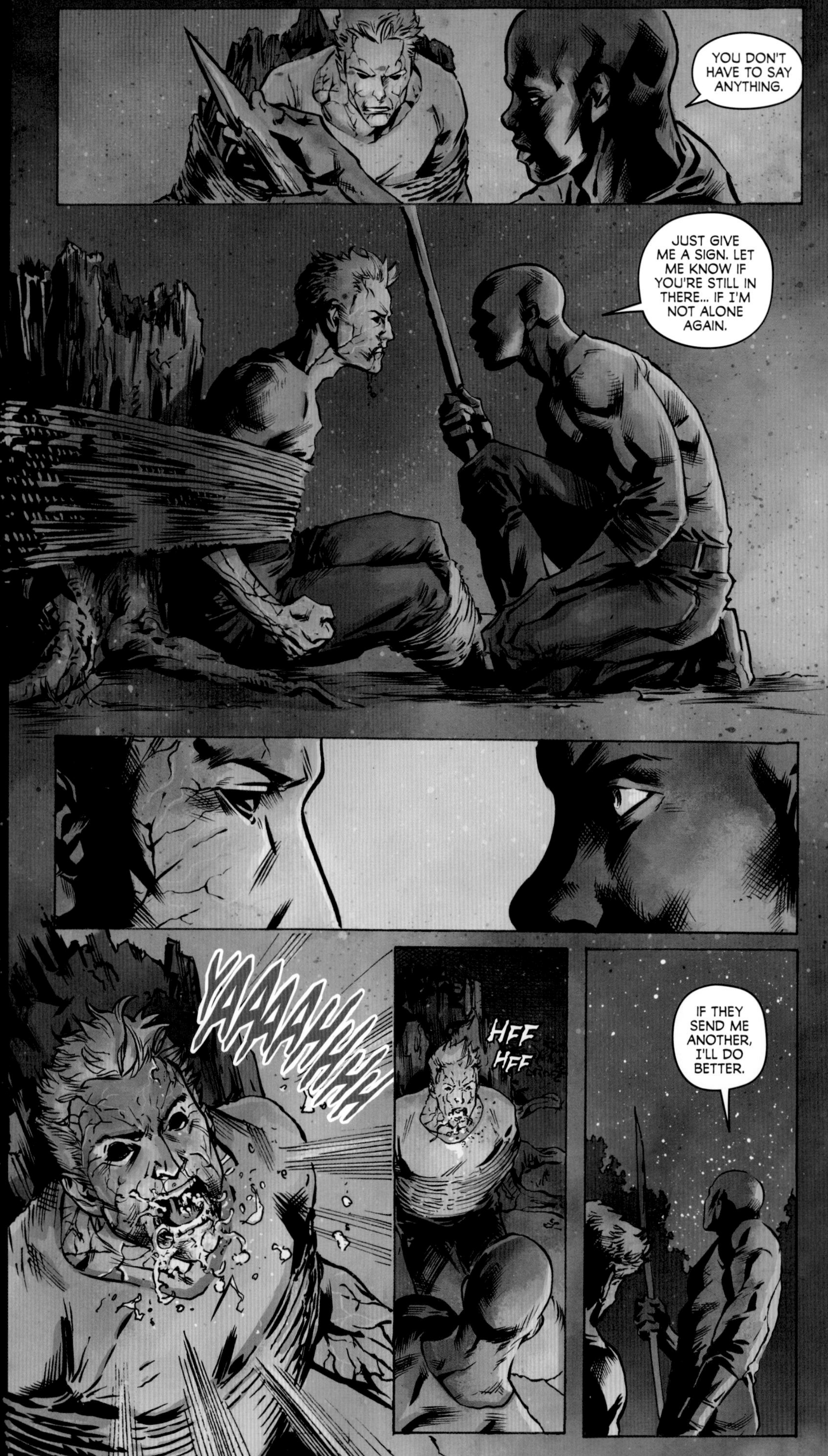
YOU DON'T HAVE TO SAY ANYTHING.
JUST GIVE ME A SIGN. LET ME KNOW IF YOU'RE STILL IN THERE... IF I'M NOT ALONE AGAIN.
HFF HFF
IF THEY SEND ME ANOTHER, I'LL DO BETTER.

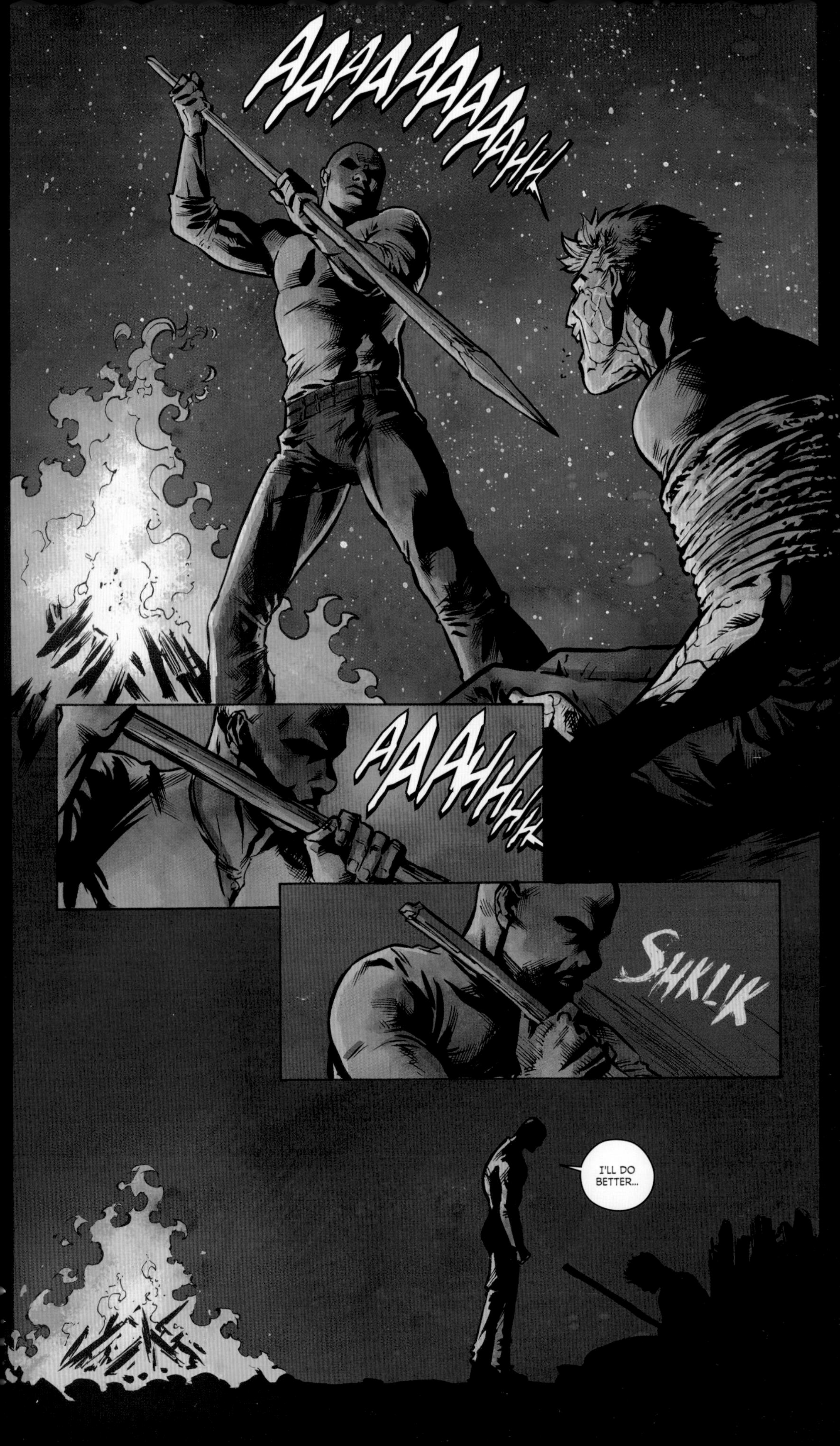
AAAAAAAAAAHH
AAAAHHHH
SHKLK
I'LL DO BETTER...

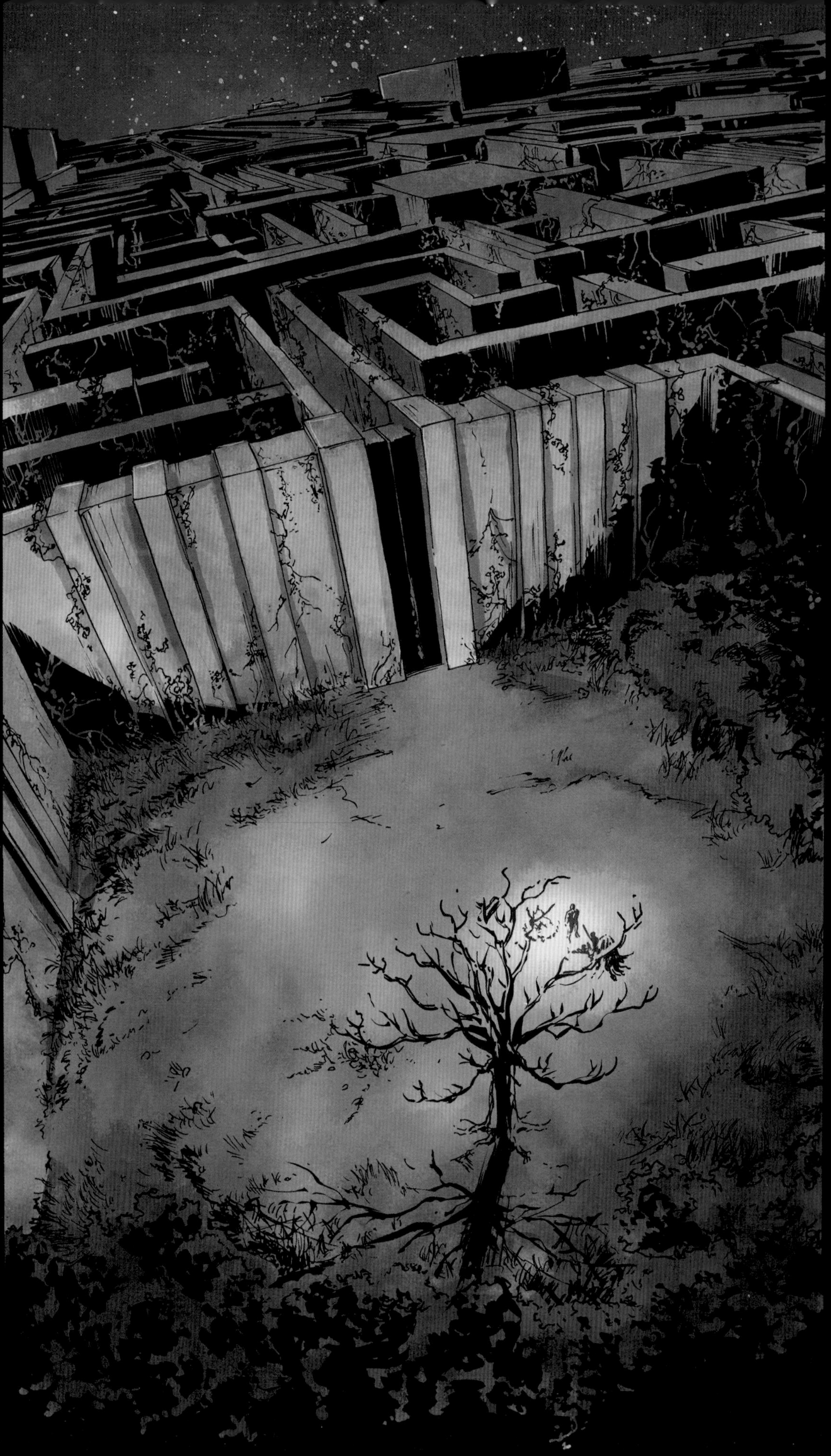

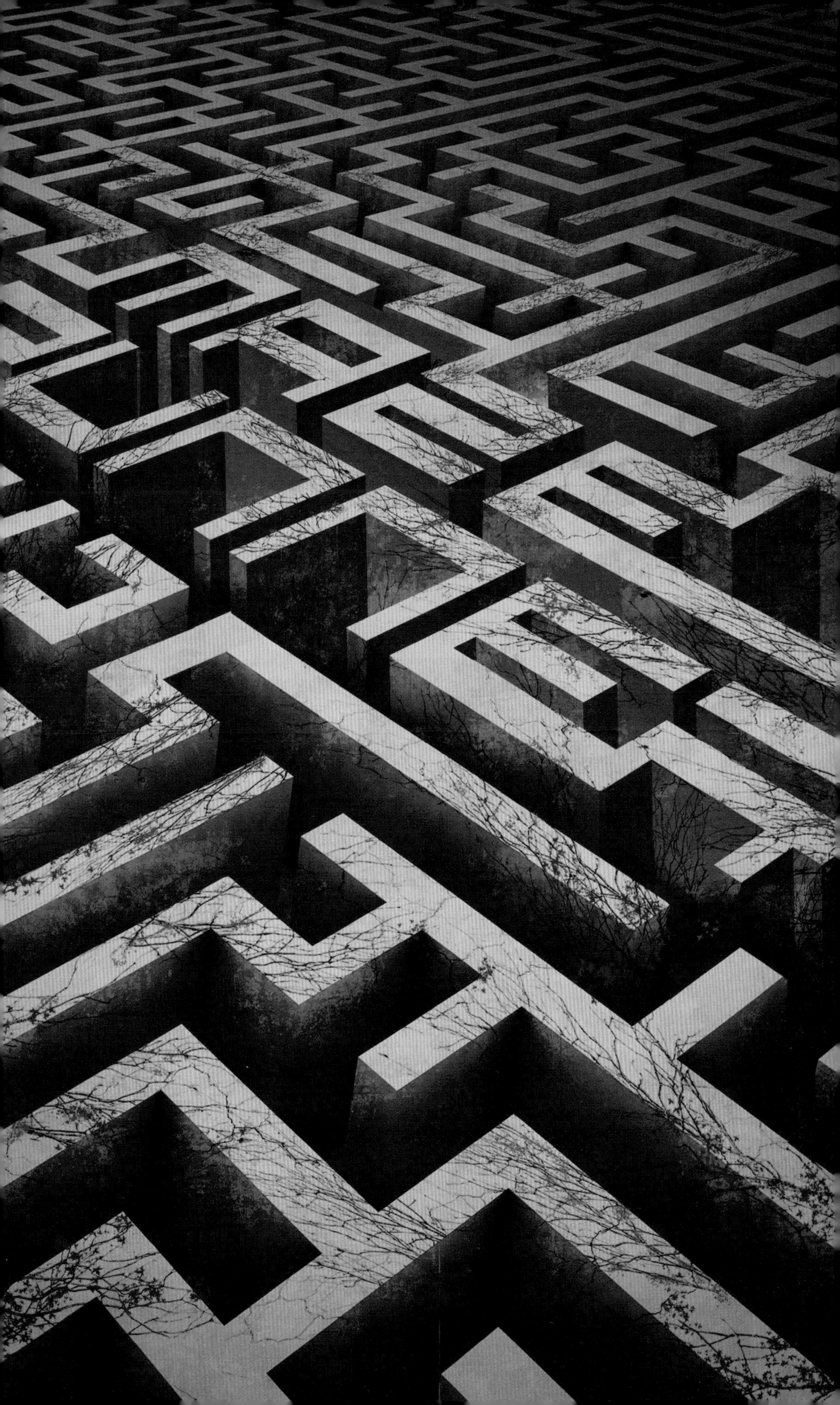

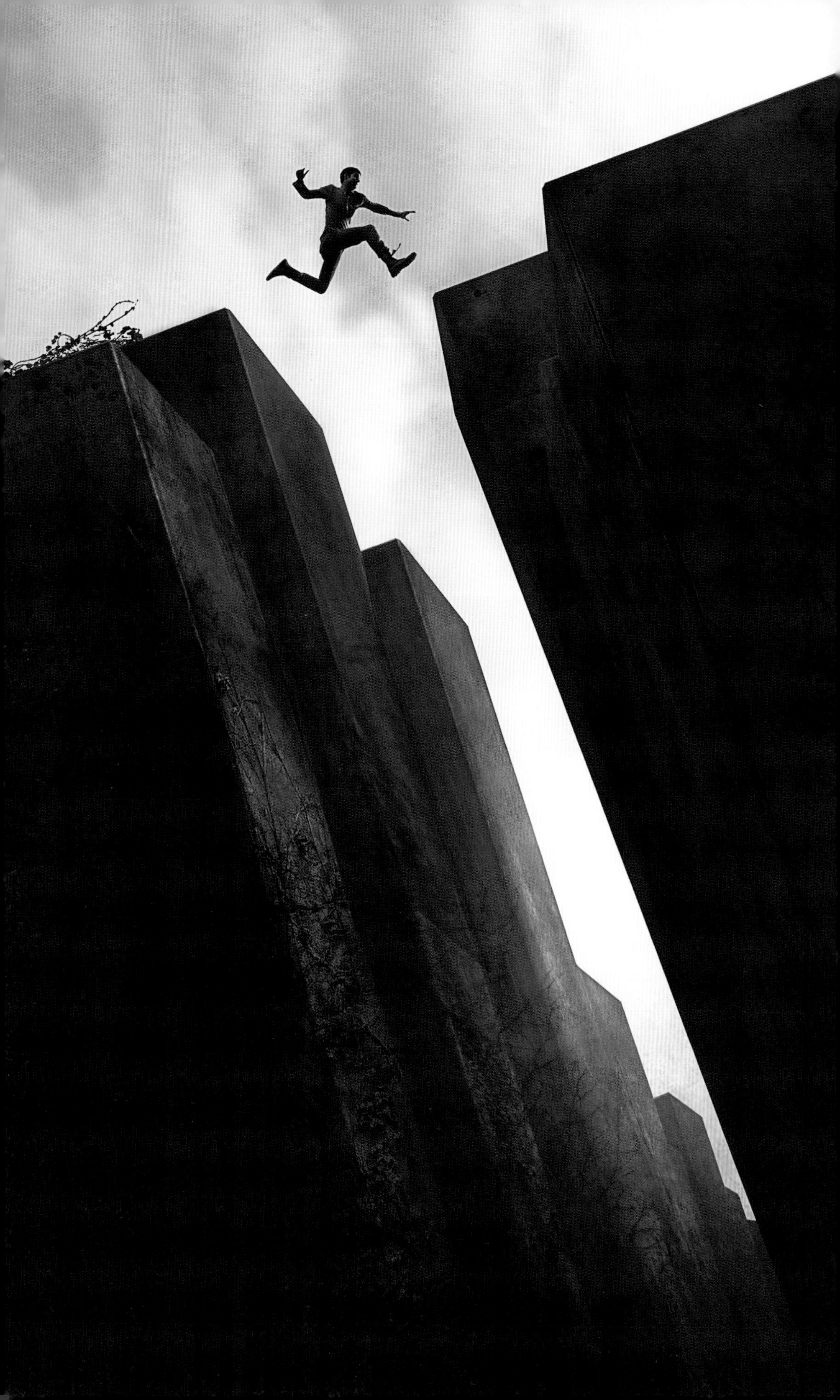

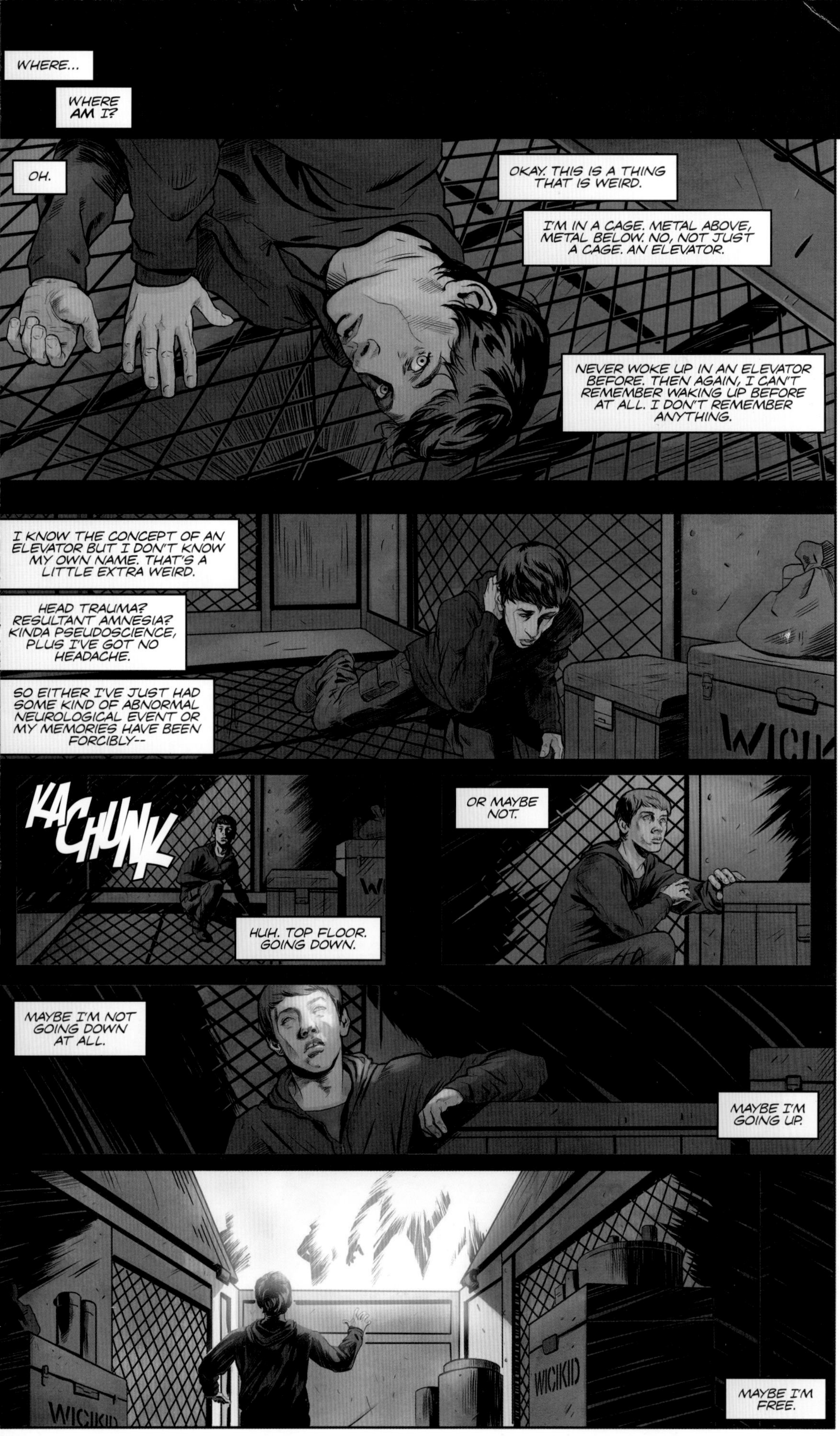
WHERE...
WHERE AM I?
OH.
OKAY. THIS IS A THING THAT IS WEIRD.
I'M IN A CAGE. METAL ABOVE, METAL BELOW. NO, NOT JUST A CAGE. AN ELEVATOR.
NEVER WOKE UP IN AN ELEVATOR BEFORE. THEN AGAIN, I CAN'T REMEMBER WAKING UP BEFORE AT ALL. I DON'T REMEMBER ANYTHING.
I KNOW THE CONCEPT OF AN ELEVATOR BUT I DON'T KNOW MY OWN NAME. THAT'S A LITTLE EXTRA WEIRD.
HEAD TRAUMA? RESULTANT AMNESIA? KINDA PSEUDOSCIENCE, PLUS I'VE GOT NO HEADACHE.
SO EITHER I'VE JUST HAD SOME KIND OF ABNORMAL NEUROLOGICAL EVENT OR MY MEMORIES HAVE BEEN FORCIBLY--
KACHUNK
HUH. TOP FLOOR. GOING DOWN.
OR MAYBE NOT.
MAYBE I'M NOT GOING DOWN AT ALL.
MAYBE I'M GOING UP.
MAYBE I'M FREE.

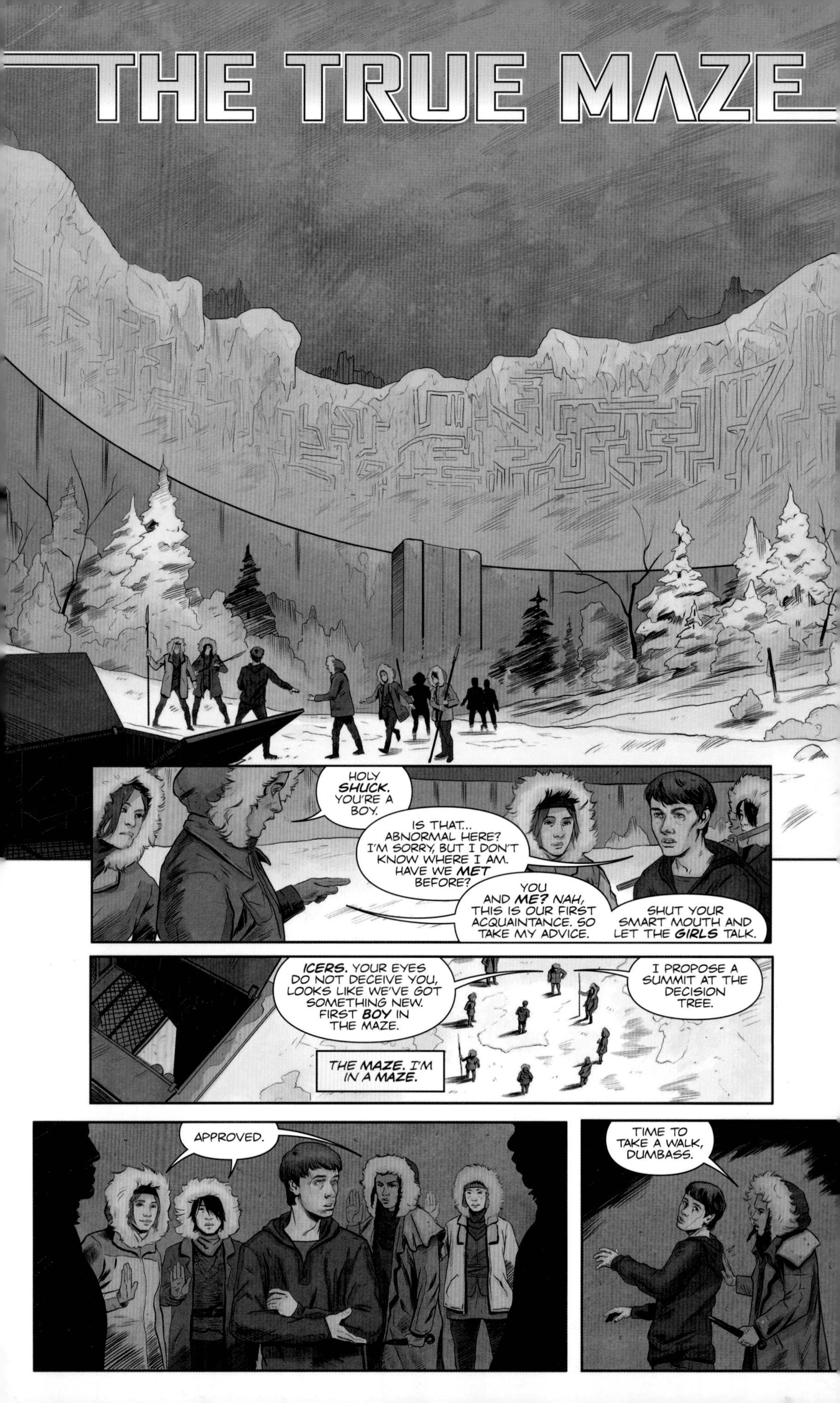
THE TRUE MAZE
HOLY SHUCK. YOU'RE A BOY.
IS THAT... ABNORMAL HERE? I'M SORRY, BUT I DON'T KNOW WHERE I AM. HAVE WE MET BEFORE?
YOU AND ME? NAH, THIS IS OUR FIRST ACQUAINTANCE. SO TAKE MY ADVICE.
SHUT YOUR SMART MOUTH AND LET THE GIRLS TALK.
ICERS. YOUR EYES DO NOT DECEIVE YOU, LOOKS LIKE WE'VE GOT SOMETHING NEW. FIRST BOY IN THE MAZE.
I PROPOSE A SUMMIT AT THE DECISION TREE.
THE MAZE. I'M IN A MAZE.
APPROVED.
TIME TO TAKE A WALK, DUMBASS.

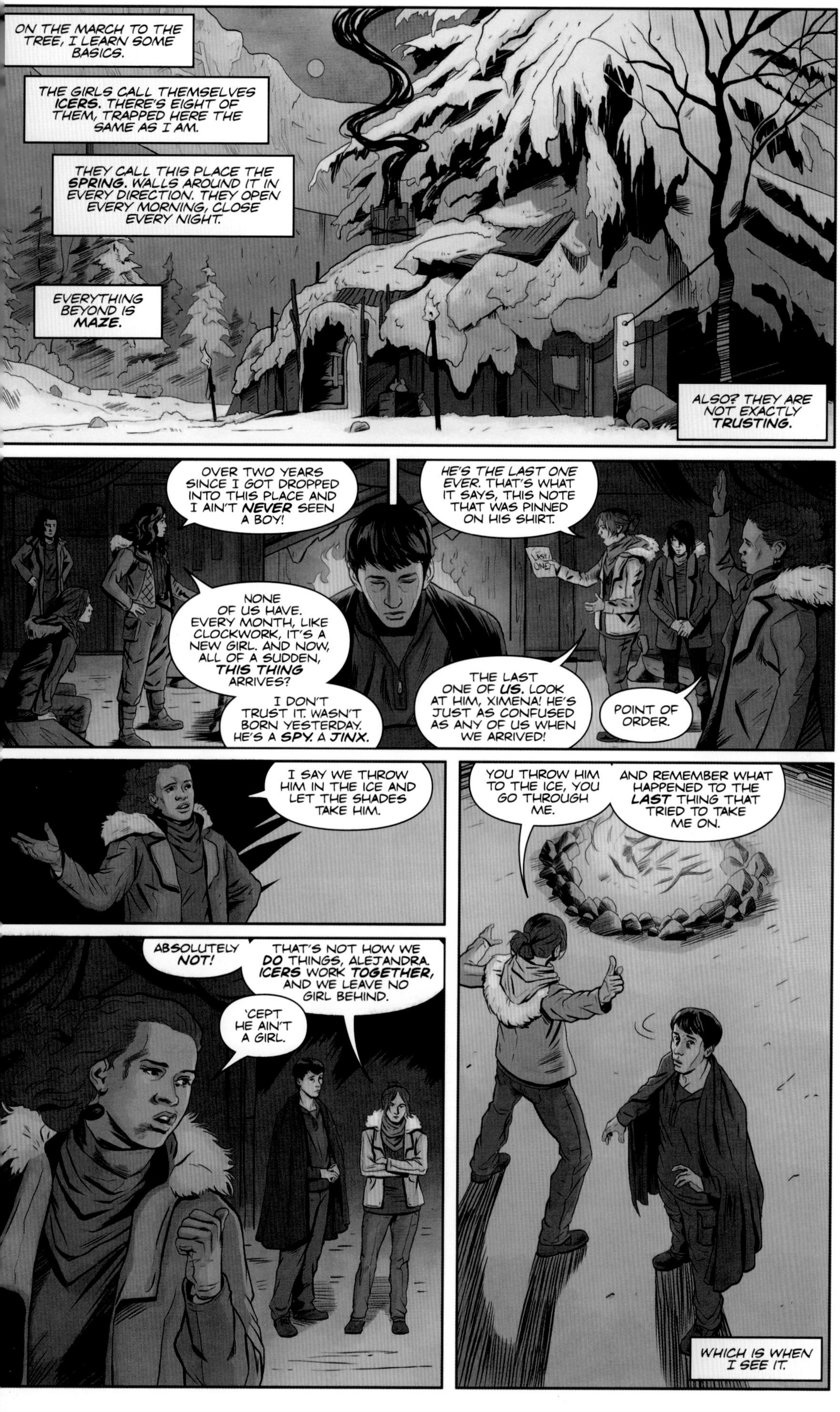
ON THE MARCH TO THE TREE, I LEARN SOME BASICS.
THE GIRLS CALL THEMSELVES ICERS. THERE'S EIGHT OF THEM, TRAPPED HERE THE SAME AS I AM.
THEY CALL THIS PLACE THE SPRING. WALLS AROUND IT IN EVERY DIRECTION. THEY OPEN EVERY MORNING, CLOSE EVERY NIGHT.
EVERYTHING BEYOND IS MAZE.
ALSO? THEY ARE NOT EXACTLY TRUSTING.
OVER TWO YEARS SINCE I GOT DROPPED INTO THIS PLACE AND I AIN'T NEVER SEEN A BOY!
HE'S THE LAST ONE EVER. THAT'S WHAT IT SAYS, THIS NOTE THAT WAS PINNED ON HIS SHIRT.
LAST ONE
NONE OF US HAVE. EVERY MONTH, LIKE CLOCKWORK, IT'S A NEW GIRL. AND NOW, ALL OF A SUDDEN, THIS THING ARRIVES?
I DON'T TRUST IT. WASN'T BORN YESTERDAY. HE'S A SPY. A JINX.
THE LAST ONE OF US. LOOK AT HIM, XIMENA! HE'S JUST AS CONFUSED AS ANY OF US WHEN WE ARRIVED!
POINT OF ORDER.
I SAY WE THROW HIM IN THE ICE AND LET THE SHADES TAKE HIM.
ABSOLUTELY NOT!
THAT'S NOT HOW WE DO THINGS, ALEJANDRA. ICERS WORK TOGETHER, AND WE LEAVE NO GIRL BEHIND.
'CEPT HE AIN'T A GIRL.
YOU THROW HIM TO THE ICE, YOU GO THROUGH ME.
AND REMEMBER WHAT HAPPENED TO THE LAST THING THAT TRIED TO TAKE ME ON.
WHICH IS WHEN I SEE IT.

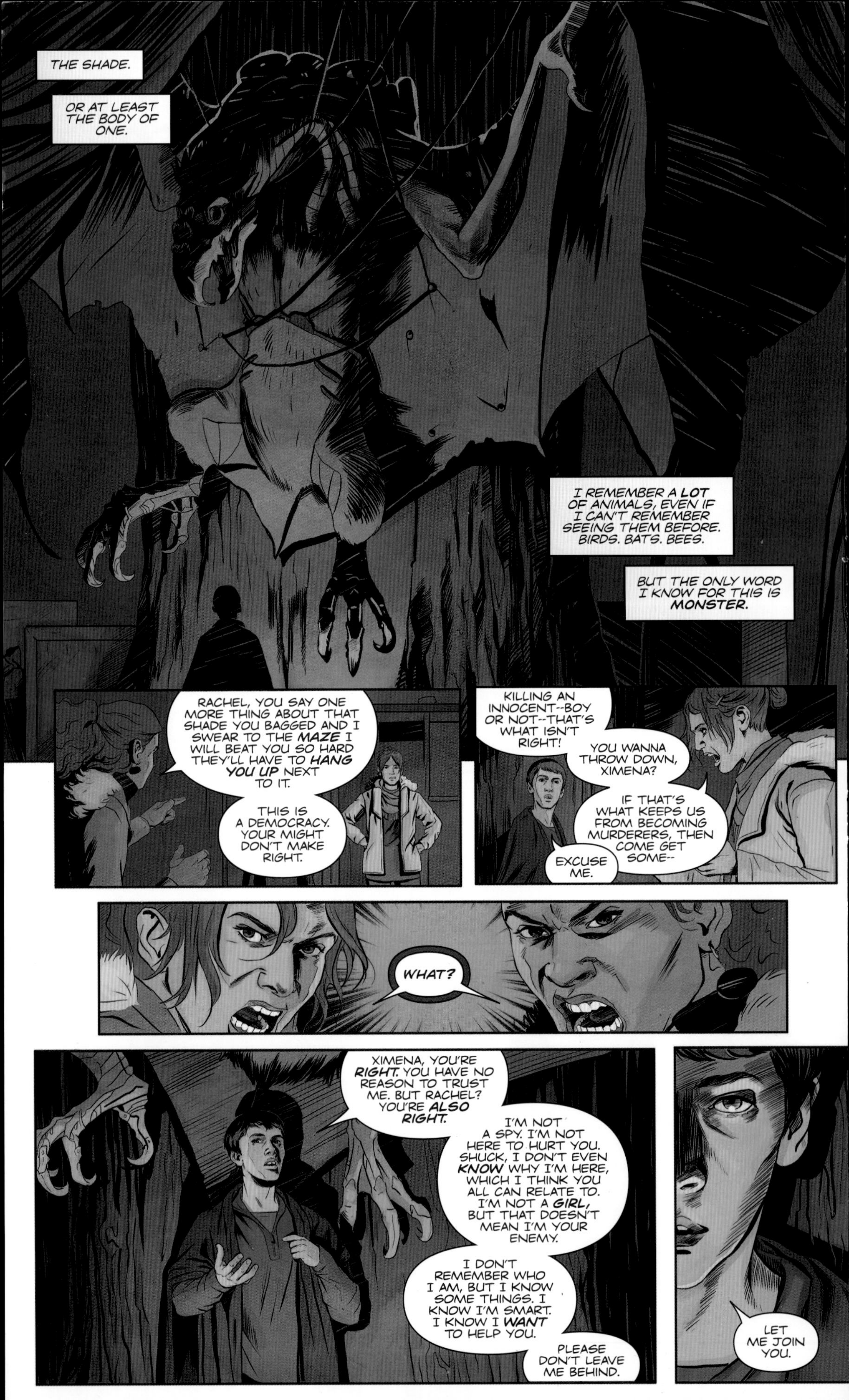

THE SHADE.
OR AT LEAST THE BODY OF ONE.
I REMEMBER A **LOT** OF ANIMALS, EVEN IF I CAN'T REMEMBER SEEING THEM BEFORE. BIRDS. BATS. BEES.
BUT THE ONLY WORD I KNOW FOR THIS IS **MONSTER.**
RACHEL, YOU SAY ONE MORE THING ABOUT THAT SHADE YOU BAGGED AND I SWEAR TO THE **MAZE** I WILL BEAT YOU SO HARD THEY'LL HAVE TO **HANG YOU UP** NEXT TO IT.
THIS IS A DEMOCRACY. YOUR MIGHT DON'T MAKE RIGHT.
KILLING AN INNOCENT--BOY OR NOT--THAT'S WHAT ISN'T RIGHT!
YOU WANNA THROW DOWN, XIMENA?
IF THAT'S WHAT KEEPS US FROM BECOMING MURDERERS, THEN COME GET SOME--
EXCUSE ME.
WHAT?
XIMENA, YOU'RE **RIGHT.** YOU HAVE NO REASON TO TRUST ME. BUT RACHEL? YOU'RE **ALSO RIGHT.**
I'M NOT A SPY. I'M NOT HERE TO HURT YOU. SHUCK, I DON'T EVEN **KNOW** WHY I'M HERE, WHICH I THINK YOU ALL CAN RELATE TO. I'M NOT A **GIRL,** BUT THAT DOESN'T MEAN I'M YOUR ENEMY.
I DON'T REMEMBER WHO I AM, BUT I KNOW SOME THINGS. I KNOW I'M SMART. I KNOW I **WANT** TO HELP YOU.
PLEASE DON'T LEAVE ME BEHIND.
LET ME JOIN YOU.

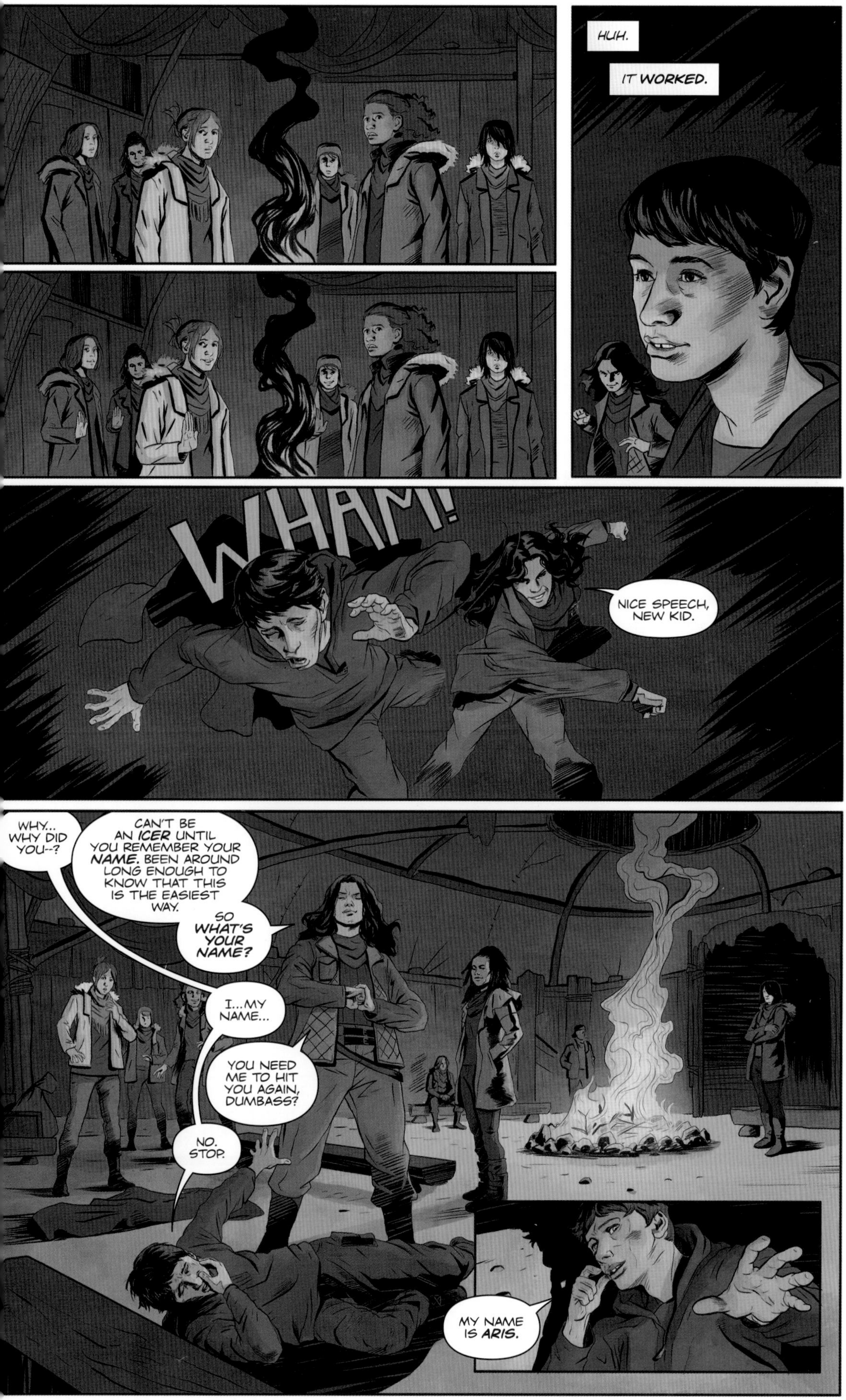
HUH.
IT WORKED.
WHAM!
NICE SPEECH, NEW KID.
WHY... WHY DID YOU--?
CAN'T BE AN ICER UNTIL YOU REMEMBER YOUR NAME. BEEN AROUND LONG ENOUGH TO KNOW THAT THIS IS THE EASIEST WAY.
SO WHAT'S YOUR NAME?
I...MY NAME...
YOU NEED ME TO HIT YOU AGAIN, DUMBASS?
NO. STOP.
MY NAME IS ARIS.

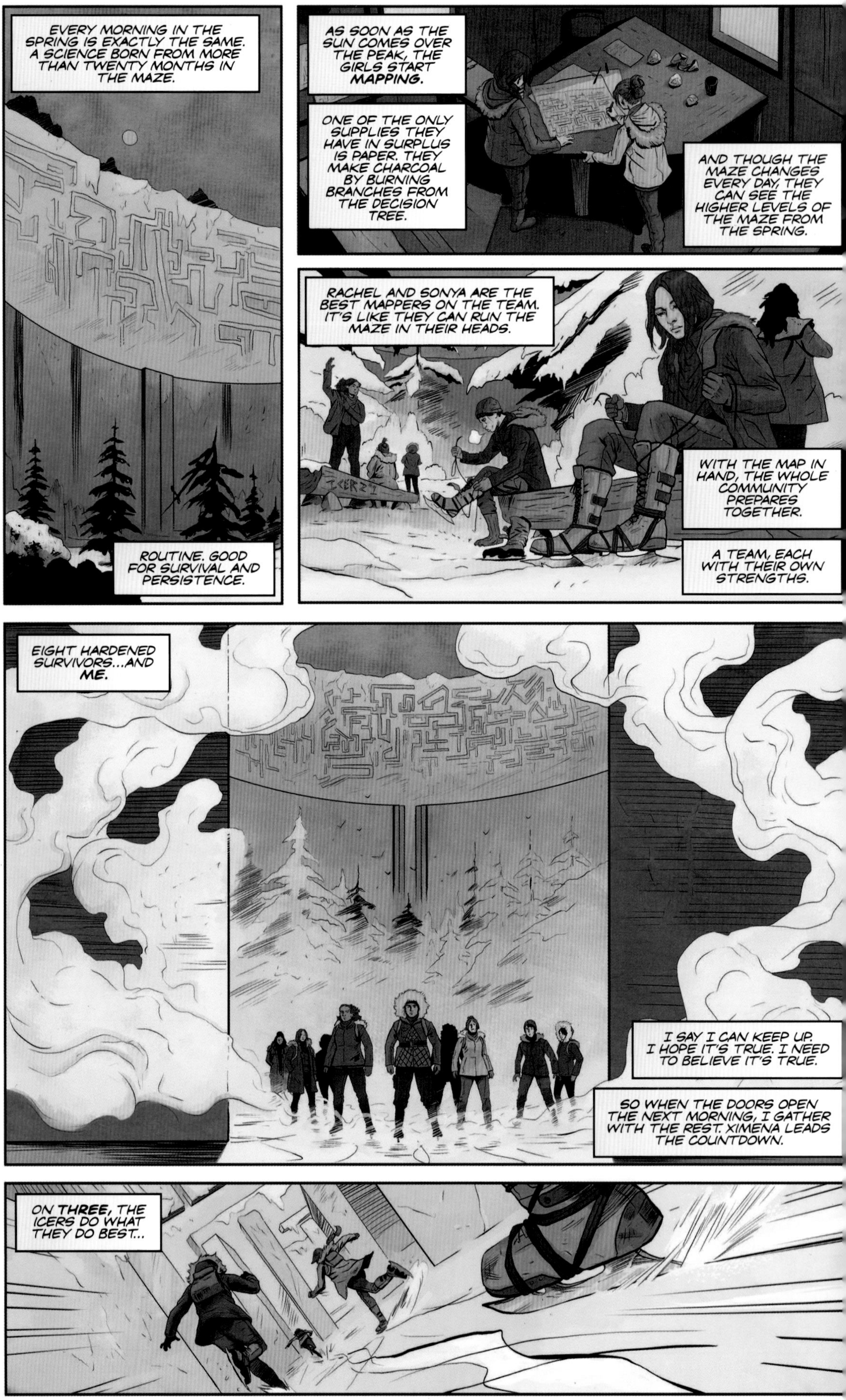
EVERY MORNING IN THE SPRING IS EXACTLY THE SAME. A SCIENCE BORN FROM MORE THAN TWENTY MONTHS IN THE MAZE.
ROUTINE. GOOD FOR SURVIVAL AND PERSISTENCE.
AS SOON AS THE SUN COMES OVER THE PEAK, THE GIRLS START MAPPING.
ONE OF THE ONLY SUPPLIES THEY HAVE IN SURPLUS IS PAPER. THEY MAKE CHARCOAL BY BURNING BRANCHES FROM THE DECISION TREE.
AND THOUGH THE MAZE CHANGES EVERY DAY, THEY CAN SEE THE HIGHER LEVELS OF THE MAZE FROM THE SPRING.
RACHEL AND SONYA ARE THE BEST MAPPERS ON THE TEAM. IT'S LIKE THEY CAN RUN THE MAZE IN THEIR HEADS.
WITH THE MAP IN HAND, THE WHOLE COMMUNITY PREPARES TOGETHER.
A TEAM, EACH WITH THEIR OWN STRENGTHS.
EIGHT HARDENED SURVIVORS...AND ME.
I SAY I CAN KEEP UP. I HOPE IT'S TRUE. I NEED TO BELIEVE IT'S TRUE.
SO WHEN THE DOORS OPEN THE NEXT MORNING, I GATHER WITH THE REST. XIMENA LEADS THE COUNTDOWN.
ON THREE, THE ICERS DO WHAT THEY DO BEST...

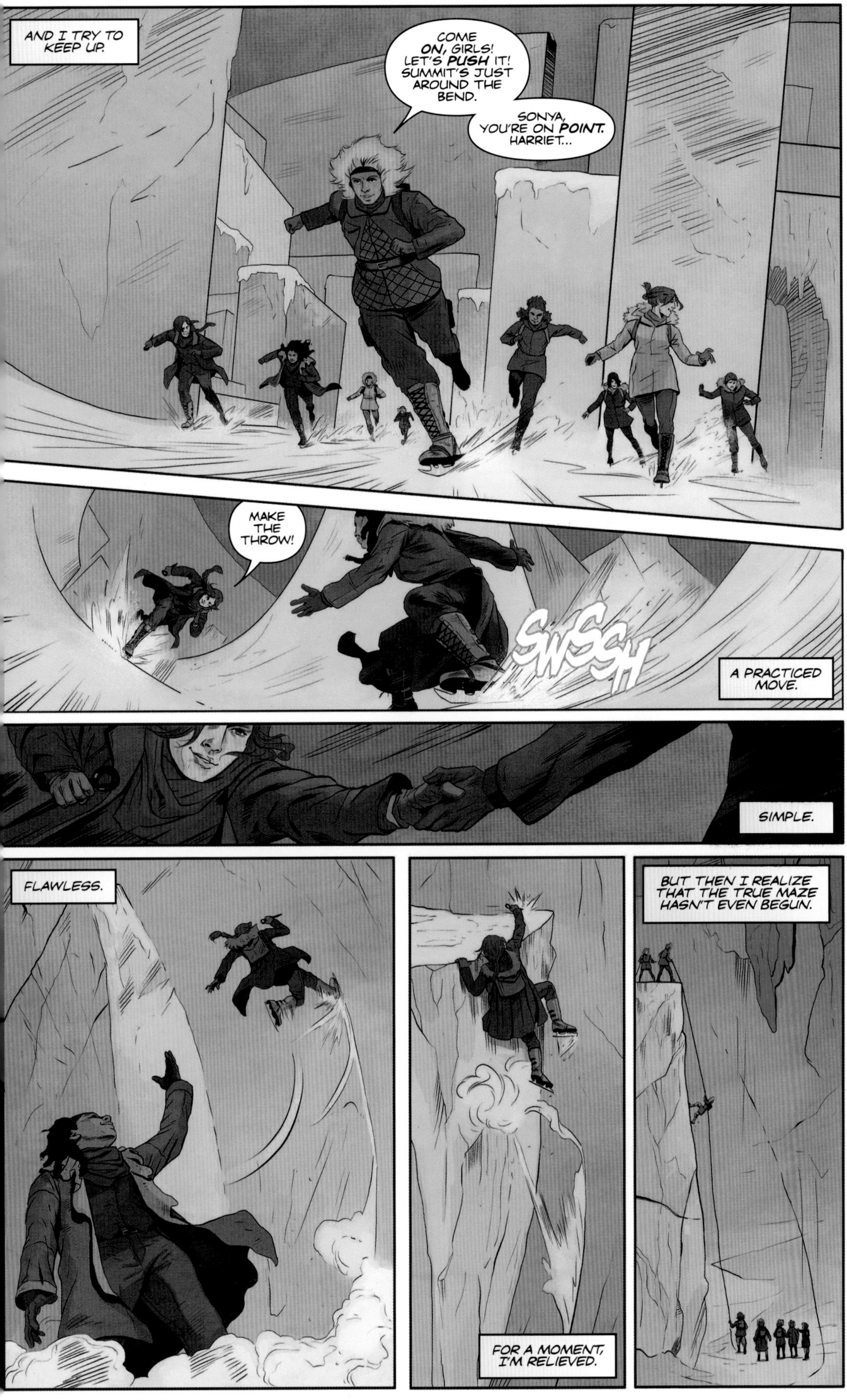
AND I TRY TO KEEP UP.
COME ON, GIRLS! LET'S PUSH IT! SUMMIT'S JUST AROUND THE BEND.
SONYA, YOU'RE ON POINT. HARRIET...
MAKE THE THROW!
SWSSH
A PRACTICED MOVE.
SIMPLE.
FLAWLESS.
FOR A MOMENT, I'M RELIEVED.
BUT THEN I REALIZE THAT THE TRUE MAZE HASN'T EVEN BEGUN.

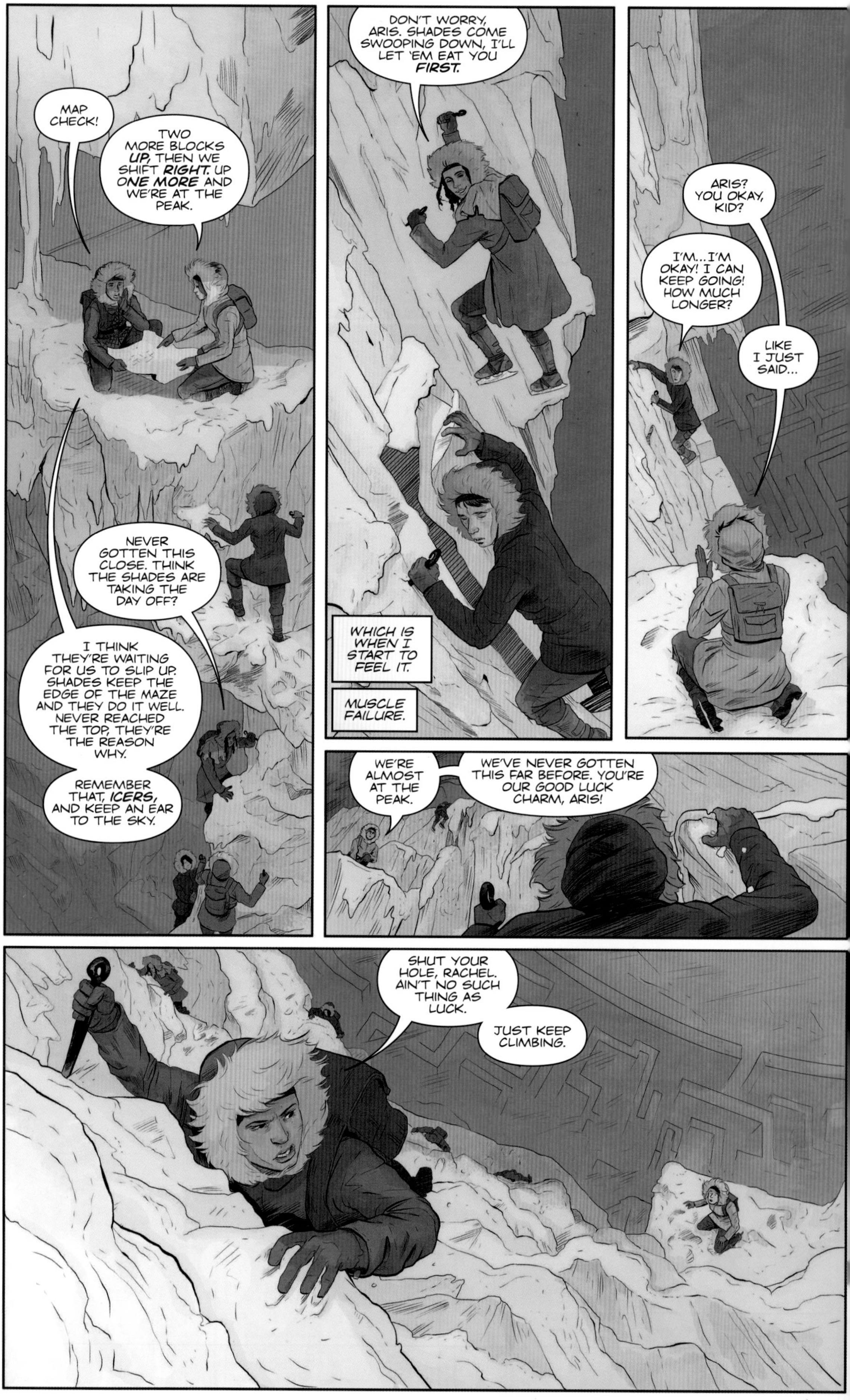
MAP CHECK!
TWO MORE BLOCKS UP, THEN WE SHIFT RIGHT. UP ONE MORE AND WE'RE AT THE PEAK.
NEVER GOTTEN THIS CLOSE. THINK THE SHADES ARE TAKING THE DAY OFF?
I THINK THEY'RE WAITING FOR US TO SLIP UP. SHADES KEEP THE EDGE OF THE MAZE AND THEY DO IT WELL. NEVER REACHED THE TOP, THEY'RE THE REASON WHY.
REMEMBER THAT, ICERS, AND KEEP AN EAR TO THE SKY.
DON'T WORRY, ARIS. SHADES COME SWOOPING DOWN, I'LL LET 'EM EAT YOU FIRST.
WHICH IS WHEN I START TO FEEL IT.
MUSCLE FAILURE.
ARIS? YOU OKAY, KID?
I'M...I'M OKAY! I CAN KEEP GOING! HOW MUCH LONGER?
LIKE I JUST SAID...
WE'RE ALMOST AT THE PEAK.
WE'VE NEVER GOTTEN THIS FAR BEFORE. YOU'RE OUR GOOD LUCK CHARM, ARIS!
SHUT YOUR HOLE, RACHEL. AIN'T NO SUCH THING AS LUCK.
JUST KEEP CLIMBING.

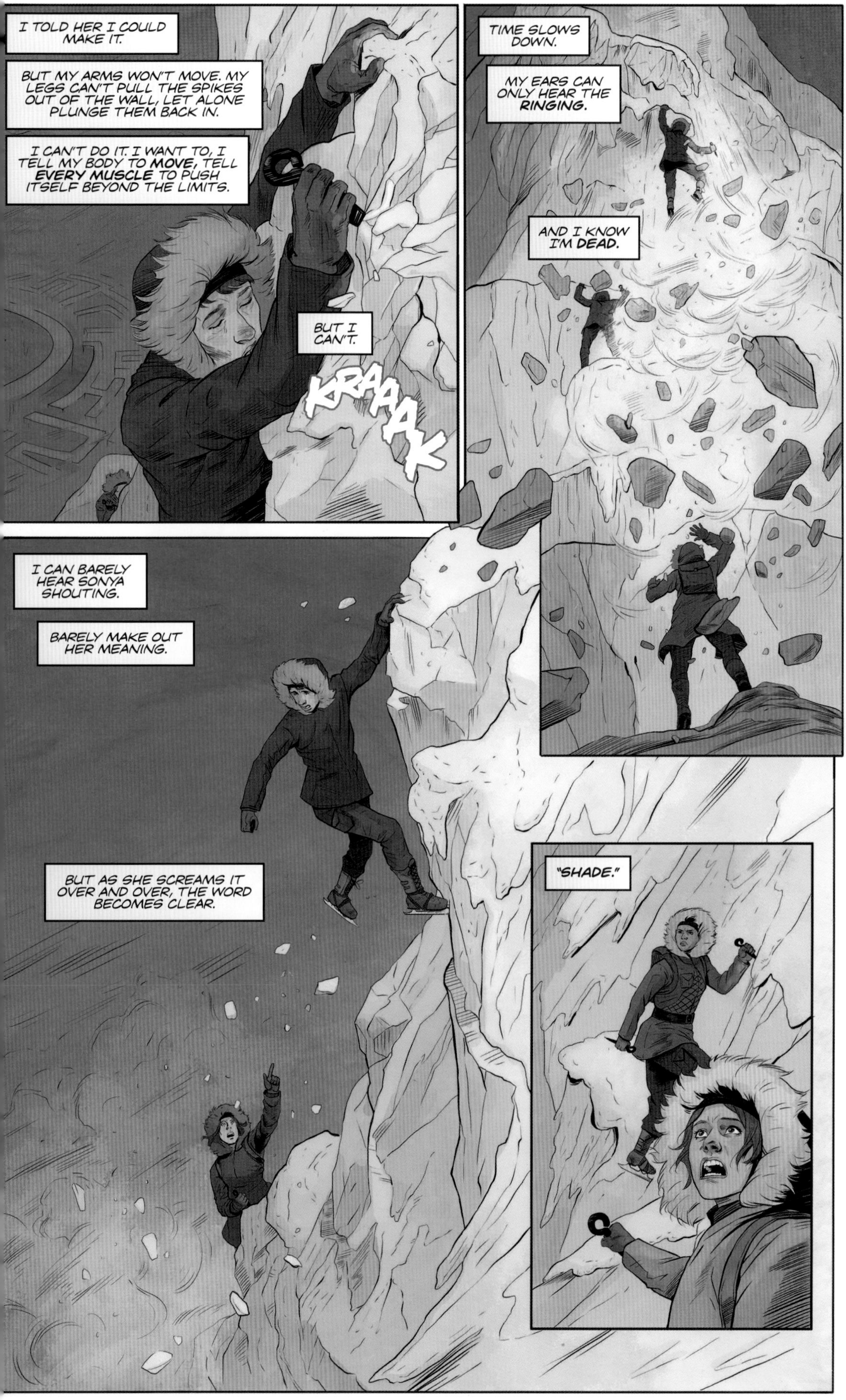
I TOLD HER I COULD MAKE IT.
BUT MY ARMS WON'T MOVE. MY LEGS CAN'T PULL THE SPIKES OUT OF THE WALL, LET ALONE PLUNGE THEM BACK IN.
I CAN'T DO IT. I WANT TO, I TELL MY BODY TO MOVE, TELL EVERY MUSCLE TO PUSH ITSELF BEYOND THE LIMITS.
BUT I CAN'T.
KRAAAAK
TIME SLOWS DOWN.
MY EARS CAN ONLY HEAR THE RINGING.
AND I KNOW I'M DEAD.
I CAN BARELY HEAR SONYA SHOUTING.
BARELY MAKE OUT HER MEANING.
BUT AS SHE SCREAMS IT OVER AND OVER, THE WORD BECOMES CLEAR.
"SHADE."

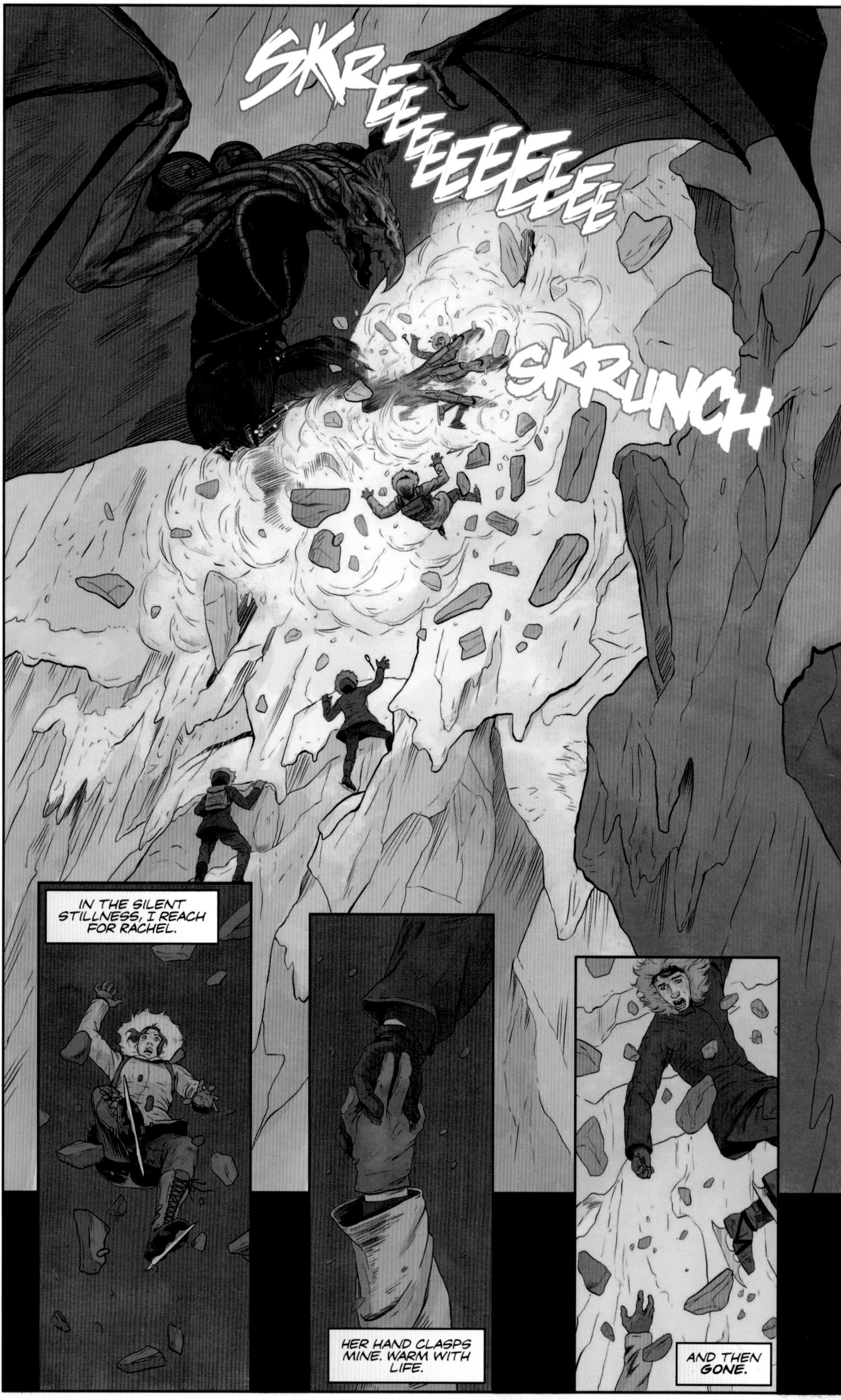
SKREEEEEEEEEEEE
SKRUNCH
IN THE SILENT STILLNESS, I REACH FOR RACHEL.
HER HAND CLASPS MINE. WARM WITH LIFE.
AND THEN GONE.

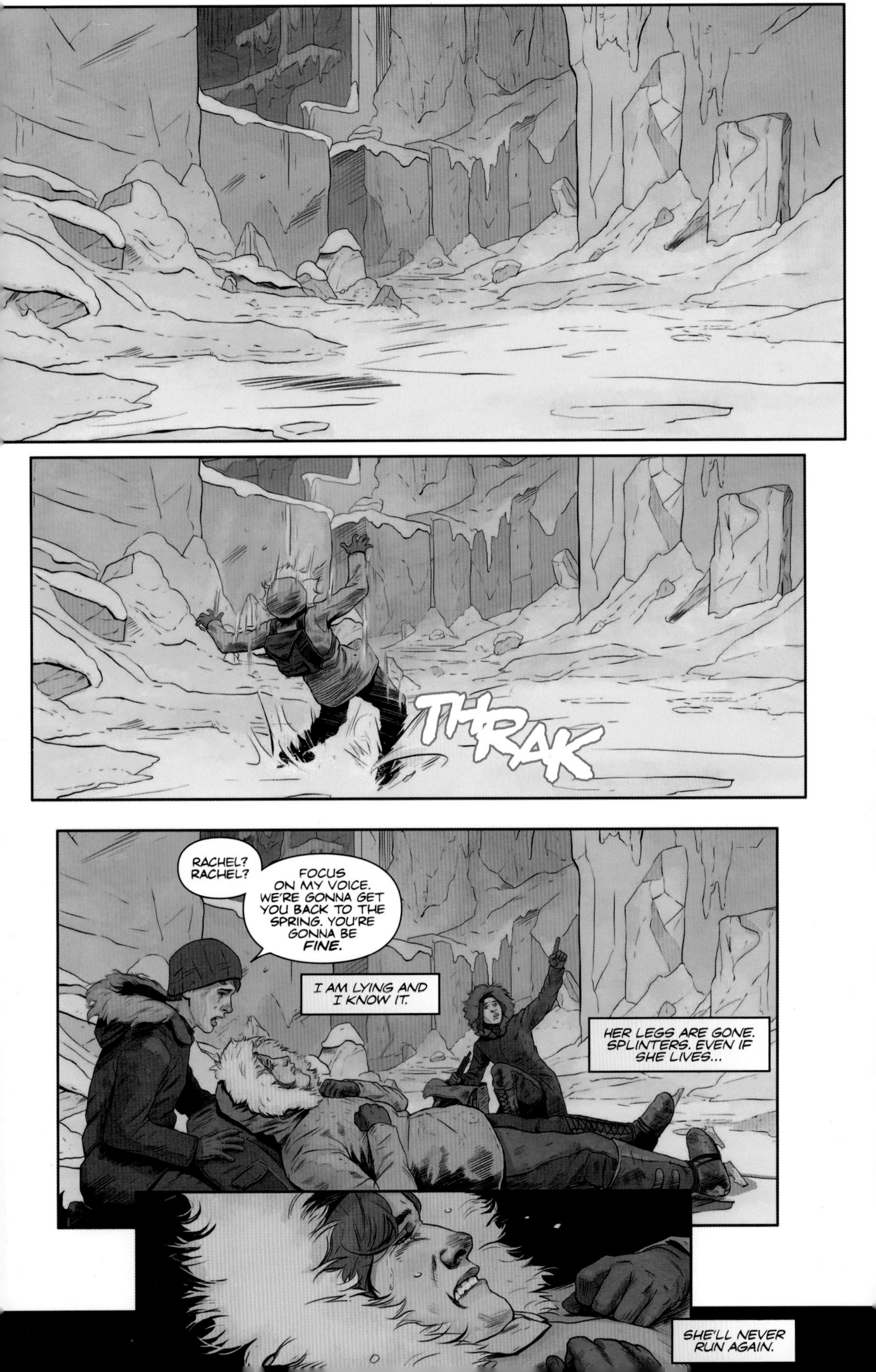
THRAK
RACHEL? RACHEL?
FOCUS ON MY VOICE. WE'RE GONNA GET YOU BACK TO THE SPRING. YOU'RE GONNA BE FINE.
I AM LYING AND I KNOW IT.
HER LEGS ARE GONE. SPLINTERS. EVEN IF SHE LIVES...
SHE'LL NEVER RUN AGAIN.

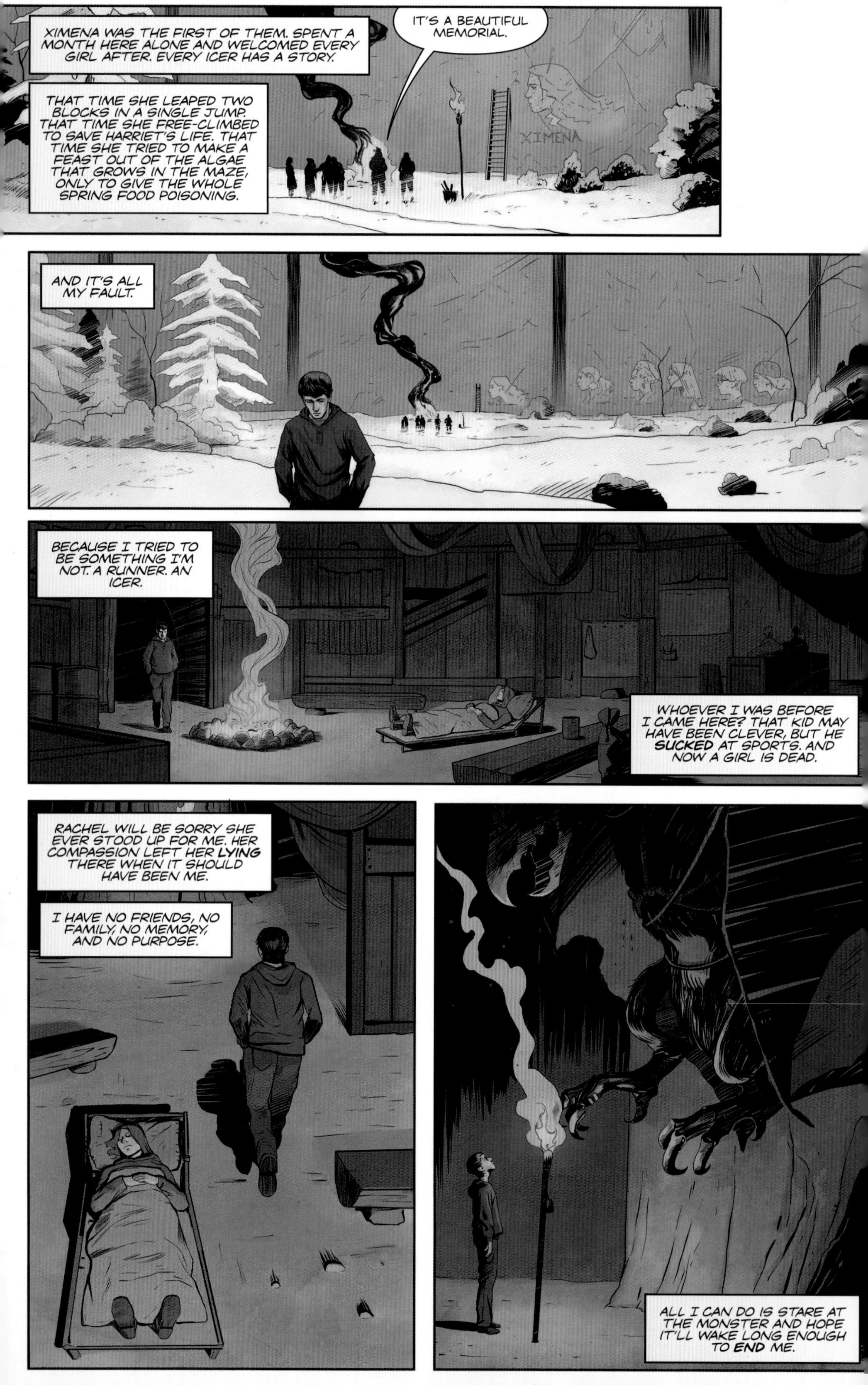
XIMENA WAS THE FIRST OF THEM. SPENT A MONTH HERE ALONE AND WELCOMED EVERY GIRL AFTER. EVERY ICER HAS A STORY.
IT'S A BEAUTIFUL MEMORIAL.
THAT TIME SHE LEAPED TWO BLOCKS IN A SINGLE JUMP. THAT TIME SHE FREE-CLIMBED TO SAVE HARRIET'S LIFE. THAT TIME SHE TRIED TO MAKE A FEAST OUT OF THE ALGAE THAT GROWS IN THE MAZE, ONLY TO GIVE THE WHOLE SPRING FOOD POISONING.
XIMENA
AND IT'S ALL MY FAULT.
BECAUSE I TRIED TO BE SOMETHING I'M NOT. A RUNNER. AN ICER.
WHOEVER I WAS BEFORE I CAME HERE? THAT KID MAY HAVE BEEN CLEVER, BUT HE **SUCKED** AT SPORTS. AND NOW A GIRL IS DEAD.
RACHEL WILL BE SORRY SHE EVER STOOD UP FOR ME. HER COMPASSION LEFT HER **LYING** THERE WHEN IT SHOULD HAVE BEEN ME.
I HAVE NO FRIENDS, NO FAMILY, NO MEMORY, AND NO PURPOSE.
ALL I CAN DO IS STARE AT THE MONSTER AND HOPE IT'LL WAKE LONG ENOUGH TO **END** ME.

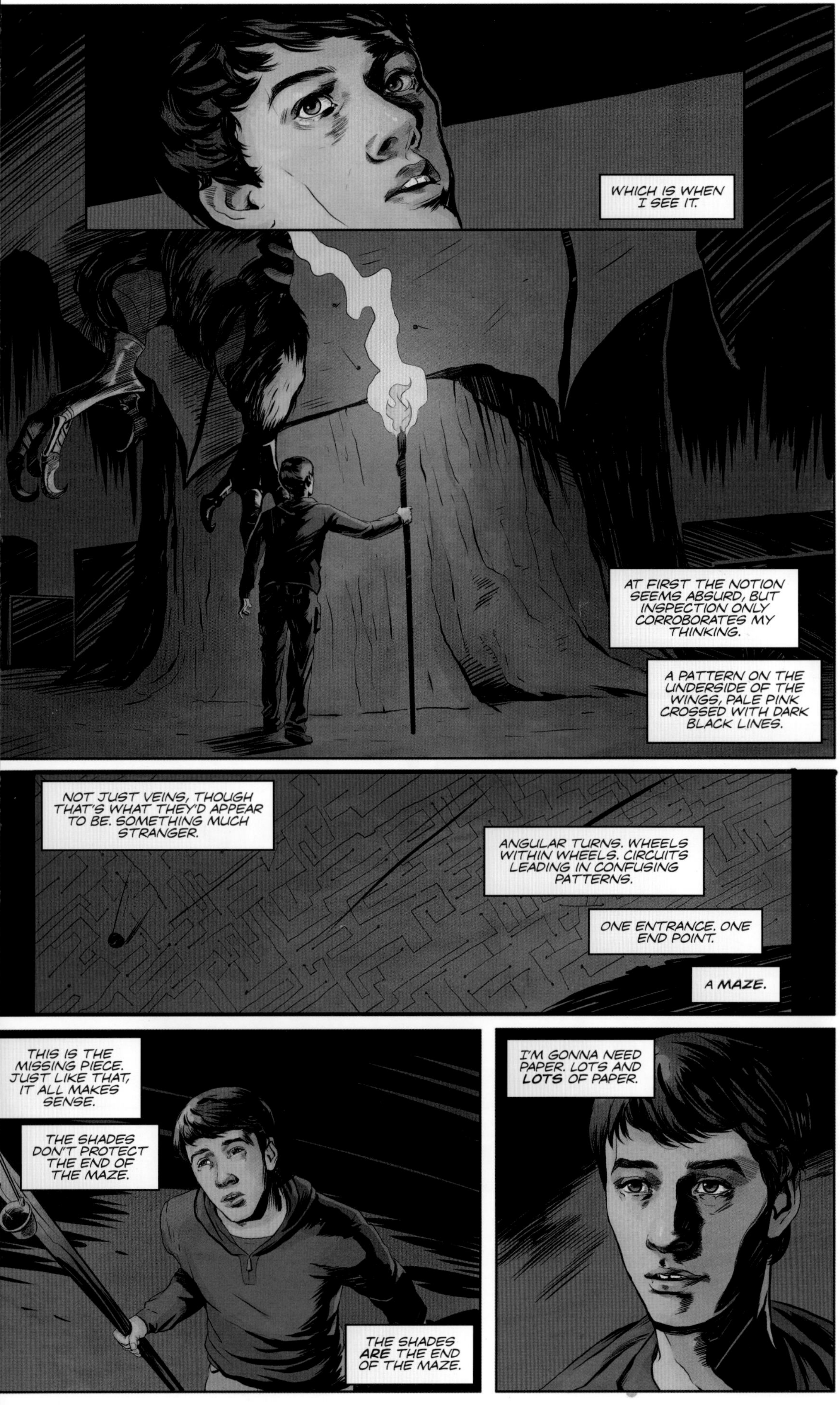
WHICH IS WHEN I SEE IT.
AT FIRST THE NOTION SEEMS ABSURD, BUT INSPECTION ONLY CORROBORATES MY THINKING.
A PATTERN ON THE UNDERSIDE OF THE WINGS, PALE PINK CROSSED WITH DARK BLACK LINES.
NOT JUST VEINS, THOUGH THAT'S WHAT THEY'D APPEAR TO BE. SOMETHING MUCH STRANGER.
ANGULAR TURNS. WHEELS WITHIN WHEELS. CIRCUITS LEADING IN CONFUSING PATTERNS.
ONE ENTRANCE. ONE END POINT.
A **MAZE.**
THIS IS THE MISSING PIECE. JUST LIKE THAT, IT ALL MAKES SENSE.
THE SHADES DON'T PROTECT THE END OF THE MAZE.
THE SHADES **ARE** THE END OF THE MAZE.
I'M GONNA NEED PAPER. LOTS AND **LOTS** OF PAPER.

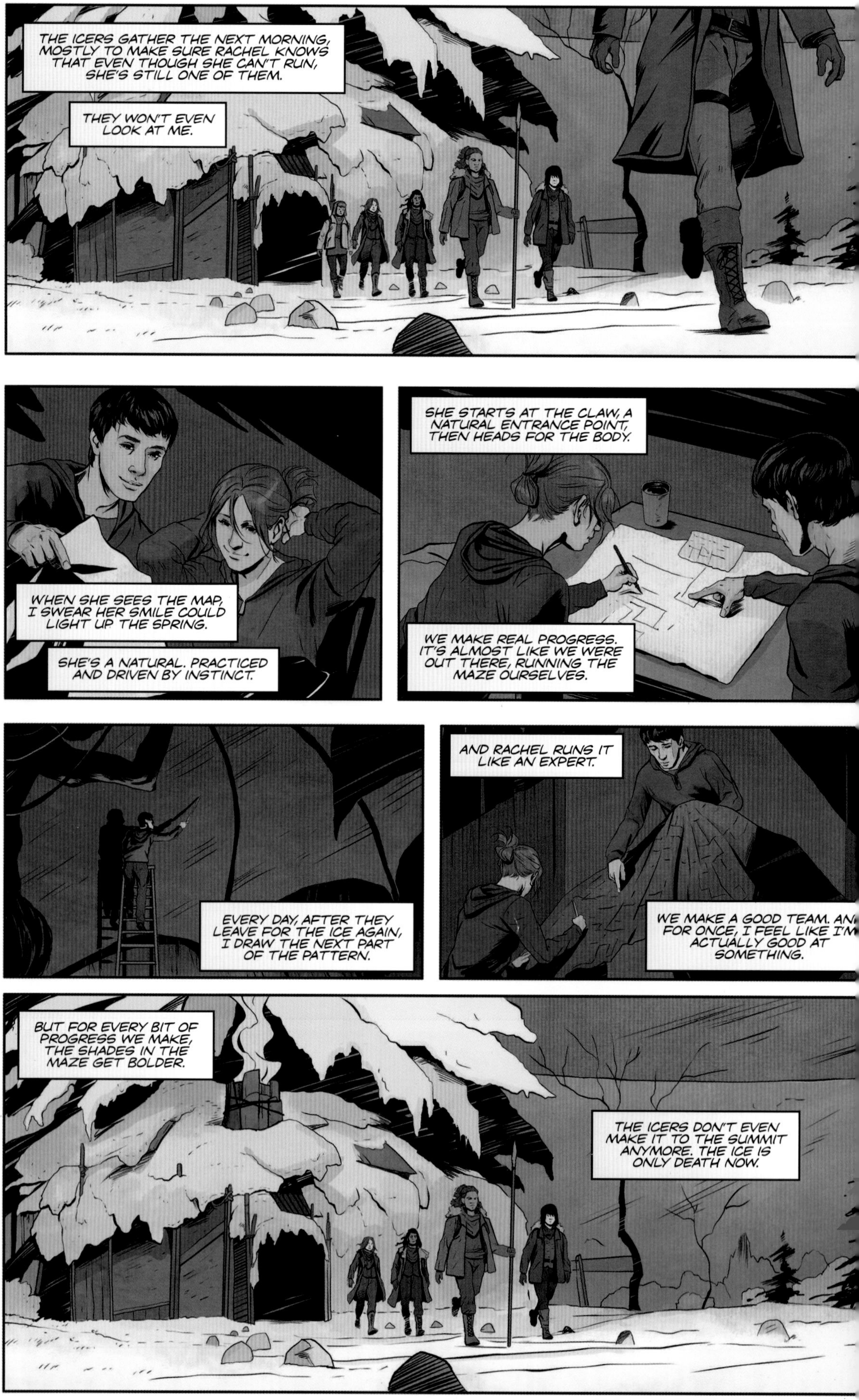
THE ICERS GATHER THE NEXT MORNING, MOSTLY TO MAKE SURE RACHEL KNOWS THAT EVEN THOUGH SHE CAN'T RUN, SHE'S STILL ONE OF THEM.
THEY WON'T EVEN LOOK AT ME.
WHEN SHE SEES THE MAP, I SWEAR HER SMILE COULD LIGHT UP THE SPRING.
SHE'S A NATURAL. PRACTICED AND DRIVEN BY INSTINCT.
SHE STARTS AT THE CLAW, A NATURAL ENTRANCE POINT, THEN HEADS FOR THE BODY.
WE MAKE REAL PROGRESS. IT'S ALMOST LIKE WE WERE OUT THERE, RUNNING THE MAZE OURSELVES.
EVERY DAY, AFTER THEY LEAVE FOR THE ICE AGAIN, I DRAW THE NEXT PART OF THE PATTERN.
AND RACHEL RUNS IT LIKE AN EXPERT.
WE MAKE A GOOD TEAM. AN
FOR ONCE, I FEEL LIKE I'M
ACTUALLY GOOD AT SOMETHING.
BUT FOR EVERY BIT OF PROGRESS WE MAKE, THE SHADES IN THE MAZE GET BOLDER.
THE ICERS DON'T EVEN MAKE IT TO THE SUMMIT ANYMORE. THE ICE IS ONLY DEATH NOW.

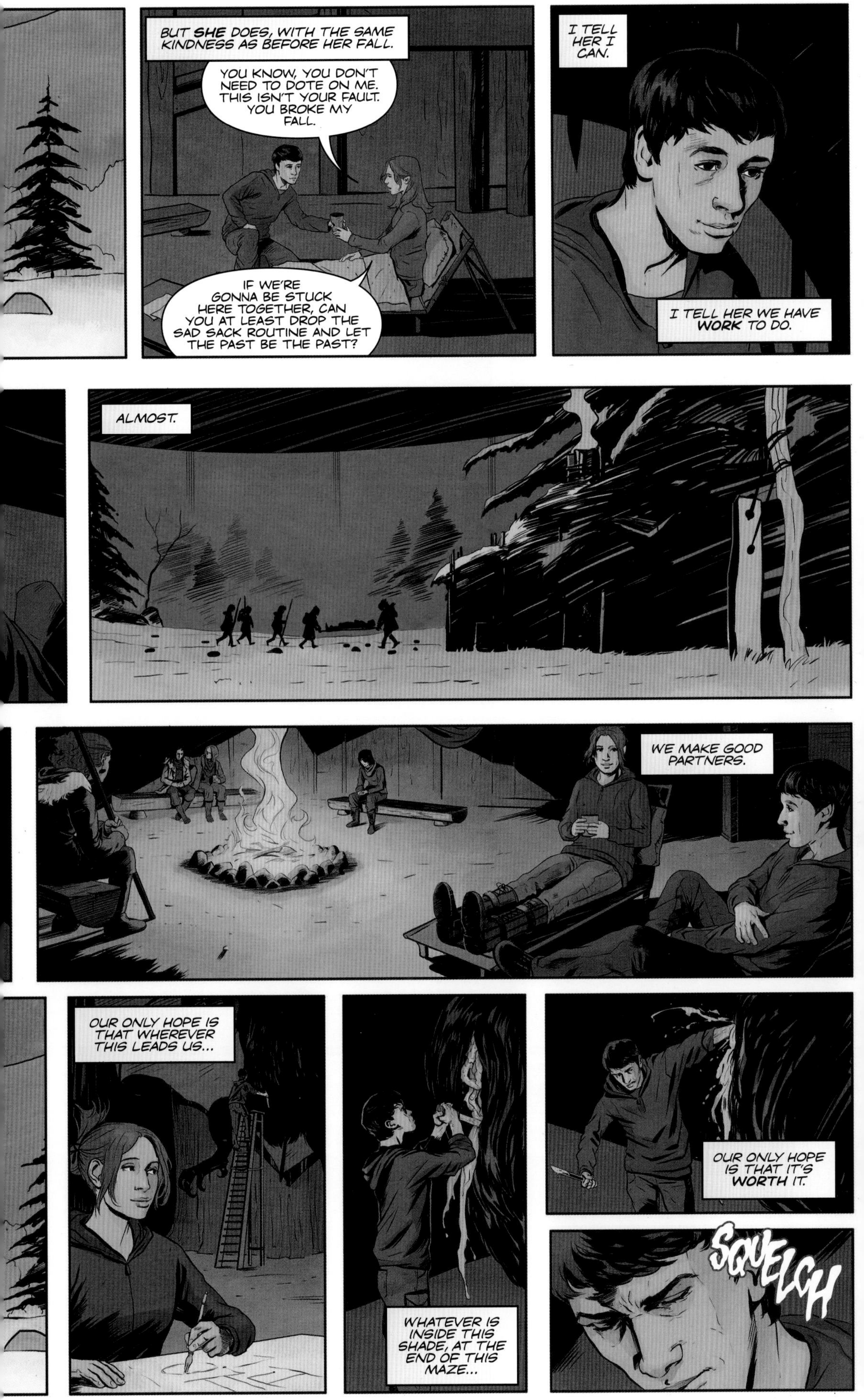

BUT SHE DOES, WITH THE SAME KINDNESS AS BEFORE HER FALL.
YOU KNOW, YOU DON'T NEED TO DOTE ON ME. THIS ISN'T YOUR FAULT. YOU BROKE MY FALL.
IF WE'RE GONNA BE STUCK HERE TOGETHER, CAN YOU AT LEAST DROP THE SAD SACK ROUTINE AND LET THE PAST BE THE PAST?
I TELL HER I CAN.
I TELL HER WE HAVE WORK TO DO.
ALMOST.
WE MAKE GOOD PARTNERS.
OUR ONLY HOPE IS THAT WHEREVER THIS LEADS US...
WHATEVER IS INSIDE THIS SHADE, AT THE END OF THIS MAZE...
OUR ONLY HOPE IS THAT IT'S WORTH IT.
SQUELCH

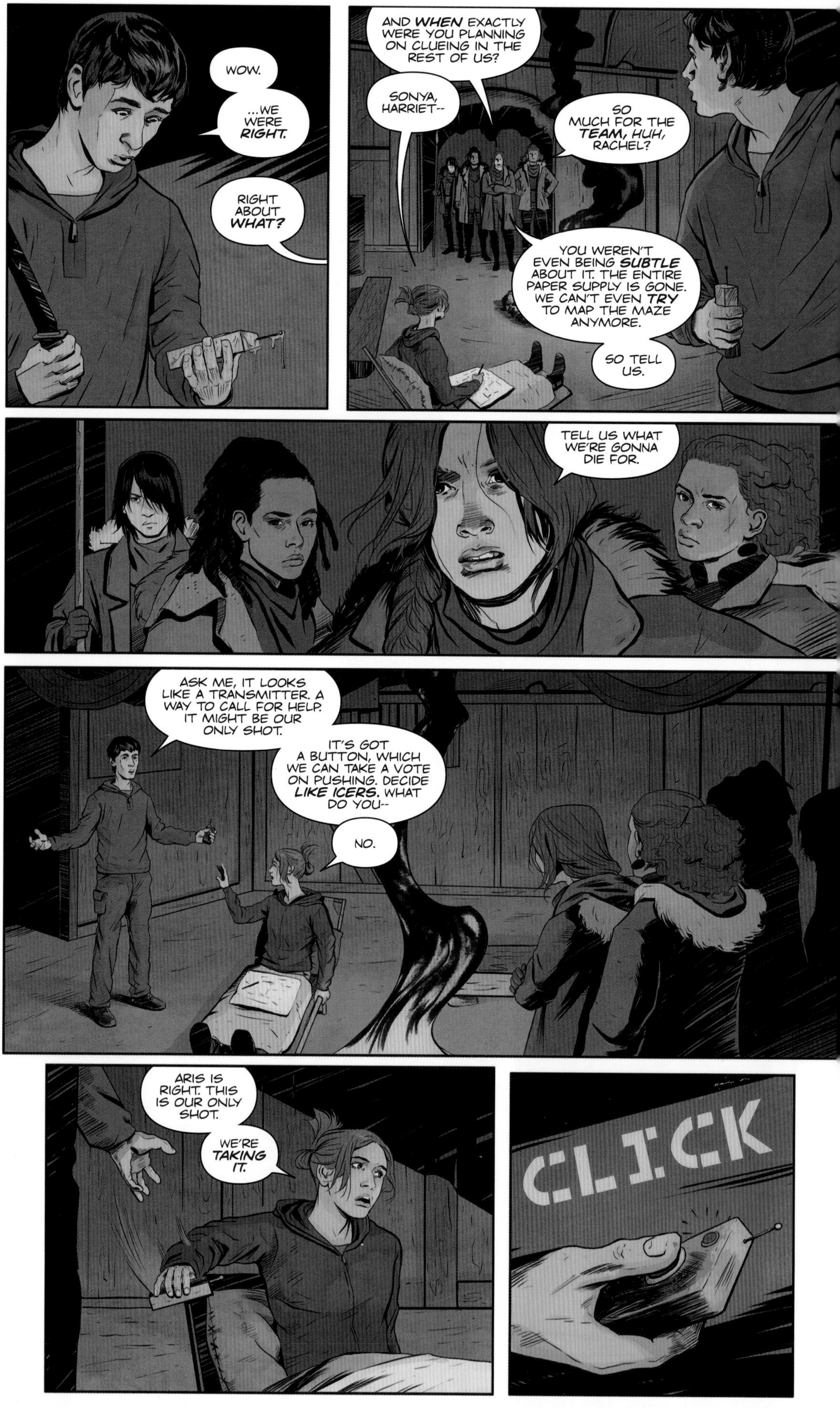

WOW.
...WE WERE RIGHT.
RIGHT ABOUT WHAT?
AND WHEN EXACTLY WERE YOU PLANNING ON CLUEING IN THE REST OF US?
SONYA, HARRIET--
SO MUCH FOR THE TEAM, HUH, RACHEL?
YOU WEREN'T EVEN BEING SUBTLE ABOUT IT. THE ENTIRE PAPER SUPPLY IS GONE. WE CAN'T EVEN TRY TO MAP THE MAZE ANYMORE.
SO TELL US.
TELL US WHAT WE'RE GONNA DIE FOR.
ASK ME, IT LOOKS LIKE A TRANSMITTER. A WAY TO CALL FOR HELP. IT MIGHT BE OUR ONLY SHOT.
IT'S GOT A BUTTON, WHICH WE CAN TAKE A VOTE ON PUSHING. DECIDE LIKE ICERS. WHAT DO YOU--
NO.
ARIS IS RIGHT. THIS IS OUR ONLY SHOT.
WE'RE TAKING IT.
CLICK

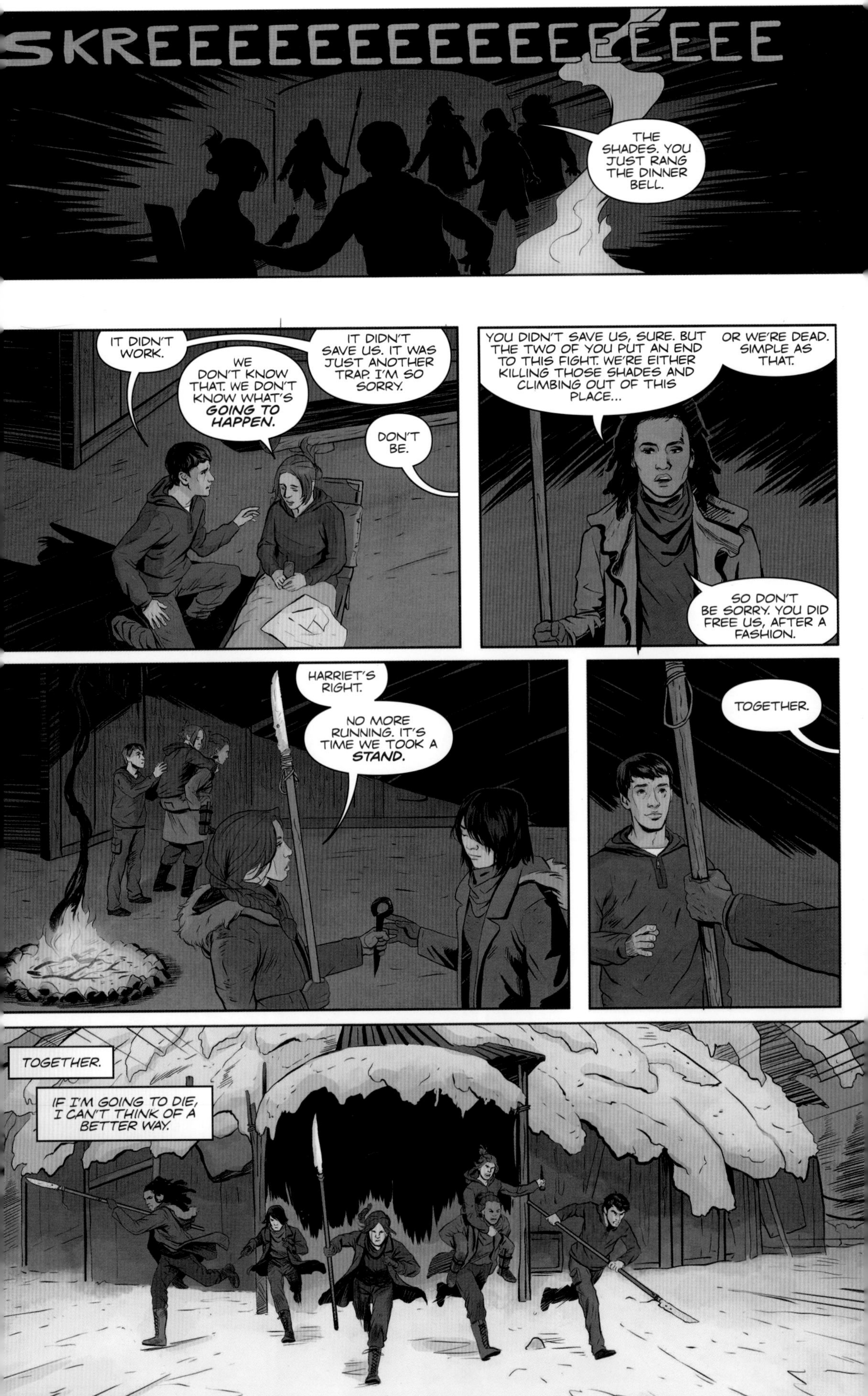
SKREEEEEEEEEEEEEEEEE
THE SHADES. YOU JUST RANG THE DINNER BELL.
IT DIDN'T WORK.
WE DON'T KNOW THAT. WE DON'T KNOW WHAT'S GOING TO HAPPEN.
IT DIDN'T SAVE US. IT WAS JUST ANOTHER TRAP. I'M SO SORRY.
DON'T BE.
YOU DIDN'T SAVE US, SURE. BUT THE TWO OF YOU PUT AN END TO THIS FIGHT. WE'RE EITHER KILLING THOSE SHADES AND CLIMBING OUT OF THIS PLACE...
OR WE'RE DEAD. SIMPLE AS THAT.
SO DON'T BE SORRY. YOU DID FREE US, AFTER A FASHION.
HARRIET'S RIGHT.
NO MORE RUNNING. IT'S TIME WE TOOK A STAND.
TOGETHER.
TOGETHER.
IF I'M GOING TO DIE, I CAN'T THINK OF A BETTER WAY.

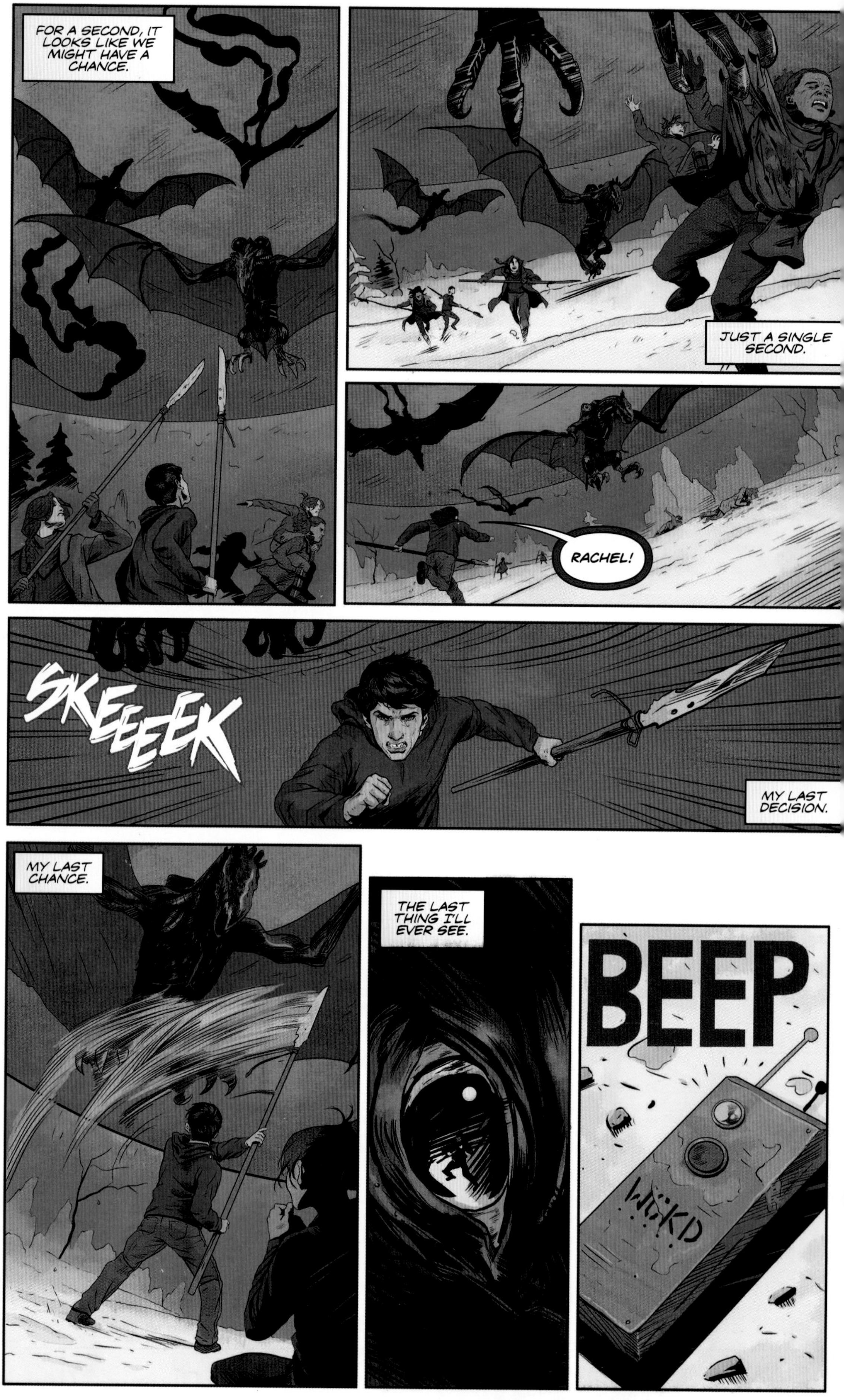
FOR A SECOND, IT LOOKS LIKE WE MIGHT HAVE A CHANCE.
JUST A SINGLE SECOND.
RACHEL!
SKEEEEEK
MY LAST DECISION.
MY LAST CHANCE.
THE LAST THING I'LL EVER SEE.
BEEP

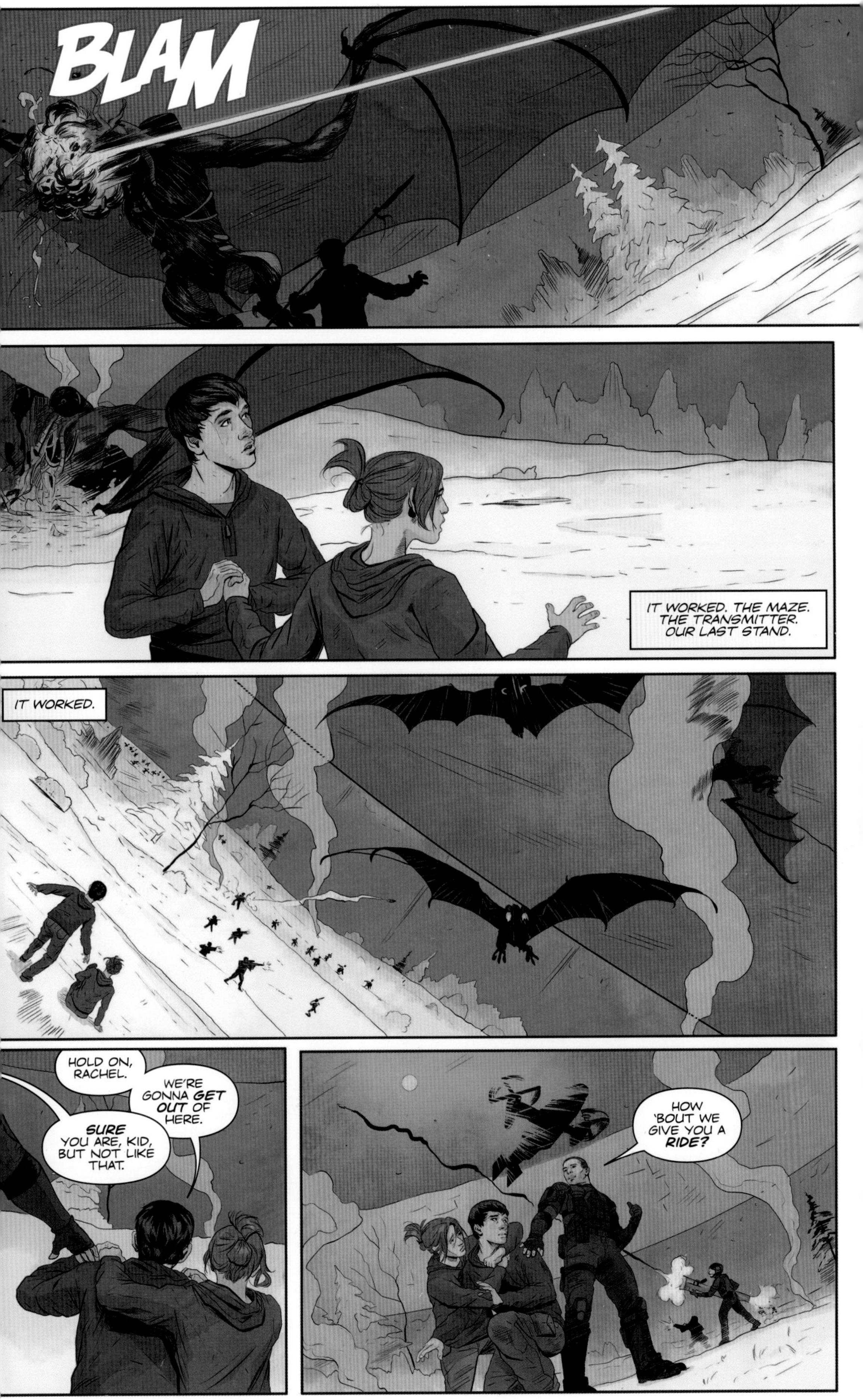
BLAM
IT WORKED. THE MAZE. THE TRANSMITTER. OUR LAST STAND.
IT WORKED.
HOLD ON, RACHEL.
WE'RE GONNA GET OUT OF HERE.
SURE YOU ARE, KID, BUT NOT LIKE THAT.
HOW 'BOUT WE GIVE YOU A RIDE?

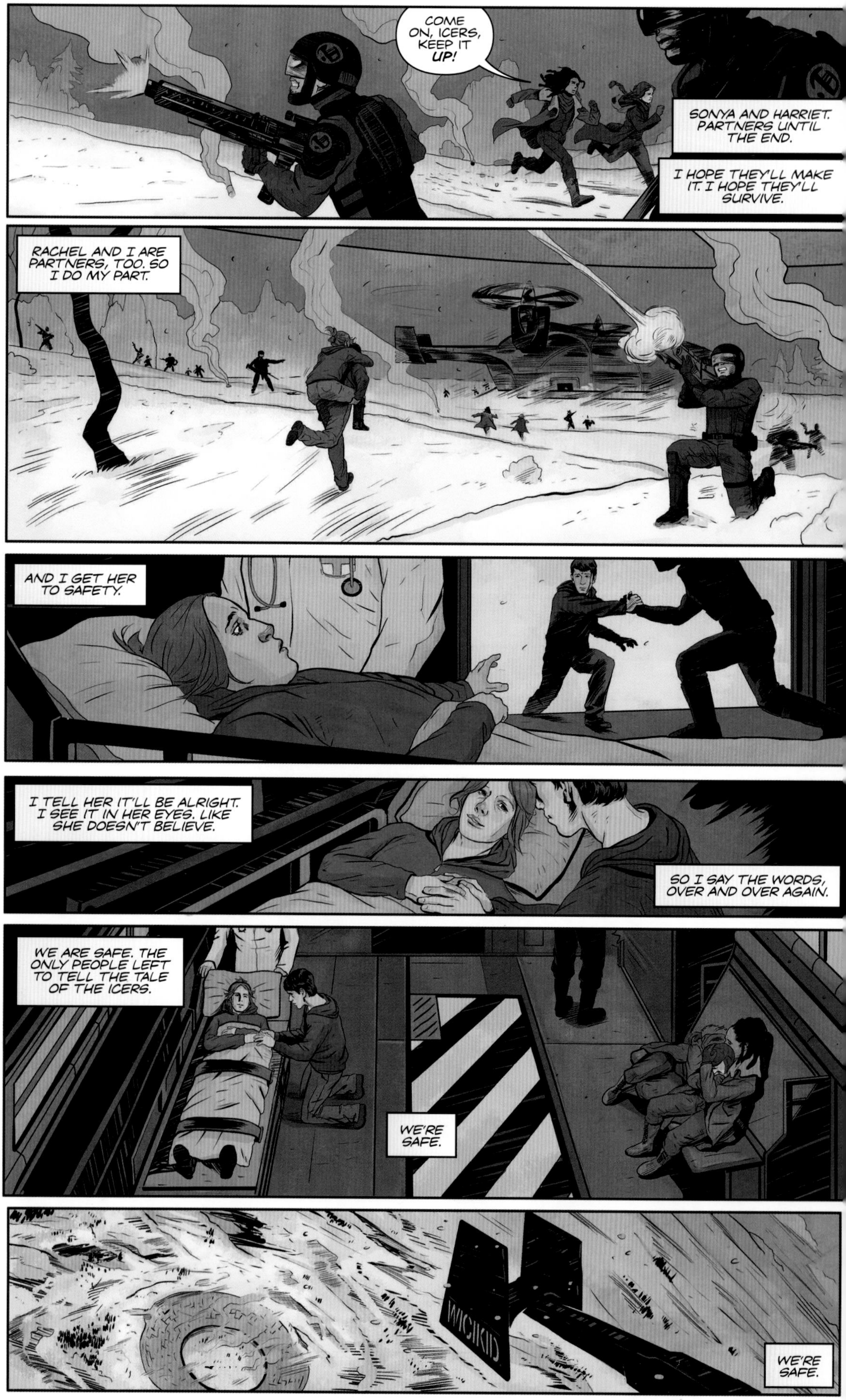
COME ON, ICERS, KEEP IT UP!
SONYA AND HARRIET. PARTNERS UNTIL THE END.
I HOPE THEY'LL MAKE IT. I HOPE THEY'LL SURVIVE.
RACHEL AND I ARE PARTNERS, TOO. SO I DO MY PART.
AND I GET HER TO SAFETY.
I TELL HER IT'LL BE ALRIGHT. I SEE IT IN HER EYES. LIKE SHE DOESN'T BELIEVE.
SO I SAY THE WORDS, OVER AND OVER AGAIN.
WE ARE SAFE. THE ONLY PEOPLE LEFT TO TELL THE TALE OF THE ICERS.
WE'RE SAFE.
WE'RE SAFE.

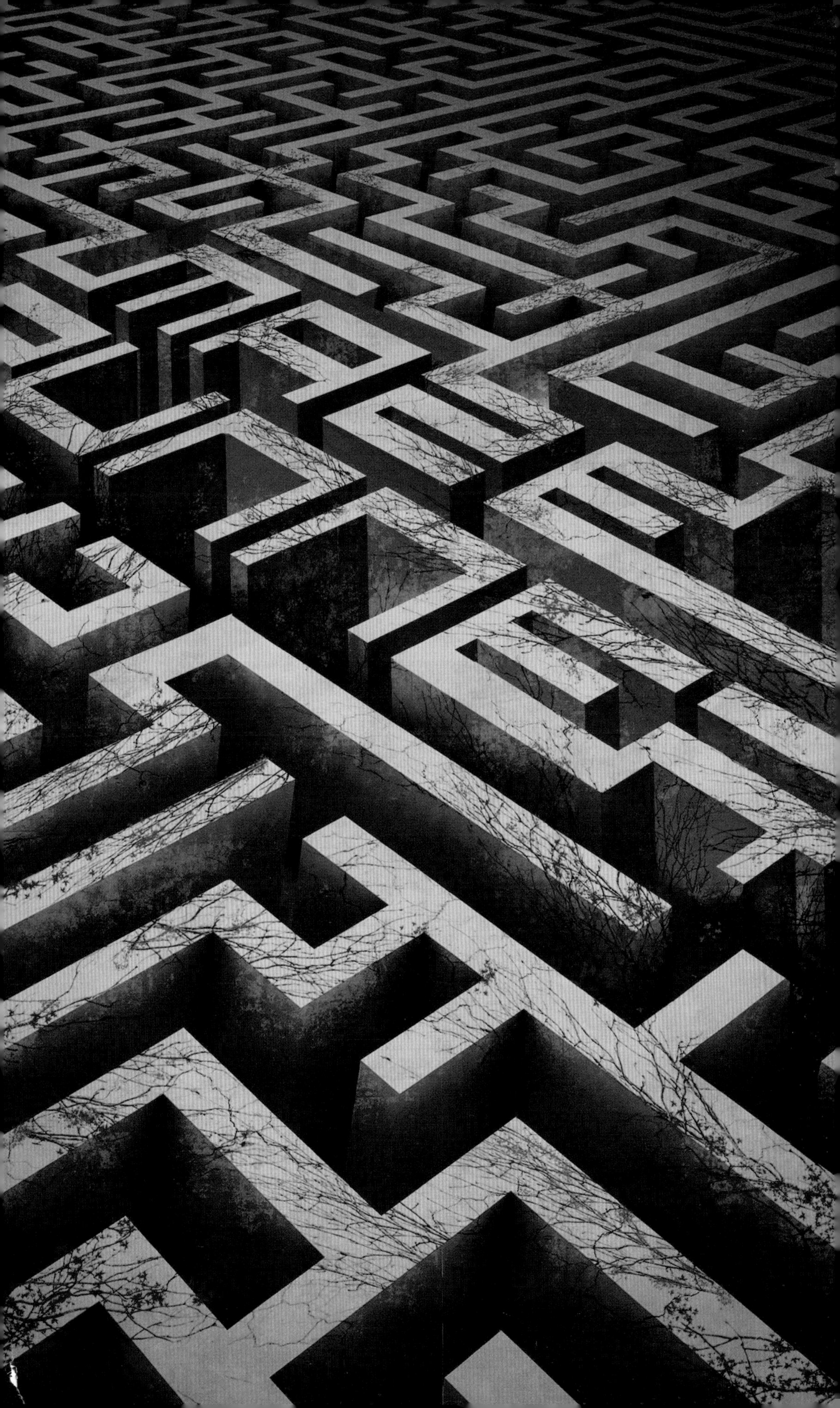

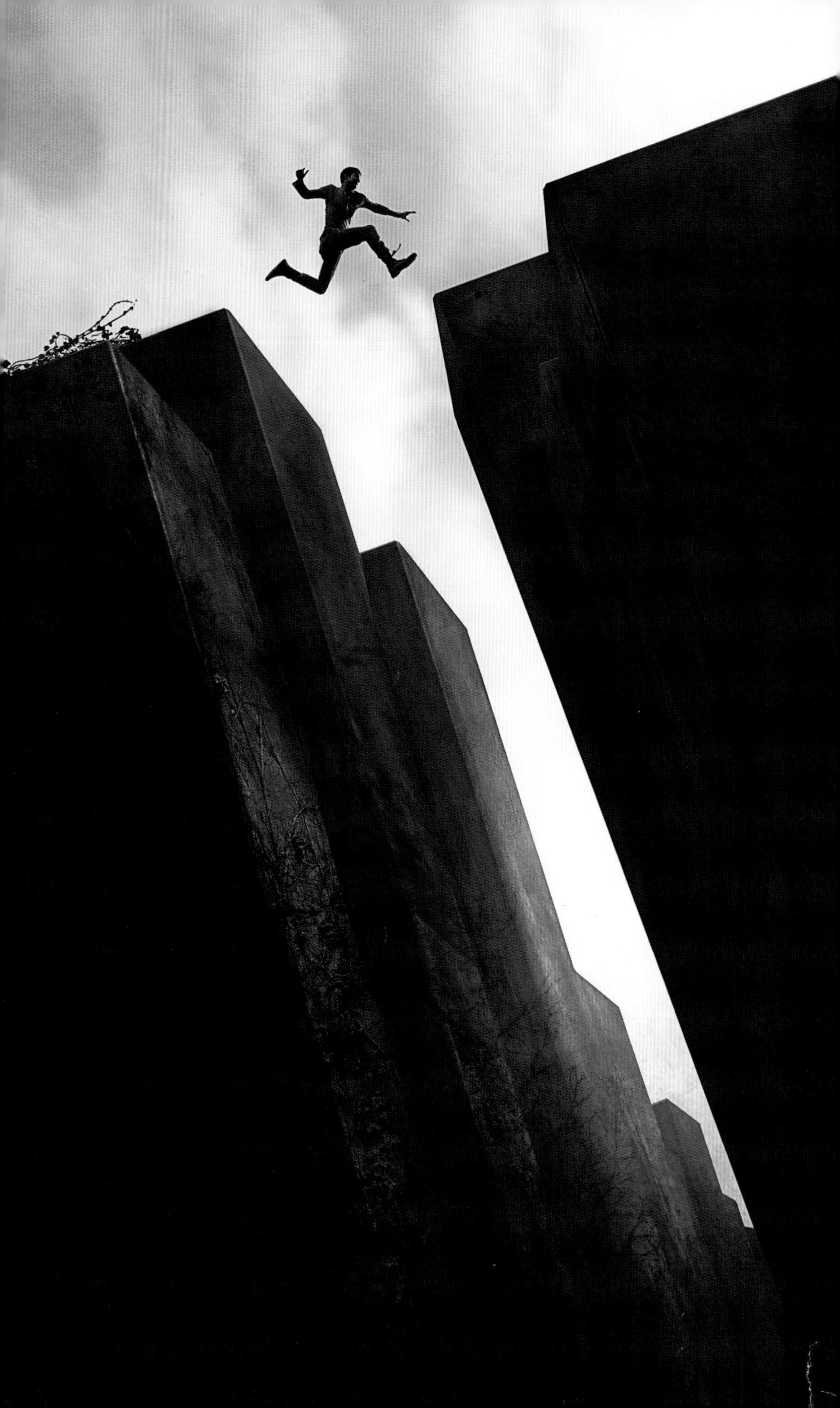

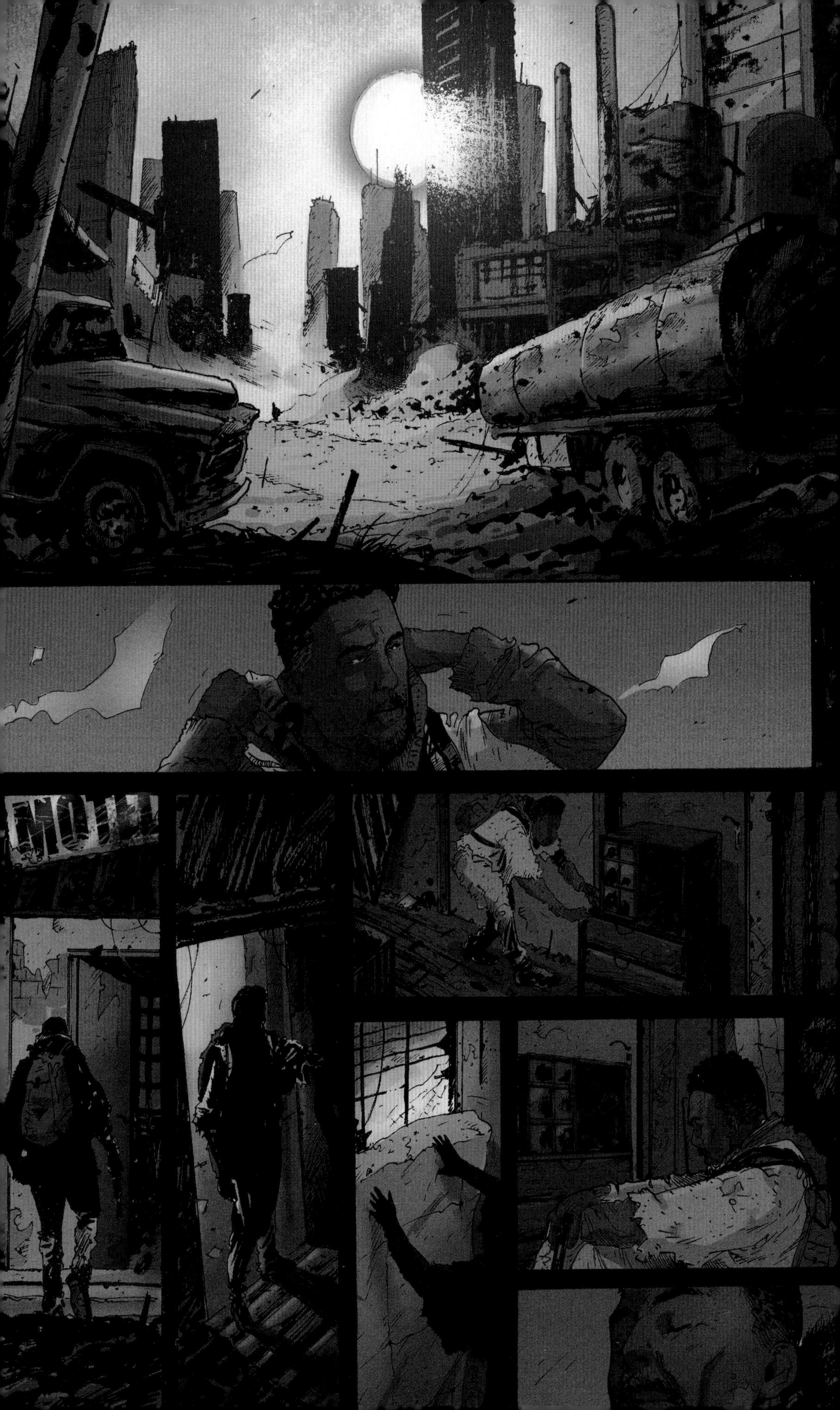
MO

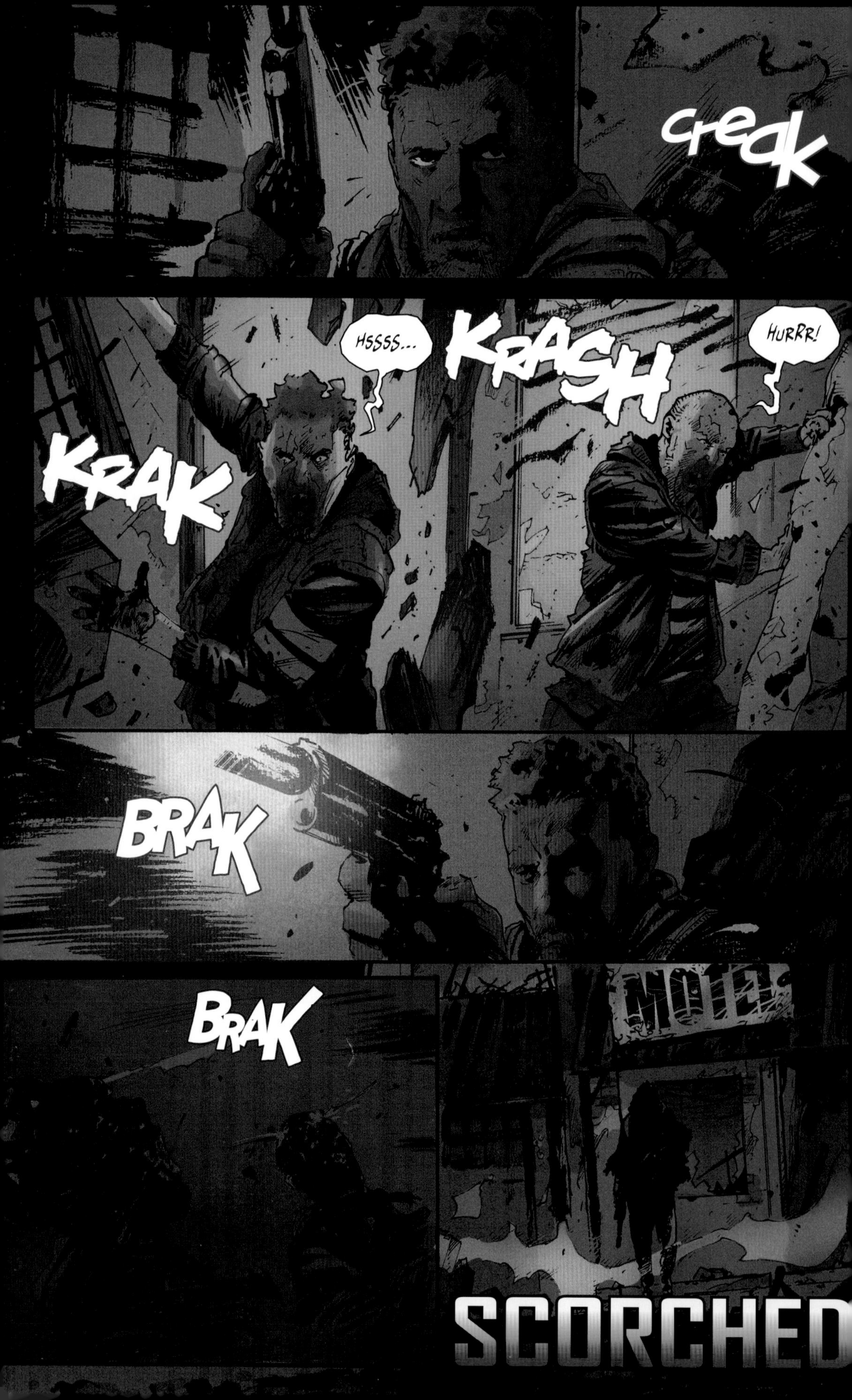
creak
KRAK
HSSSS...
KRASH
HURRR!
BRAK
BRAK
MOTEL
SCORCHED

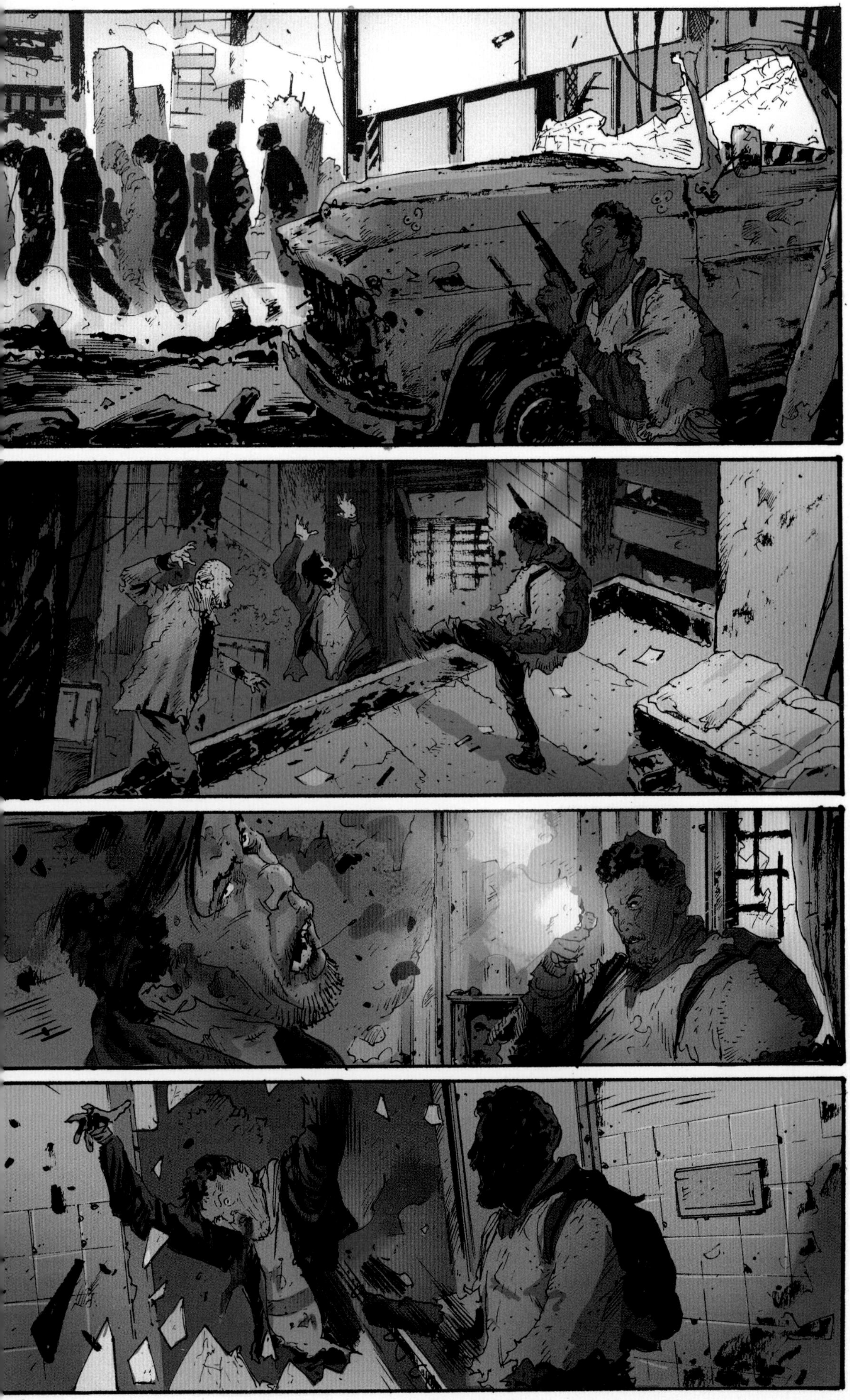

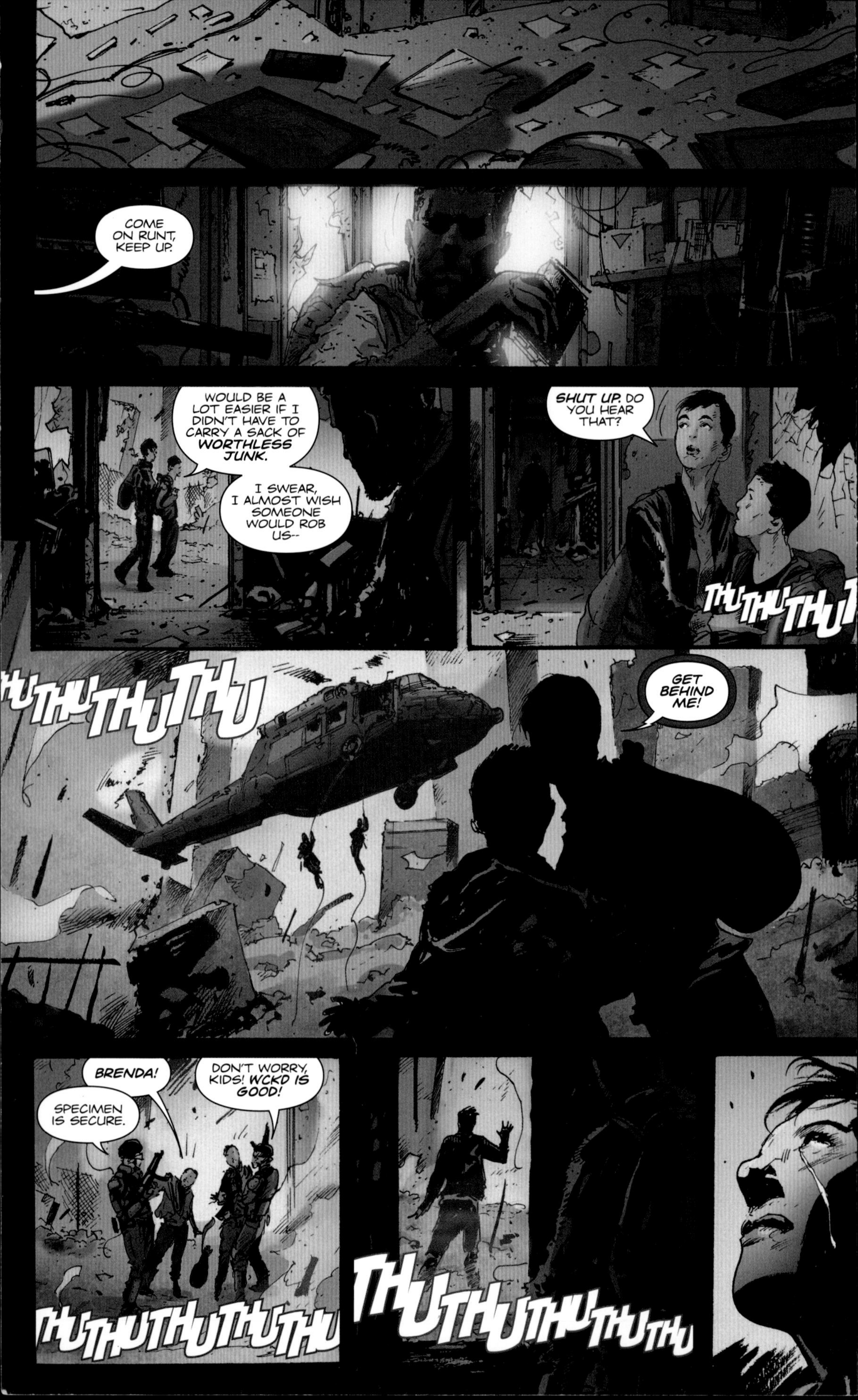
COME ON RUNT, KEEP UP.
WOULD BE A LOT EASIER IF I DIDN'T HAVE TO CARRY A SACK OF WORTHLESS JUNK.
I SWEAR, I ALMOST WISH SOMEONE WOULD ROB US--
SHUT UP. DO YOU HEAR THAT?
THUTHUTHU
THUTHUTHUTHU
GET BEHIND ME!
BRENDA!
SPECIMEN IS SECURE.
DON'T WORRY, KIDS! WCKD IS GOOD!
THUTHUTHUTHUTHU
THUTHUTHUTHUTHU

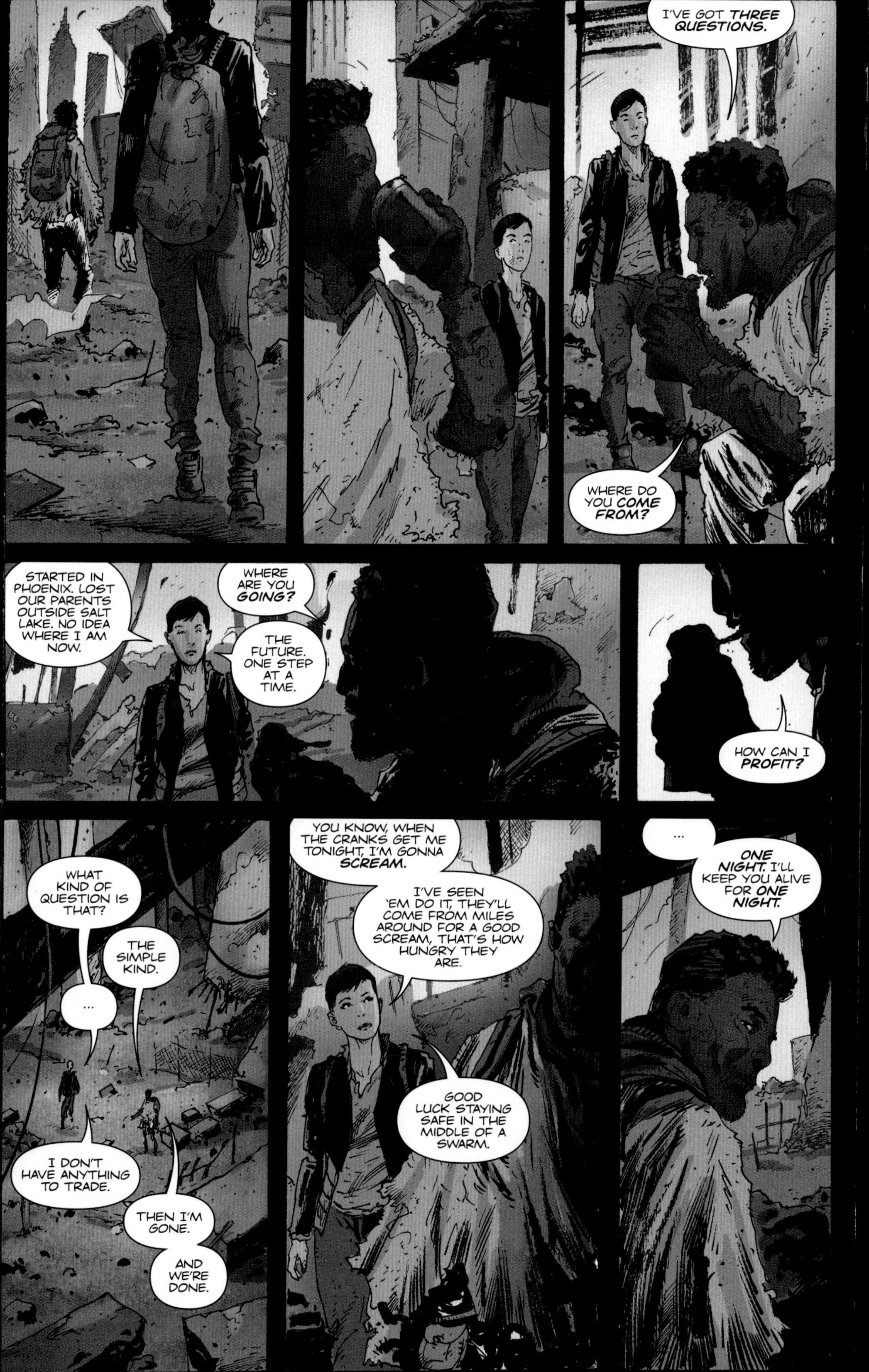
I'VE GOT THREE QUESTIONS.
WHERE DO YOU COME FROM?
STARTED IN PHOENIX. LOST OUR PARENTS OUTSIDE SALT LAKE. NO IDEA WHERE I AM NOW.
WHERE ARE YOU GOING?
THE FUTURE. ONE STEP AT A TIME.
HOW CAN I PROFIT?
WHAT KIND OF QUESTION IS THAT?
THE SIMPLE KIND.
...
I DON'T HAVE ANYTHING TO TRADE.
THEN I'M GONE.
AND WE'RE DONE.
YOU KNOW, WHEN THE CRANKS GET ME TONIGHT, I'M GONNA SCREAM.
I'VE SEEN 'EM DO IT, THEY'LL COME FROM MILES AROUND FOR A GOOD SCREAM, THAT'S HOW HUNGRY THEY ARE.
GOOD LUCK STAYING SAFE IN THE MIDDLE OF A SWARM.
...
ONE NIGHT. I'LL KEEP YOU ALIVE FOR ONE NIGHT.

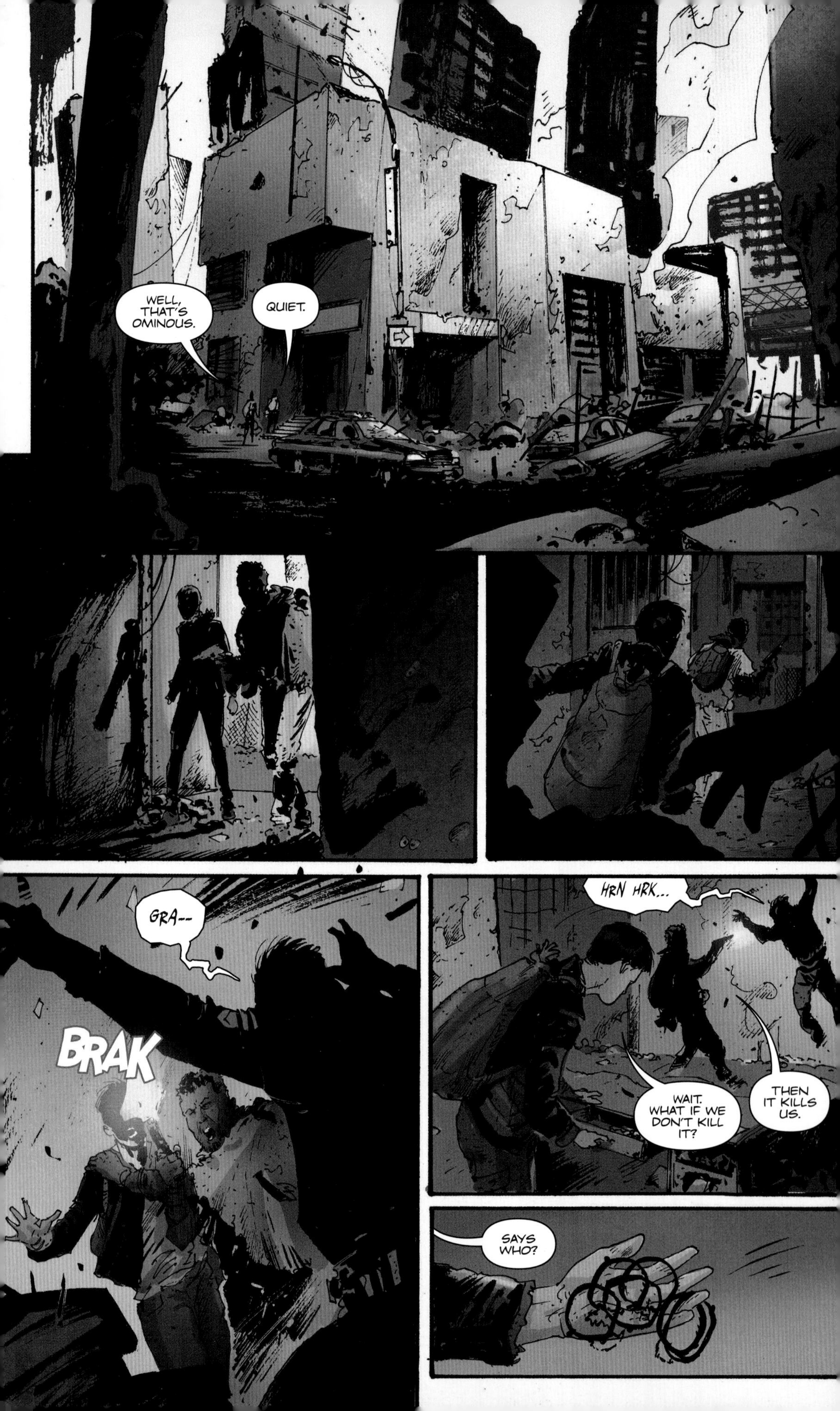
WELL, THAT'S OMINOUS.
QUIET.
GRA--
BRAK
HRN HRK...
WAIT. WHAT IF WE DON'T KILL IT?
THEN IT KILLS US.
SAYS WHO?

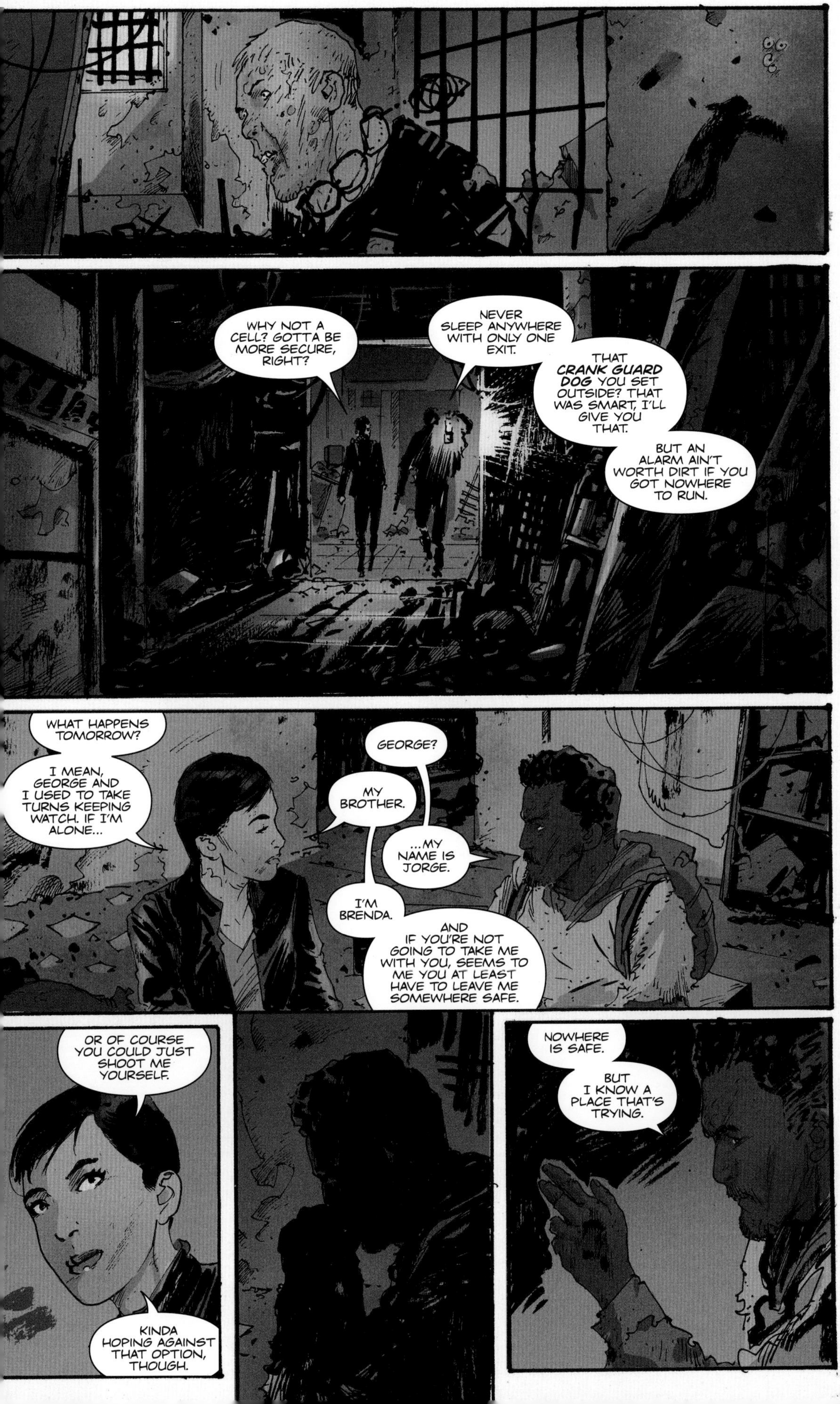
WHY NOT A CELL? GOTTA BE MORE SECURE, RIGHT?
NEVER SLEEP ANYWHERE WITH ONLY ONE EXIT.
THAT CRANK GUARD DOG YOU SET OUTSIDE? THAT WAS SMART, I'LL GIVE YOU THAT.
BUT AN ALARM AIN'T WORTH DIRT IF YOU GOT NOWHERE TO RUN.
WHAT HAPPENS TOMORROW?
I MEAN, GEORGE AND I USED TO TAKE TURNS KEEPING WATCH. IF I'M ALONE...
GEORGE?
MY BROTHER.
...MY NAME IS JORGE.
I'M BRENDA.
AND IF YOU'RE NOT GOING TO TAKE ME WITH YOU, SEEMS TO ME YOU AT LEAST HAVE TO LEAVE ME SOMEWHERE SAFE.
OR OF COURSE YOU COULD JUST SHOOT ME YOURSELF.
KINDA HOPING AGAINST THAT OPTION, THOUGH.
NOWHERE IS SAFE.
BUT I KNOW A PLACE THAT'S TRYING.

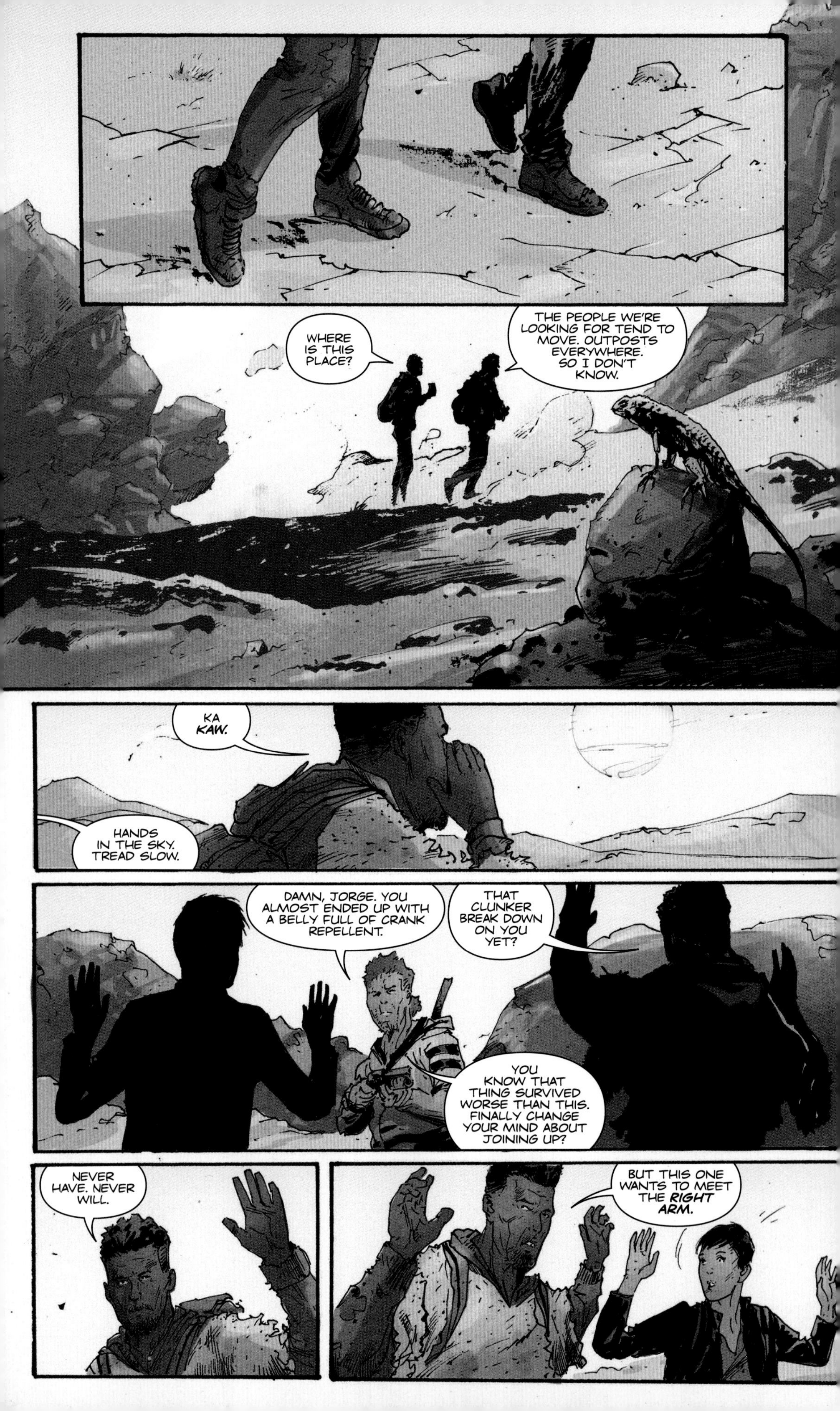
WHERE IS THIS PLACE?
THE PEOPLE WE'RE LOOKING FOR TEND TO MOVE. OUTPOSTS EVERYWHERE. SO I DON'T KNOW.
KA *KAW.*
HANDS IN THE SKY. TREAD SLOW.
DAMN, JORGE. YOU ALMOST ENDED UP WITH A BELLY FULL OF CRANK REPELLENT.
THAT CLUNKER BREAK DOWN ON YOU YET?
YOU KNOW THAT THING SURVIVED WORSE THAN THIS. FINALLY CHANGE YOUR MIND ABOUT JOINING UP?
NEVER HAVE. NEVER WILL.
BUT THIS ONE WANTS TO MEET THE ***RIGHT ARM.***

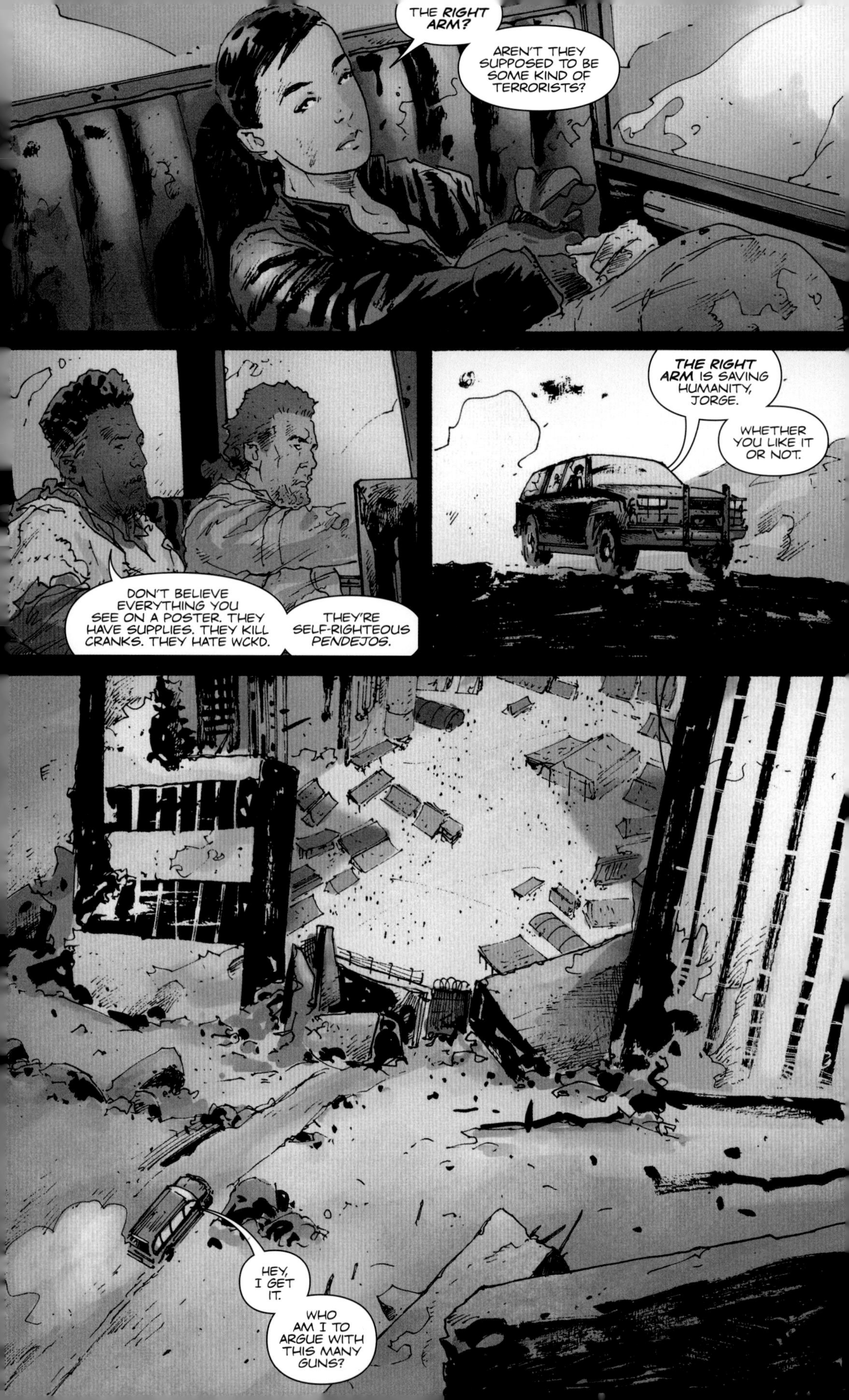
THE RIGHT ARM?
AREN'T THEY SUPPOSED TO BE SOME KIND OF TERRORISTS?
DON'T BELIEVE EVERYTHING YOU SEE ON A POSTER. THEY HAVE SUPPLIES. THEY KILL CRANKS. THEY HATE WCKD.
THEY'RE SELF-RIGHTEOUS PENDEJOS.
THE RIGHT ARM IS SAVING HUMANITY, JORGE.
WHETHER YOU LIKE IT OR NOT.
HEY, I GET IT.
WHO AM I TO ARGUE WITH THIS MANY GUNS?

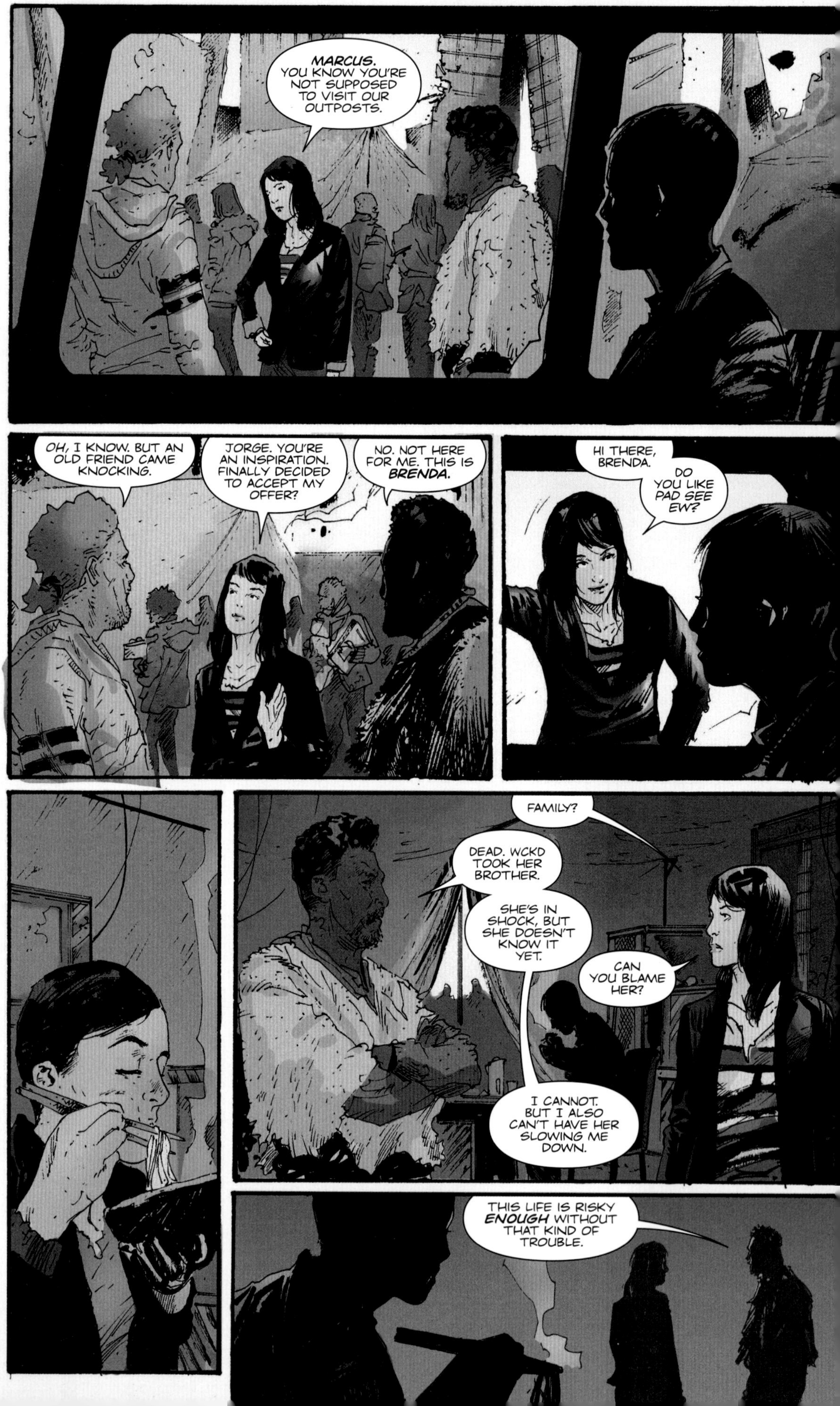

MARCUS. YOU KNOW YOU'RE NOT SUPPOSED TO VISIT OUR OUTPOSTS.
OH, I KNOW. BUT AN OLD FRIEND CAME KNOCKING.
JORGE. YOU'RE AN INSPIRATION. FINALLY DECIDED TO ACCEPT MY OFFER?
NO. NOT HERE FOR ME. THIS IS BRENDA.
HI THERE, BRENDA.
DO YOU LIKE PAD SEE EW?
FAMILY?
DEAD. WCKD TOOK HER BROTHER.
SHE'S IN SHOCK, BUT SHE DOESN'T KNOW IT YET.
CAN YOU BLAME HER?
I CANNOT. BUT I ALSO CAN'T HAVE HER SLOWING ME DOWN.
THIS LIFE IS RISKY ENOUGH WITHOUT THAT KIND OF TROUBLE.

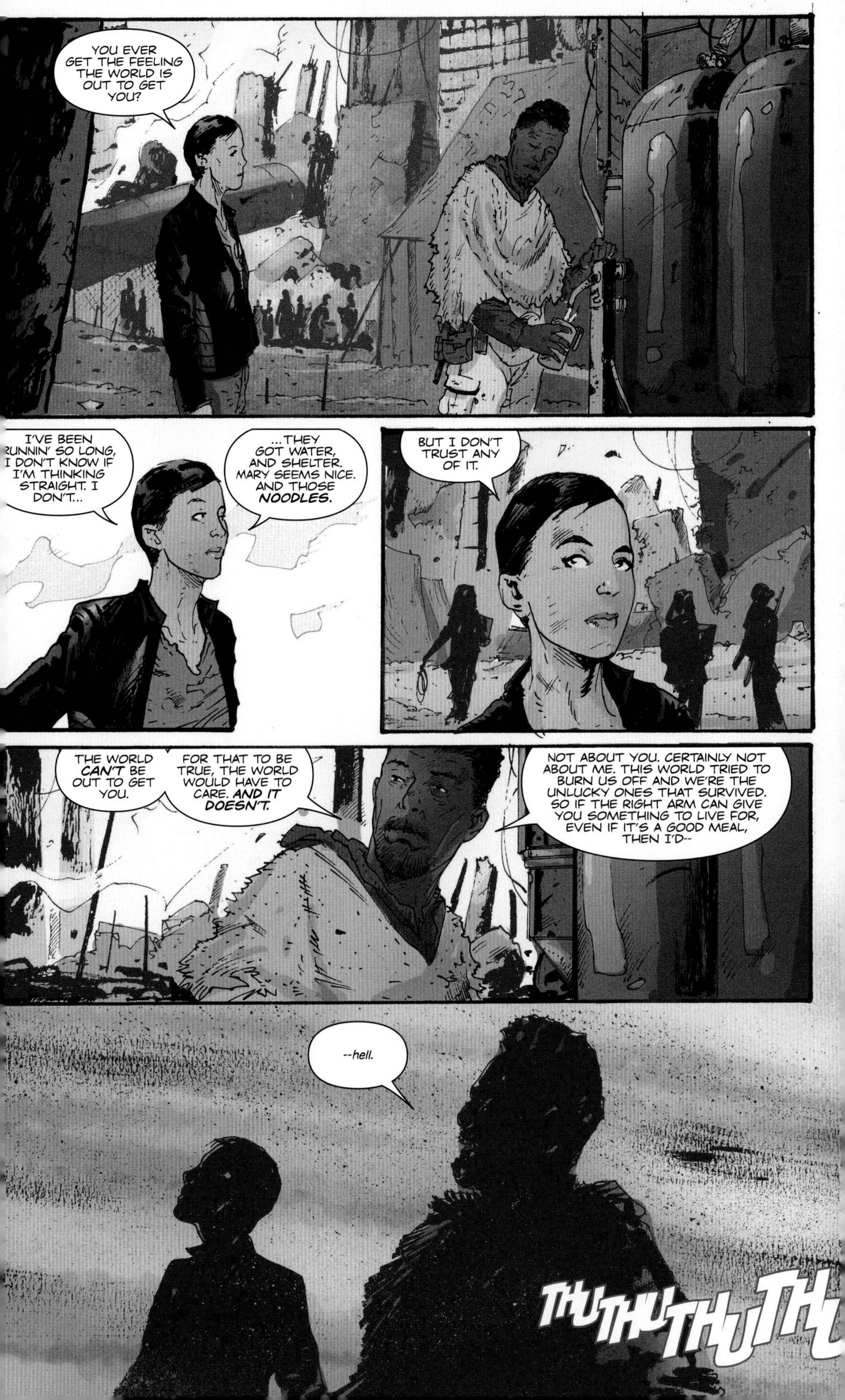

YOU EVER GET THE FEELING THE WORLD IS OUT TO GET YOU?
I'VE BEEN RUNNIN' SO LONG, I DON'T KNOW IF I'M THINKING STRAIGHT. I DON'T...
...THEY GOT WATER, AND SHELTER. MARY SEEMS NICE. AND THOSE **NOODLES.**
BUT I DON'T TRUST ANY OF IT.
THE WORLD ***CAN'T*** BE OUT TO GET YOU.
FOR THAT TO BE TRUE, THE WORLD WOULD HAVE TO CARE. ***AND IT DOESN'T.***
NOT ABOUT YOU. CERTAINLY NOT ABOUT ME. THIS WORLD TRIED TO BURN US OFF AND WE'RE THE UNLUCKY ONES THAT SURVIVED. SO IF THE RIGHT ARM CAN GIVE YOU SOMETHING TO LIVE FOR, EVEN IF IT'S A GOOD MEAL, THEN I'D--
--hell.
THU THU THU THU

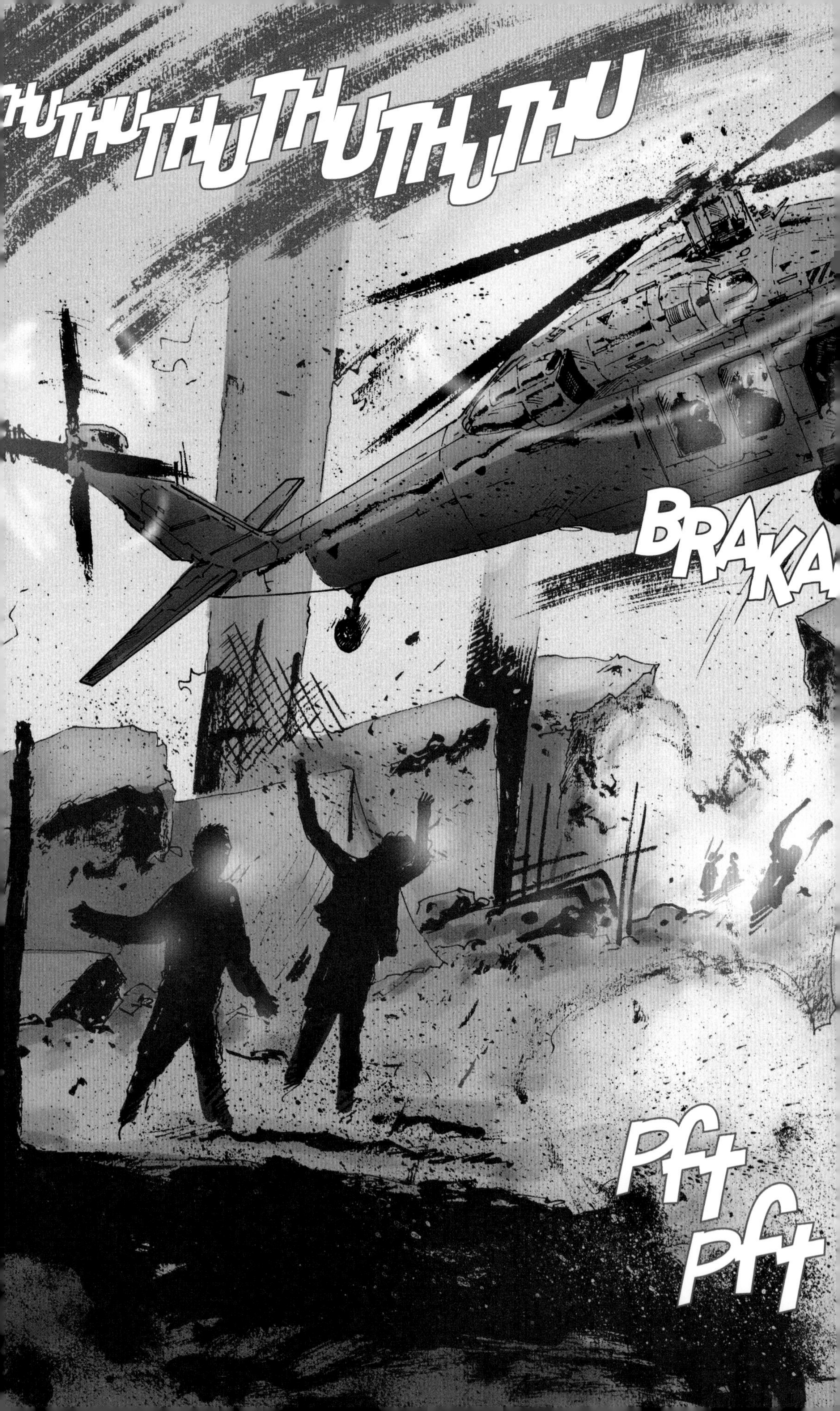
THUTHUTHUTHUTHUTHU
BRAKA
Pft
Pft

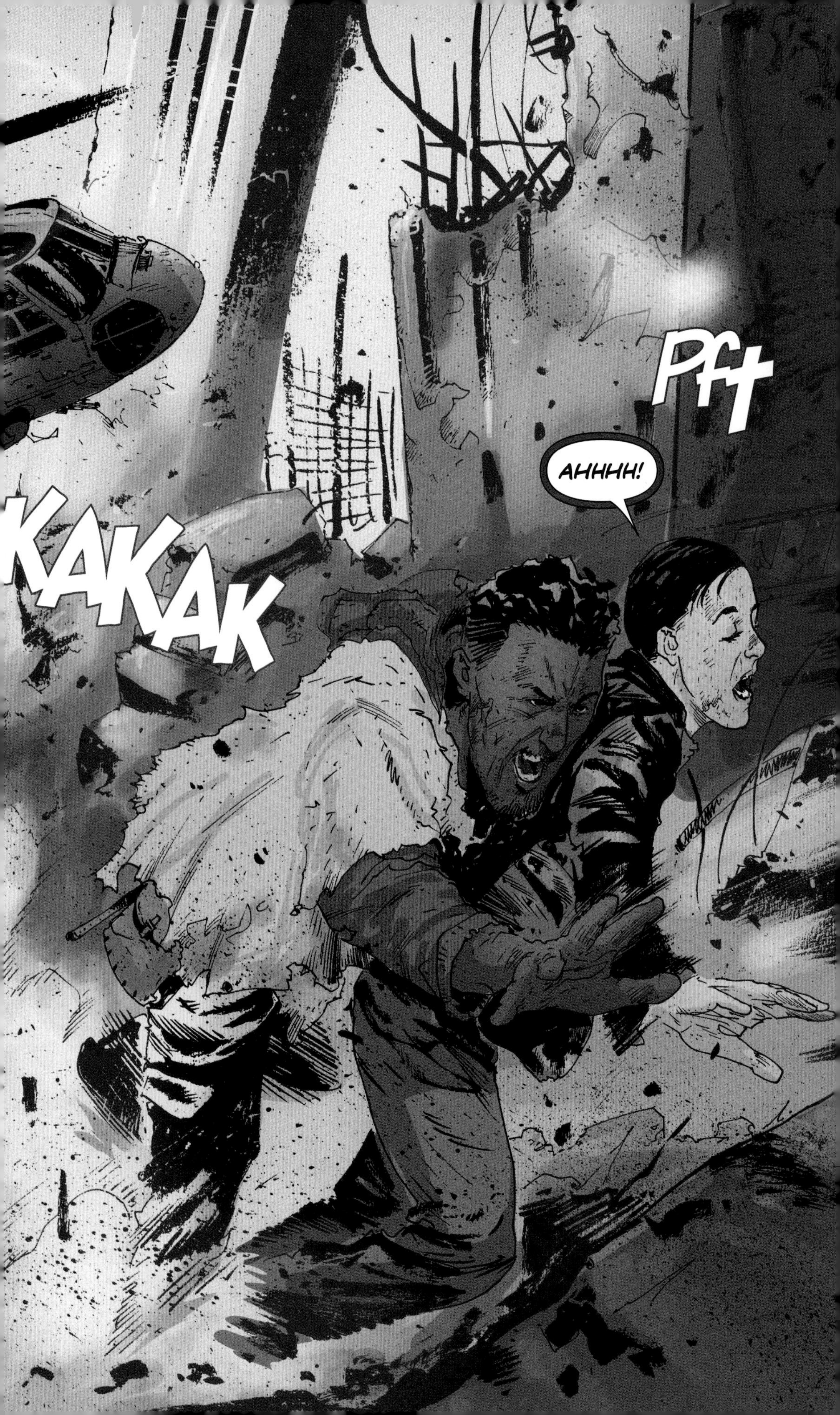
KAKAK
PFT
AHHHH!

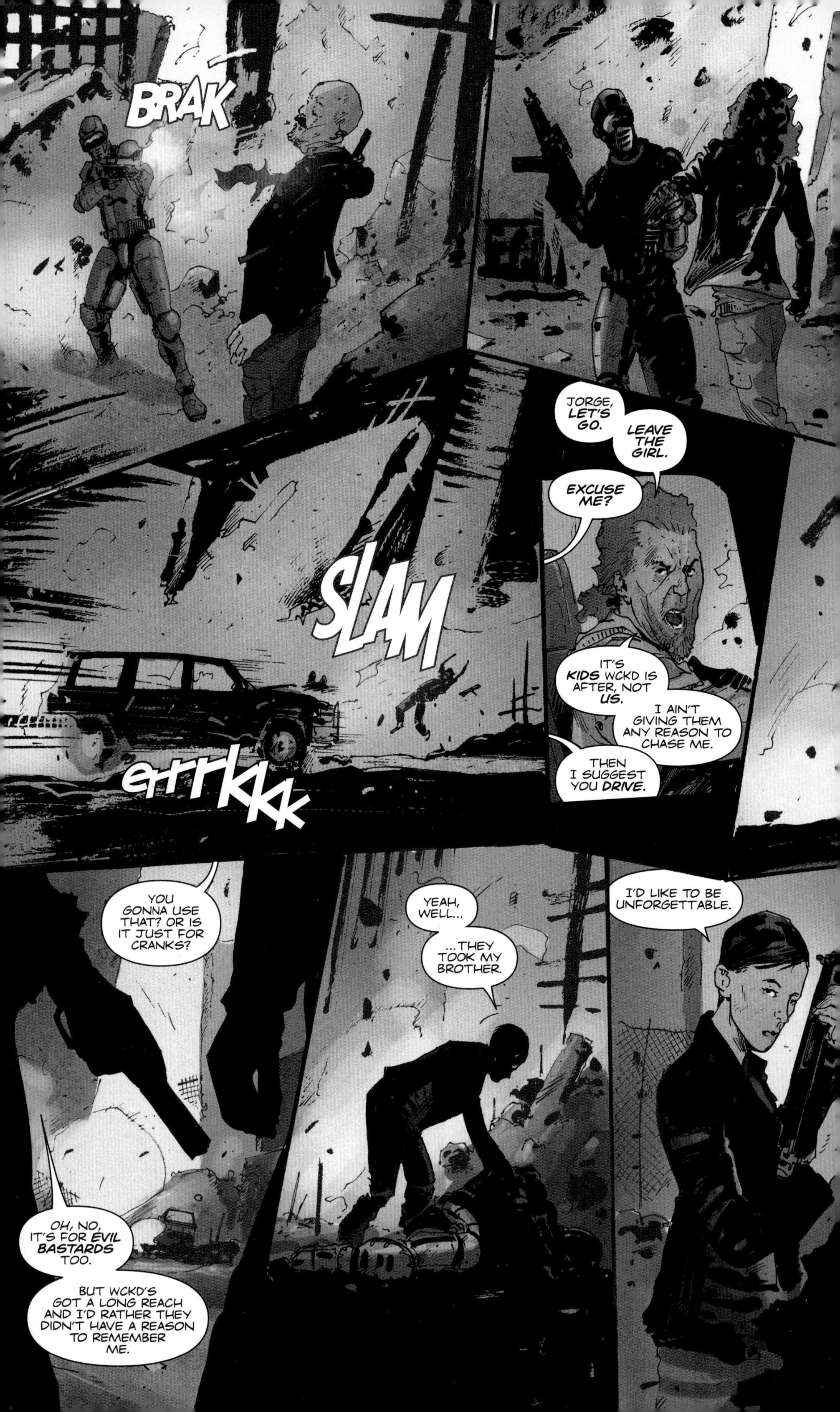
BRAK
JORGE, LET'S GO.
LEAVE THE GIRL.
EXCUSE ME?
IT'S KIDS WCKD IS AFTER, NOT US.
I AIN'T GIVING THEM ANY REASON TO CHASE ME.
THEN I SUGGEST YOU DRIVE.
SLAM
errrkkk
YOU GONNA USE THAT? OR IS IT JUST FOR CRANKS?
OH, NO, IT'S FOR EVIL BASTARDS TOO.
BUT WCKD'S GOT A LONG REACH AND I'D RATHER THEY DIDN'T HAVE A REASON TO REMEMBER ME.
YEAH, WELL...
...THEY TOOK MY BROTHER.
I'D LIKE TO BE UNFORGETTABLE.

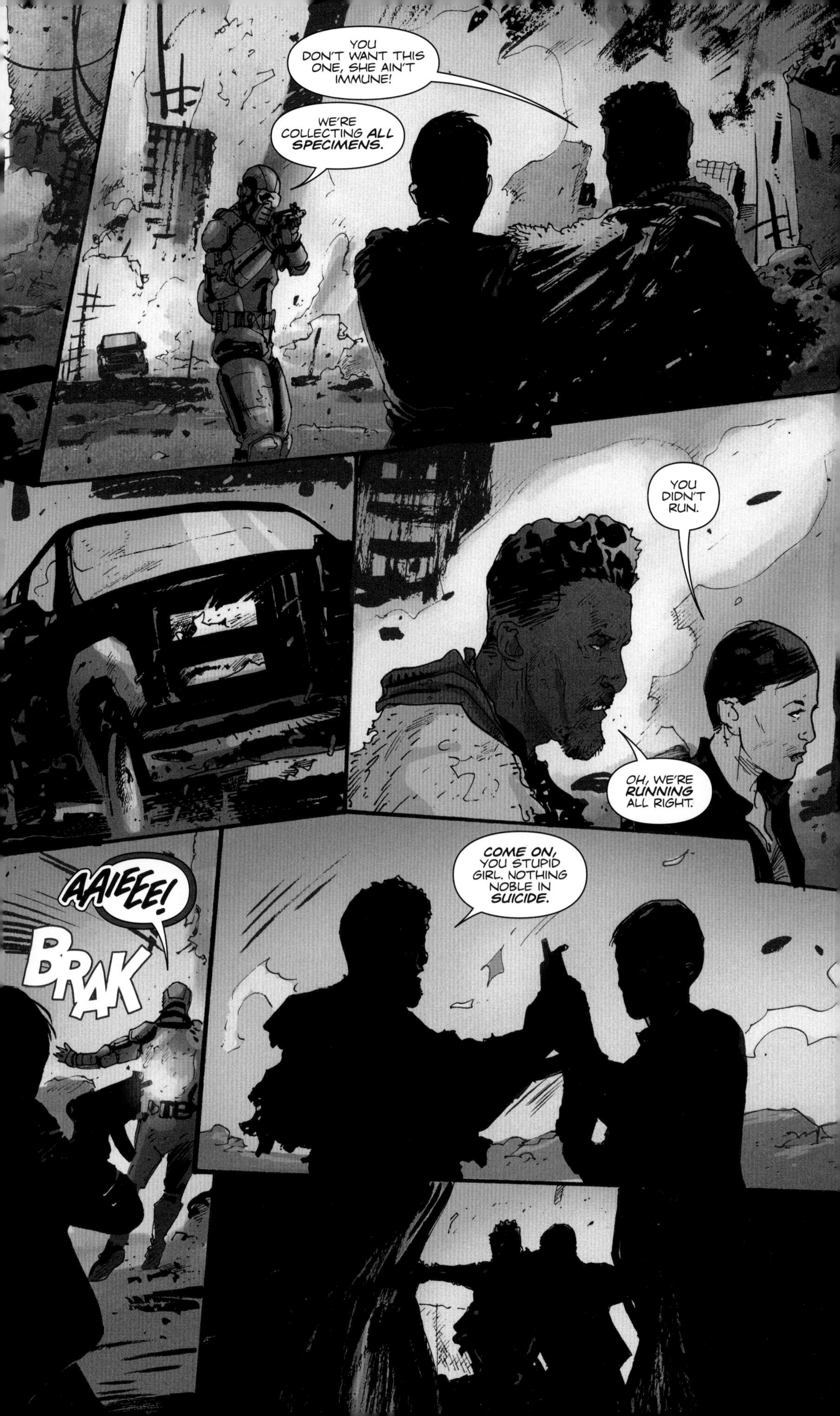

YOU DON'T WANT THIS ONE, SHE AIN'T IMMUNE!
WE'RE COLLECTING **ALL SPECIMENS.**
YOU DIDN'T RUN.
OH, WE'RE **RUNNING** ALL RIGHT.
AAIEEE!
BRAK
COME ON, YOU STUPID GIRL. NOTHING NOBLE IN **SUICIDE.**

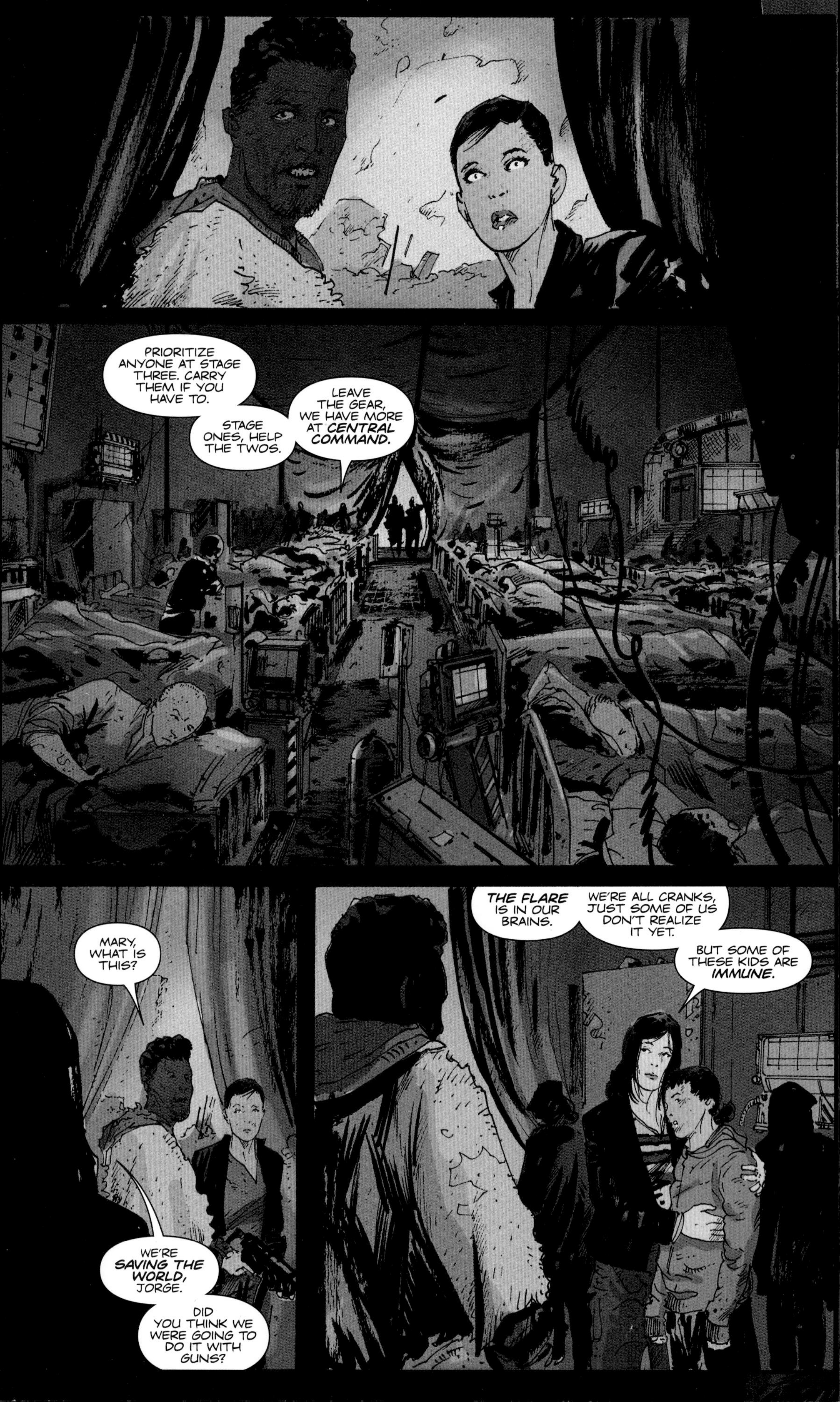
PRIORITIZE ANYONE AT STAGE THREE. CARRY THEM IF YOU HAVE TO.
STAGE ONES, HELP THE TWOS.
LEAVE THE GEAR, WE HAVE MORE AT CENTRAL COMMAND.
MARY, WHAT IS THIS?
WE'RE SAVING THE WORLD, JORGE.
DID YOU THINK WE WERE GOING TO DO IT WITH GUNS?
THE FLARE IS IN OUR BRAINS.
WE'RE ALL CRANKS, JUST SOME OF US DON'T REALIZE IT YET.
BUT SOME OF THESE KIDS ARE IMMUNE.

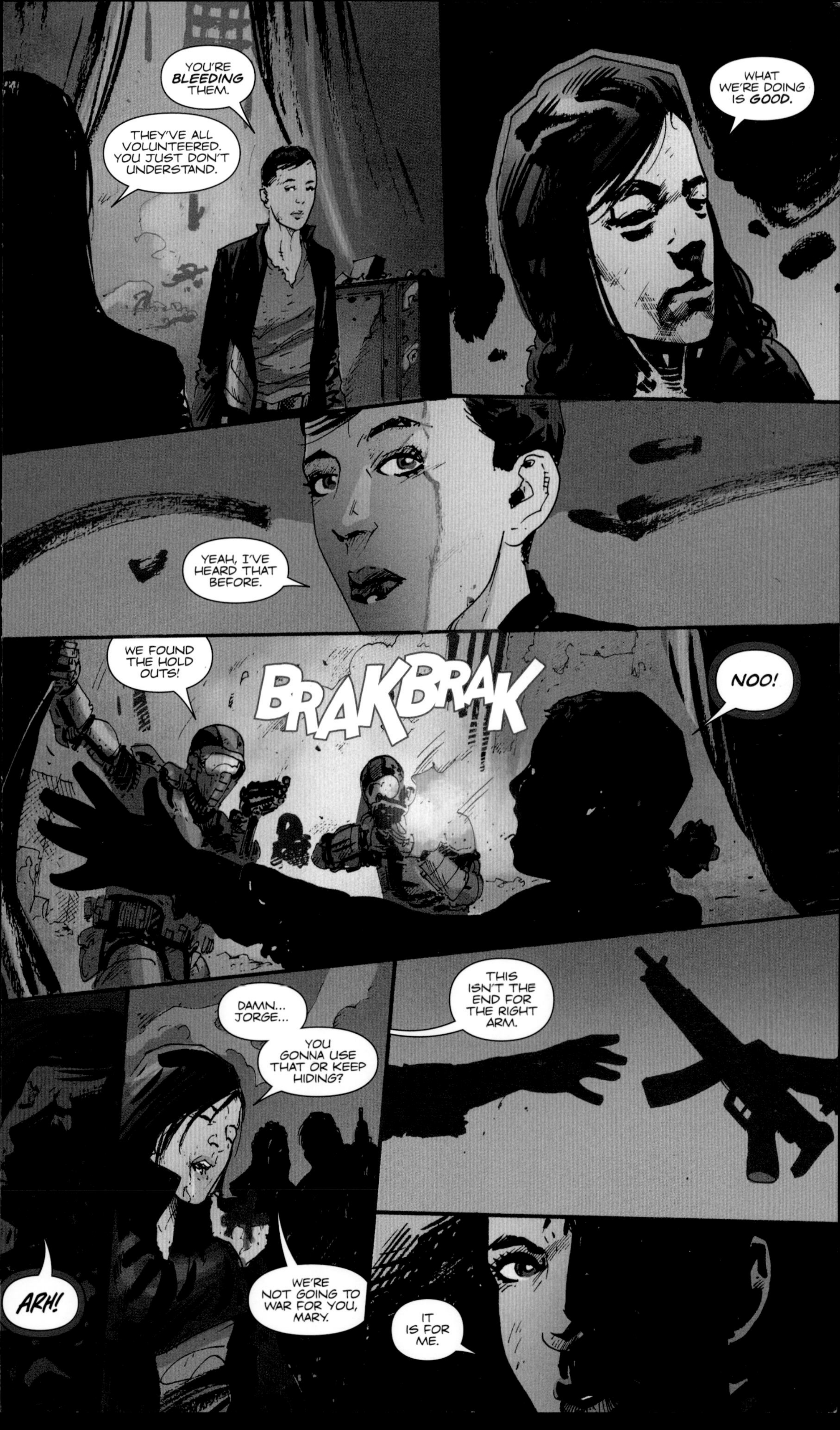

YOU'RE BLEEDING THEM.
THEY'VE ALL VOLUNTEERED. YOU JUST DON'T UNDERSTAND.
WHAT WE'RE DOING IS GOOD.
YEAH, I'VE HEARD THAT BEFORE.
WE FOUND THE HOLD OUTS!
BRAKBRAK
NOO!
DAMN... JORGE...
YOU GONNA USE THAT OR KEEP HIDING?
THIS ISN'T THE END FOR THE RIGHT ARM.
ARH!
WE'RE NOT GOING TO WAR FOR YOU, MARY.
IT IS FOR ME.

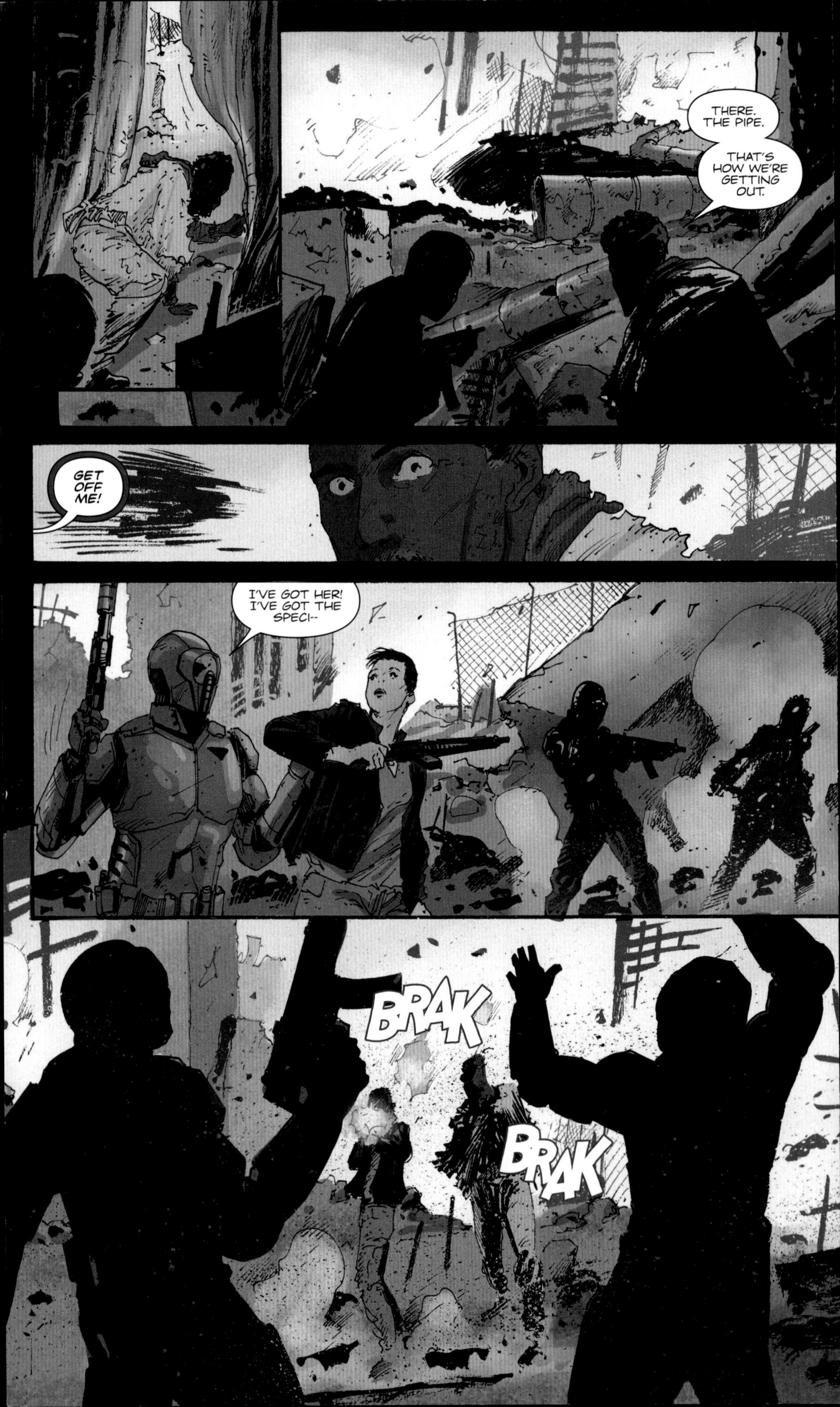
THERE. THE PIPE.
THAT'S HOW WE'RE GETTING OUT.
GET OFF ME!
I'VE GOT HER! I'VE GOT THE SPECI--
BRAK
BRAK

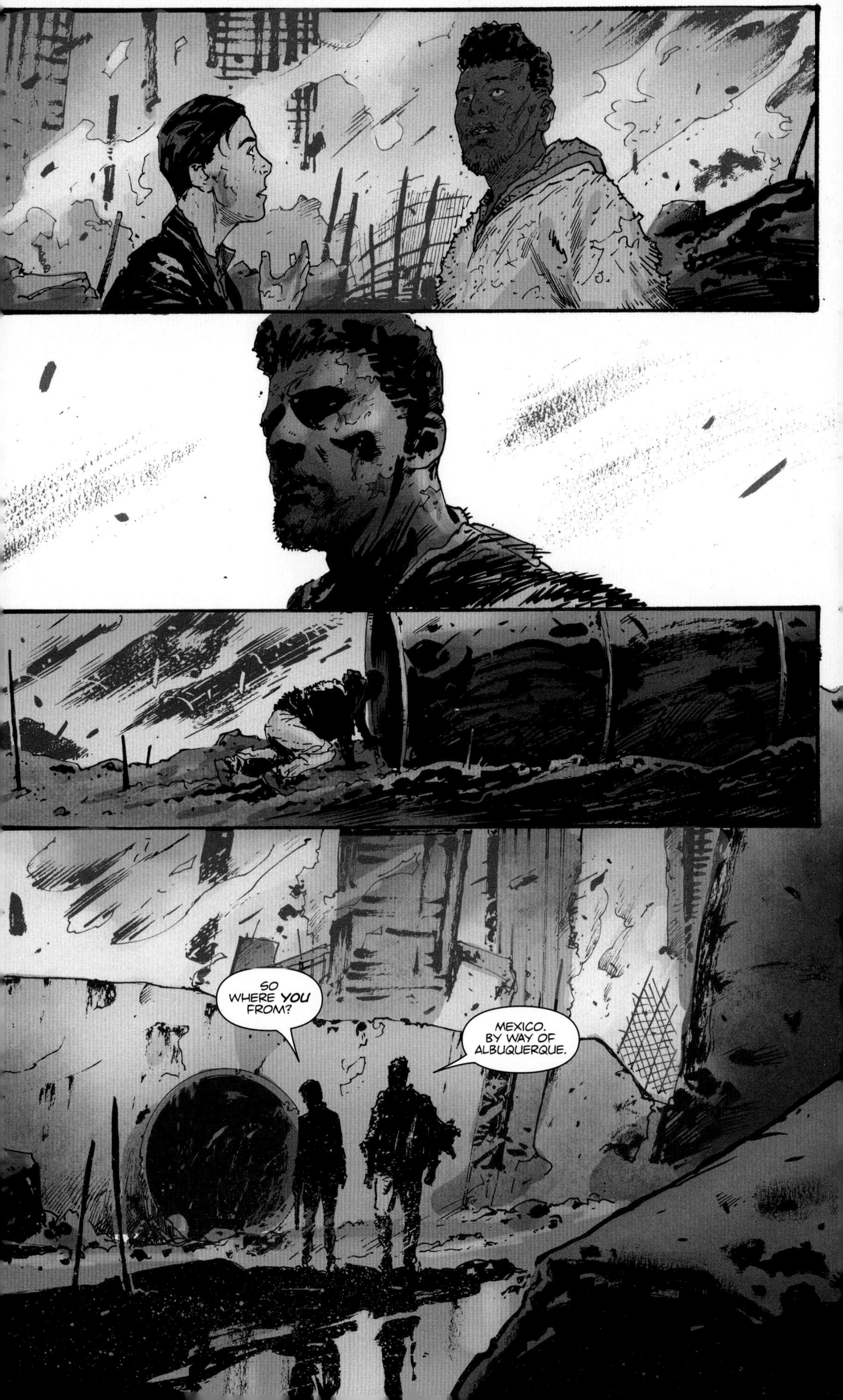
SO WHERE YOU FROM?
MEXICO. BY WAY OF ALBUQUERQUE.

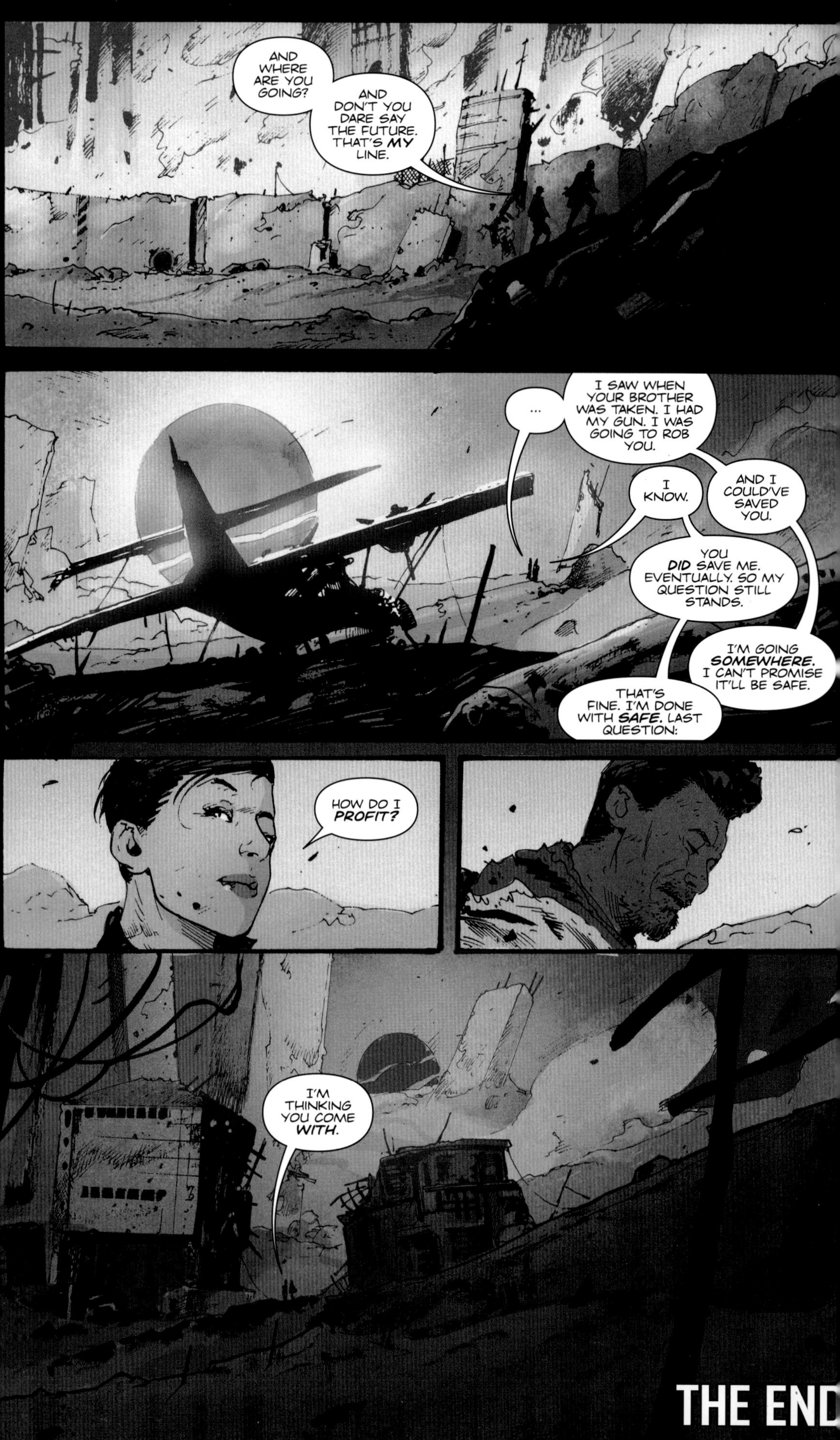
AND WHERE ARE YOU GOING?
AND DON'T YOU DARE SAY THE FUTURE. THAT'S **MY** LINE.
...
I SAW WHEN YOUR BROTHER WAS TAKEN. I HAD MY GUN. I WAS GOING TO ROB YOU.
AND I COULD'VE SAVED YOU.
I KNOW.
YOU **DID** SAVE ME. EVENTUALLY. SO MY QUESTION STILL STANDS.
I'M GOING **SOMEWHERE.** I CAN'T PROMISE IT'LL BE SAFE.
THAT'S FINE. I'M DONE WITH **SAFE.** LAST QUESTION:
HOW DO I ***PROFIT?***
I'M THINKING YOU COME ***WITH.***
THE END

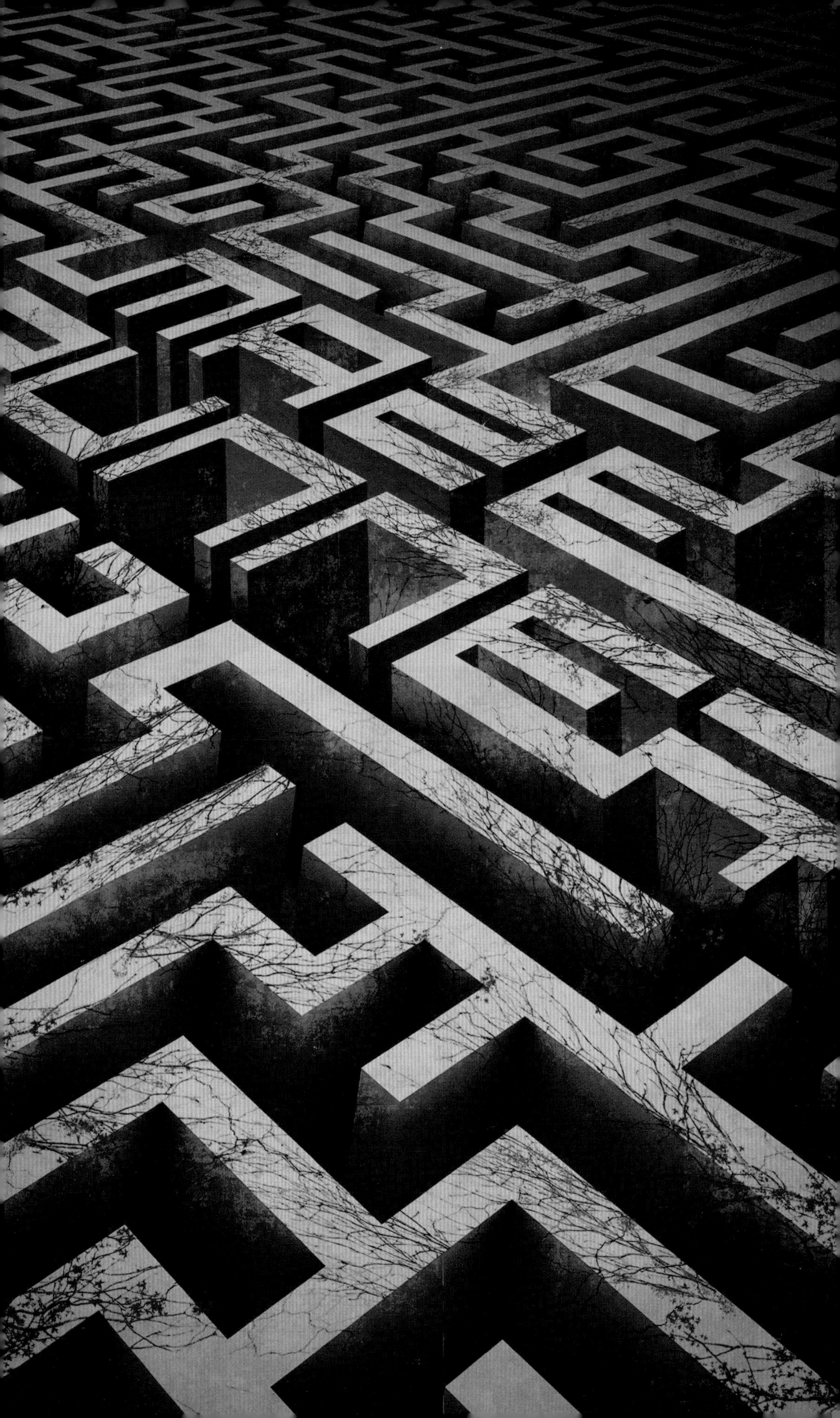

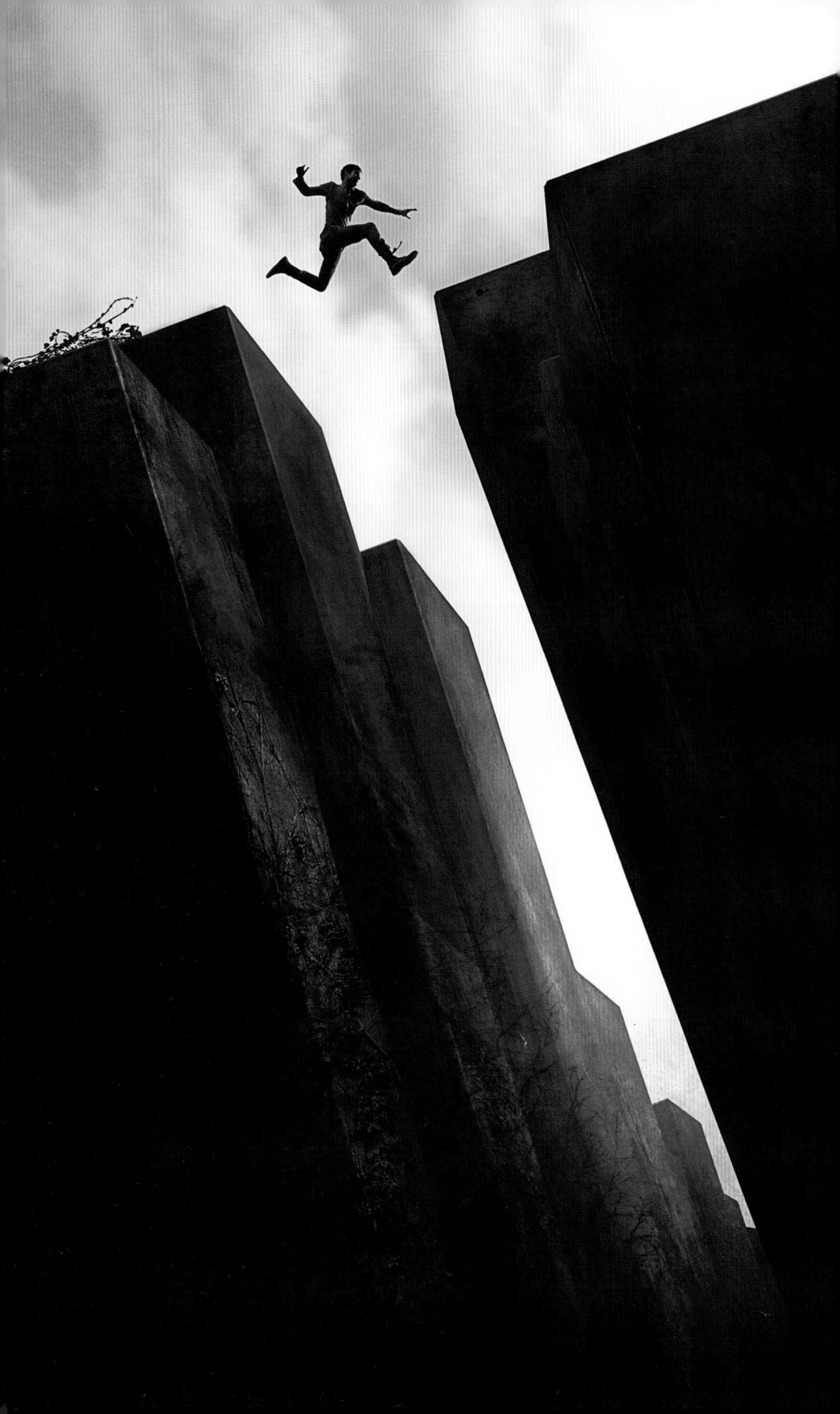

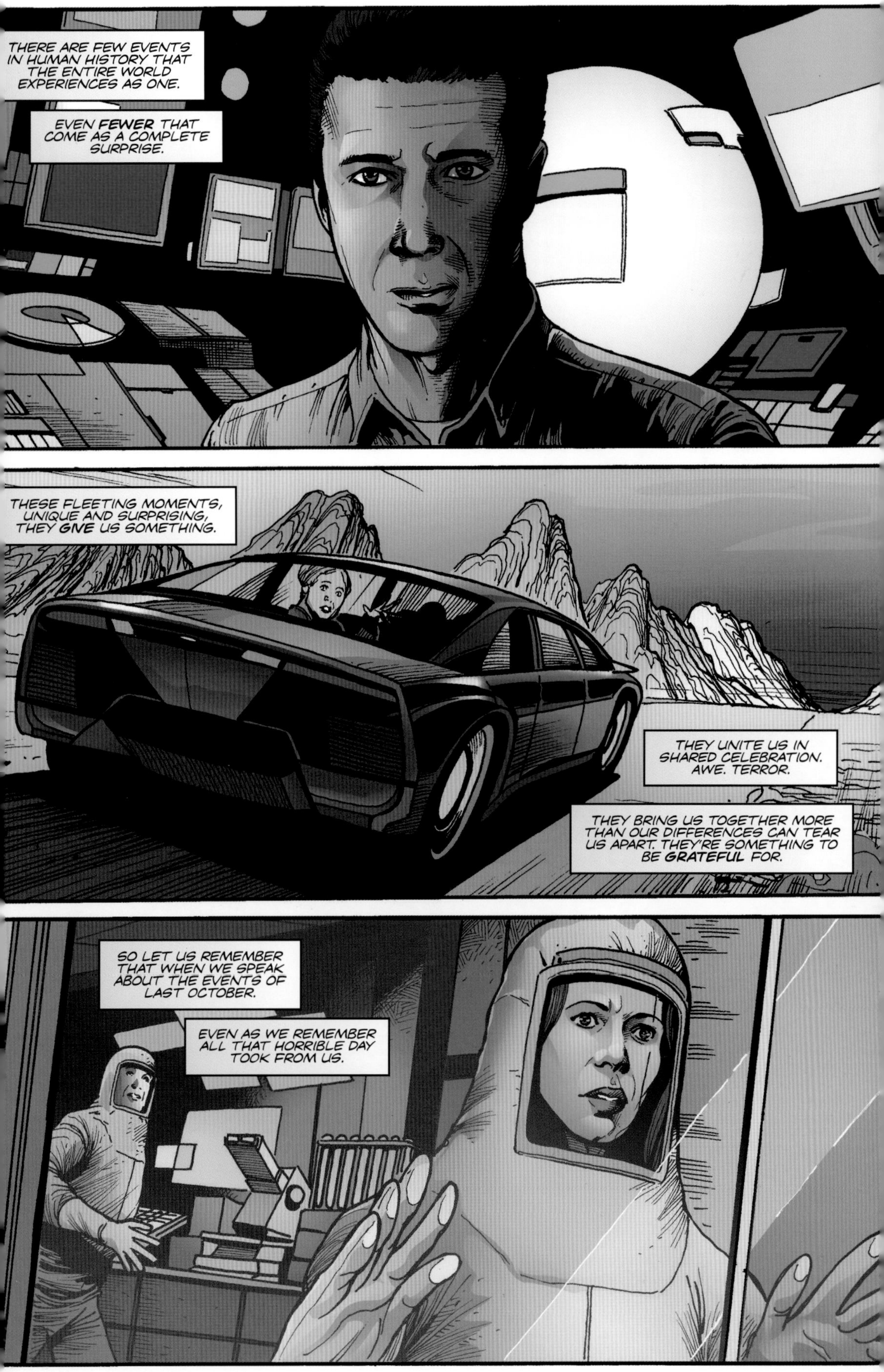
THERE ARE FEW EVENTS IN HUMAN HISTORY THAT THE ENTIRE WORLD EXPERIENCES AS ONE.
EVEN **FEWER** THAT COME AS A COMPLETE SURPRISE.
THESE FLEETING MOMENTS, UNIQUE AND SURPRISING, THEY **GIVE** US SOMETHING.
THEY UNITE US IN SHARED CELEBRATION. AWE. TERROR.
THEY BRING US TOGETHER MORE THAN OUR DIFFERENCES CAN TEAR US APART. THEY'RE SOMETHING TO BE **GRATEFUL** FOR.
SO LET US REMEMBER THAT WHEN WE SPEAK ABOUT THE EVENTS OF LAST OCTOBER.
EVEN AS WE REMEMBER ALL THAT HORRIBLE DAY TOOK FROM US.

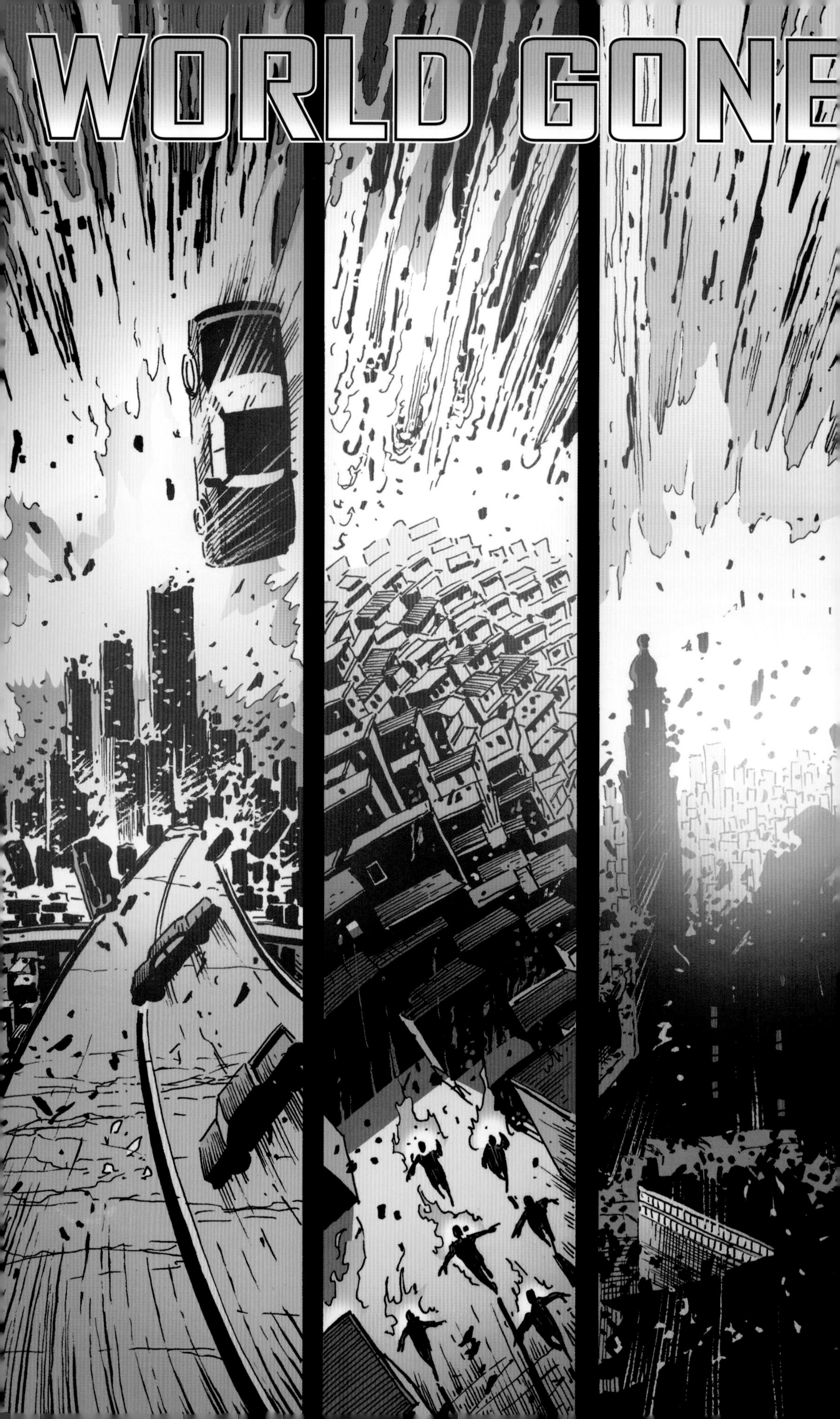

WORLD GONE

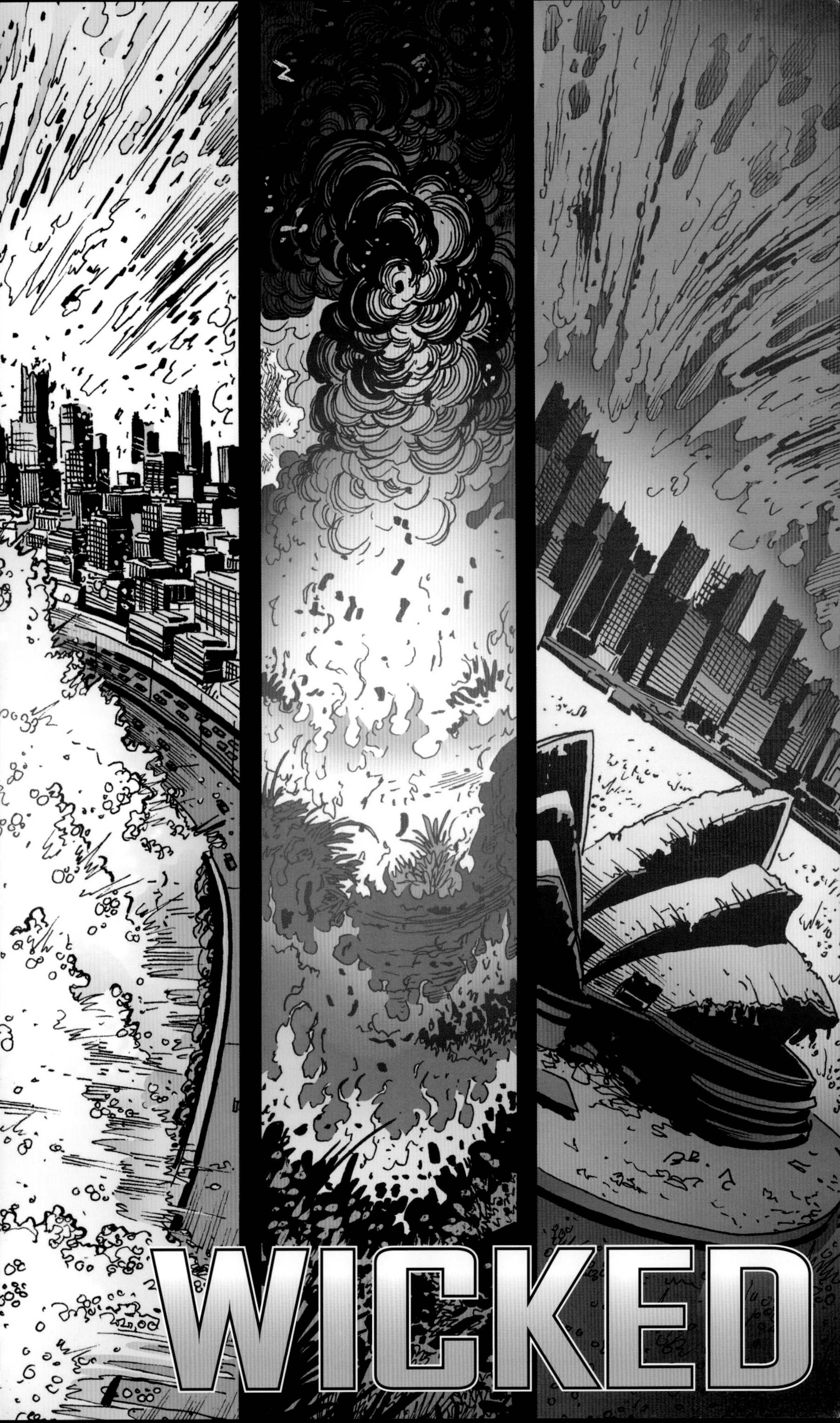
WICKED

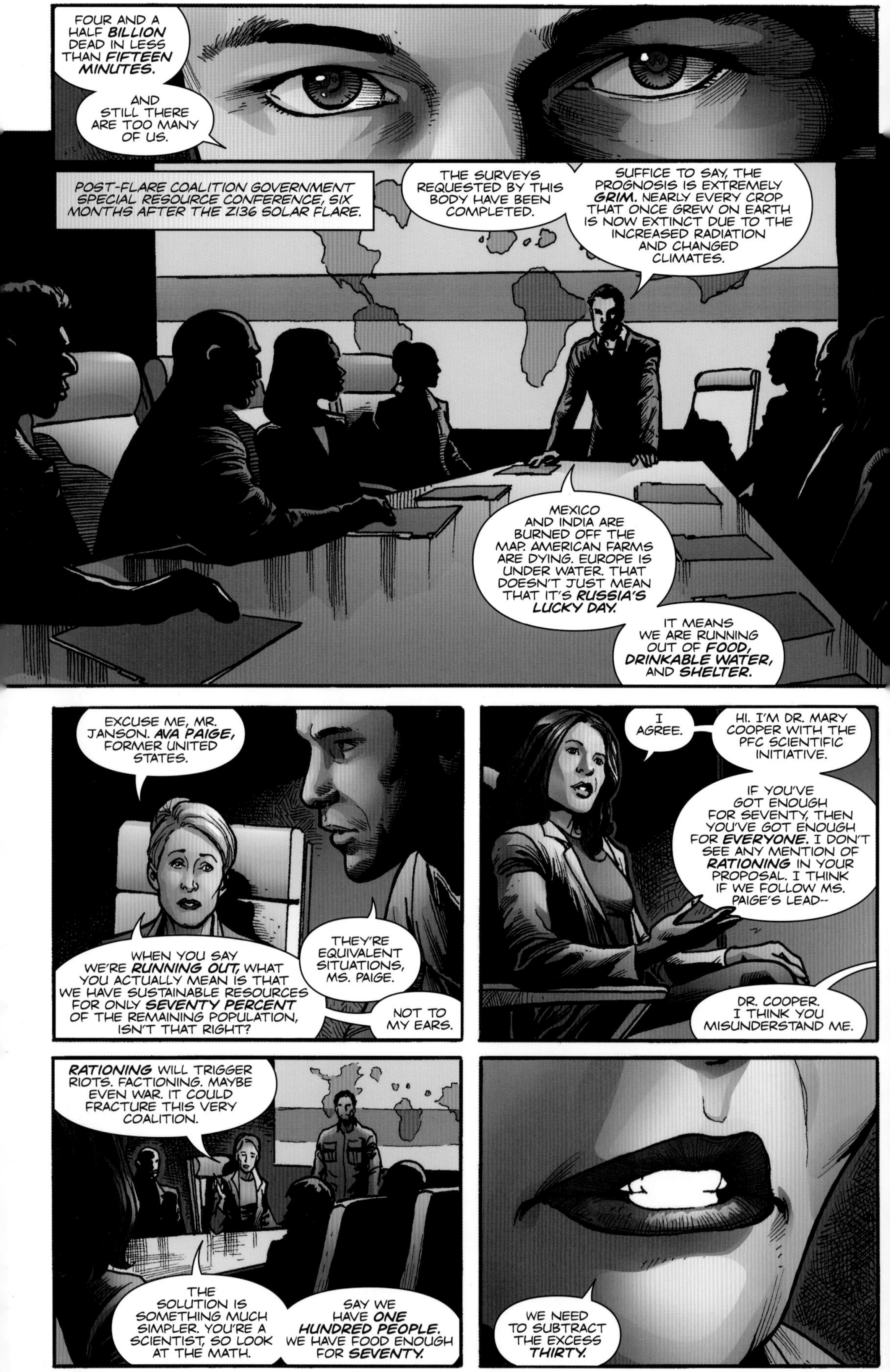
FOUR AND A HALF BILLION DEAD IN LESS THAN FIFTEEN MINUTES.
AND STILL THERE ARE TOO MANY OF US.
POST-FLARE COALITION GOVERNMENT SPECIAL RESOURCE CONFERENCE, SIX MONTHS AFTER THE Z136 SOLAR FLARE.
THE SURVEYS REQUESTED BY THIS BODY HAVE BEEN COMPLETED.
SUFFICE TO SAY, THE PROGNOSIS IS EXTREMELY GRIM. NEARLY EVERY CROP THAT ONCE GREW ON EARTH IS NOW EXTINCT DUE TO THE INCREASED RADIATION AND CHANGED CLIMATES.
MEXICO AND INDIA ARE BURNED OFF THE MAP. AMERICAN FARMS ARE DYING. EUROPE IS UNDER WATER. THAT DOESN'T JUST MEAN THAT IT'S RUSSIA'S LUCKY DAY.
IT MEANS WE ARE RUNNING OUT OF FOOD, DRINKABLE WATER, AND SHELTER.
EXCUSE ME, MR. JANSON. AVA PAIGE, FORMER UNITED STATES.
WHEN YOU SAY WE'RE RUNNING OUT, WHAT YOU ACTUALLY MEAN IS THAT WE HAVE SUSTAINABLE RESOURCES FOR ONLY SEVENTY PERCENT OF THE REMAINING POPULATION, ISN'T THAT RIGHT?
THEY'RE EQUIVALENT SITUATIONS, MS. PAIGE.
NOT TO MY EARS.
I AGREE.
HI. I'M DR. MARY COOPER WITH THE PFC SCIENTIFIC INITIATIVE.
IF YOU'VE GOT ENOUGH FOR SEVENTY, THEN YOU'VE GOT ENOUGH FOR EVERYONE. I DON'T SEE ANY MENTION OF RATIONING IN YOUR PROPOSAL. I THINK IF WE FOLLOW MS. PAIGE'S LEAD--
DR. COOPER. I THINK YOU MISUNDERSTAND ME.
RATIONING WILL TRIGGER RIOTS. FACTIONING. MAYBE EVEN WAR. IT COULD FRACTURE THIS VERY COALITION.
THE SOLUTION IS SOMETHING MUCH SIMPLER. YOU'RE A SCIENTIST, SO LOOK AT THE MATH.
SAY WE HAVE ONE HUNDRED PEOPLE. WE HAVE FOOD ENOUGH FOR SEVENTY.
WE NEED TO SUBTRACT THE EXCESS THIRTY.

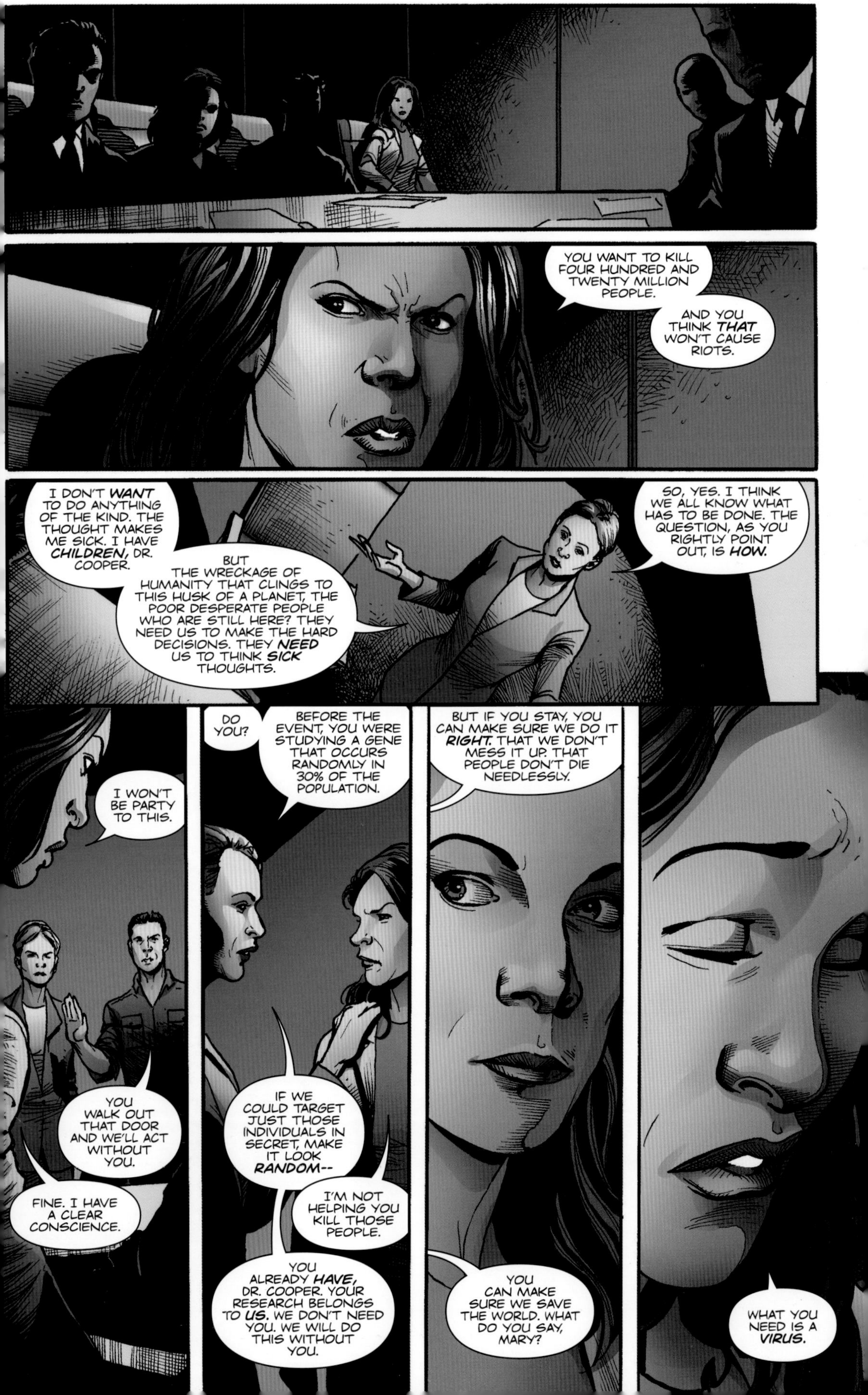
YOU WANT TO KILL FOUR HUNDRED AND TWENTY MILLION PEOPLE.
AND YOU THINK THAT WON'T CAUSE RIOTS.
I DON'T WANT TO DO ANYTHING OF THE KIND. THE THOUGHT MAKES ME SICK. I HAVE CHILDREN, DR. COOPER.
BUT THE WRECKAGE OF HUMANITY THAT CLINGS TO THIS HUSK OF A PLANET, THE POOR DESPERATE PEOPLE WHO ARE STILL HERE? THEY NEED US TO MAKE THE HARD DECISIONS. THEY NEED US TO THINK SICK THOUGHTS.
SO, YES. I THINK WE ALL KNOW WHAT HAS TO BE DONE. THE QUESTION, AS YOU RIGHTLY POINT OUT, IS HOW.
I WON'T BE PARTY TO THIS.
YOU WALK OUT THAT DOOR AND WE'LL ACT WITHOUT YOU.
FINE. I HAVE A CLEAR CONSCIENCE.
DO YOU?
BEFORE THE EVENT, YOU WERE STUDYING A GENE THAT OCCURS RANDOMLY IN 30% OF THE POPULATION.
IF WE COULD TARGET JUST THOSE INDIVIDUALS IN SECRET, MAKE IT LOOK RANDOM--
I'M NOT HELPING YOU KILL THOSE PEOPLE.
YOU ALREADY HAVE, DR. COOPER. YOUR RESEARCH BELONGS TO US. WE DON'T NEED YOU. WE WILL DO THIS WITHOUT YOU.
BUT IF YOU STAY, YOU CAN MAKE SURE WE DO IT RIGHT. THAT WE DON'T MESS IT UP. THAT PEOPLE DON'T DIE NEEDLESSLY.
YOU CAN MAKE SURE WE SAVE THE WORLD. WHAT DO YOU SAY, MARY?
WHAT YOU NEED IS A VIRUS.

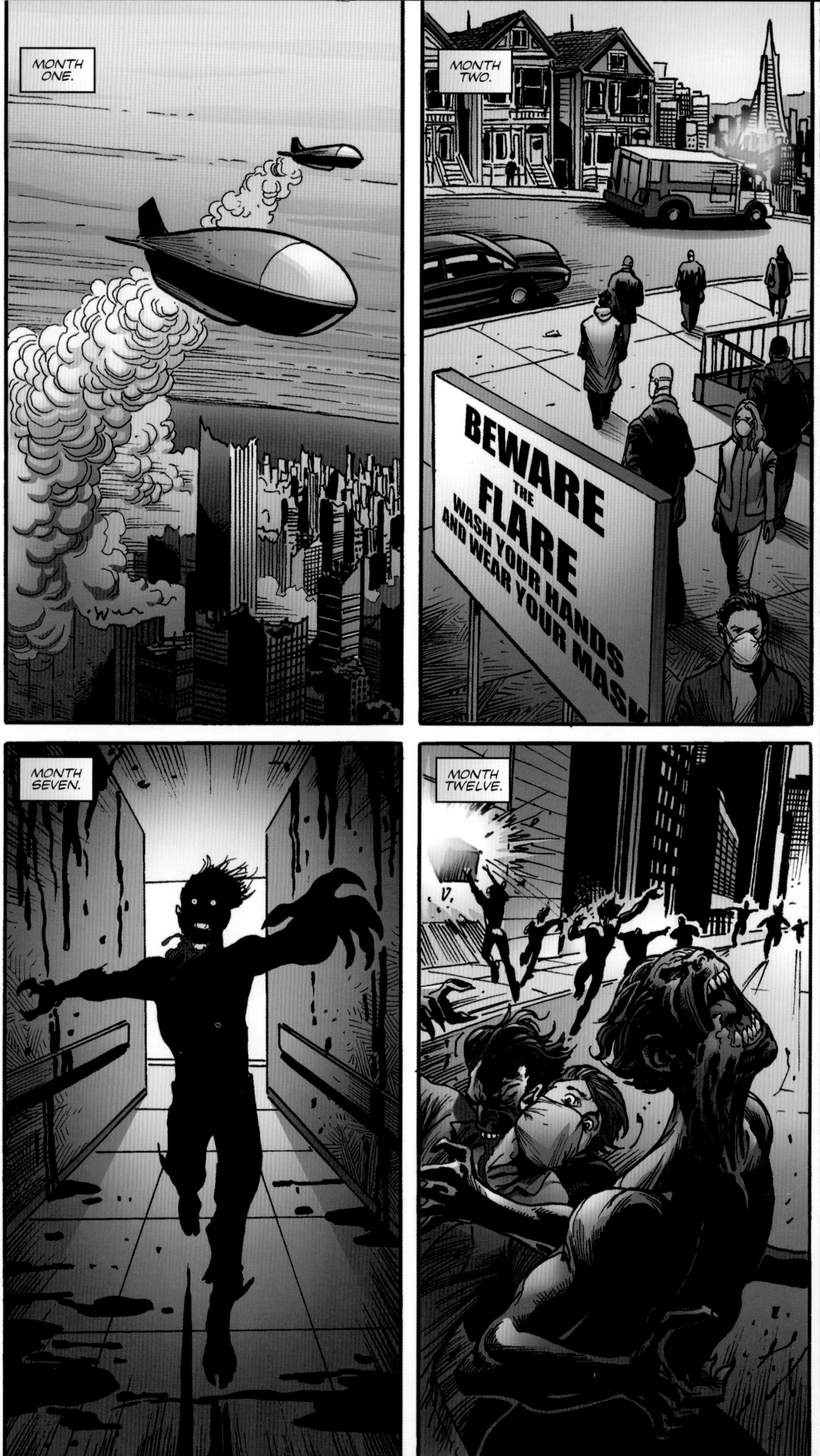
MONTH ONE.
MONTH TWO.
BEWARE THE FLARE
WASH YOUR HANDS AND WEAR YOUR MASK
MONTH SEVEN.
MONTH TWELVE.

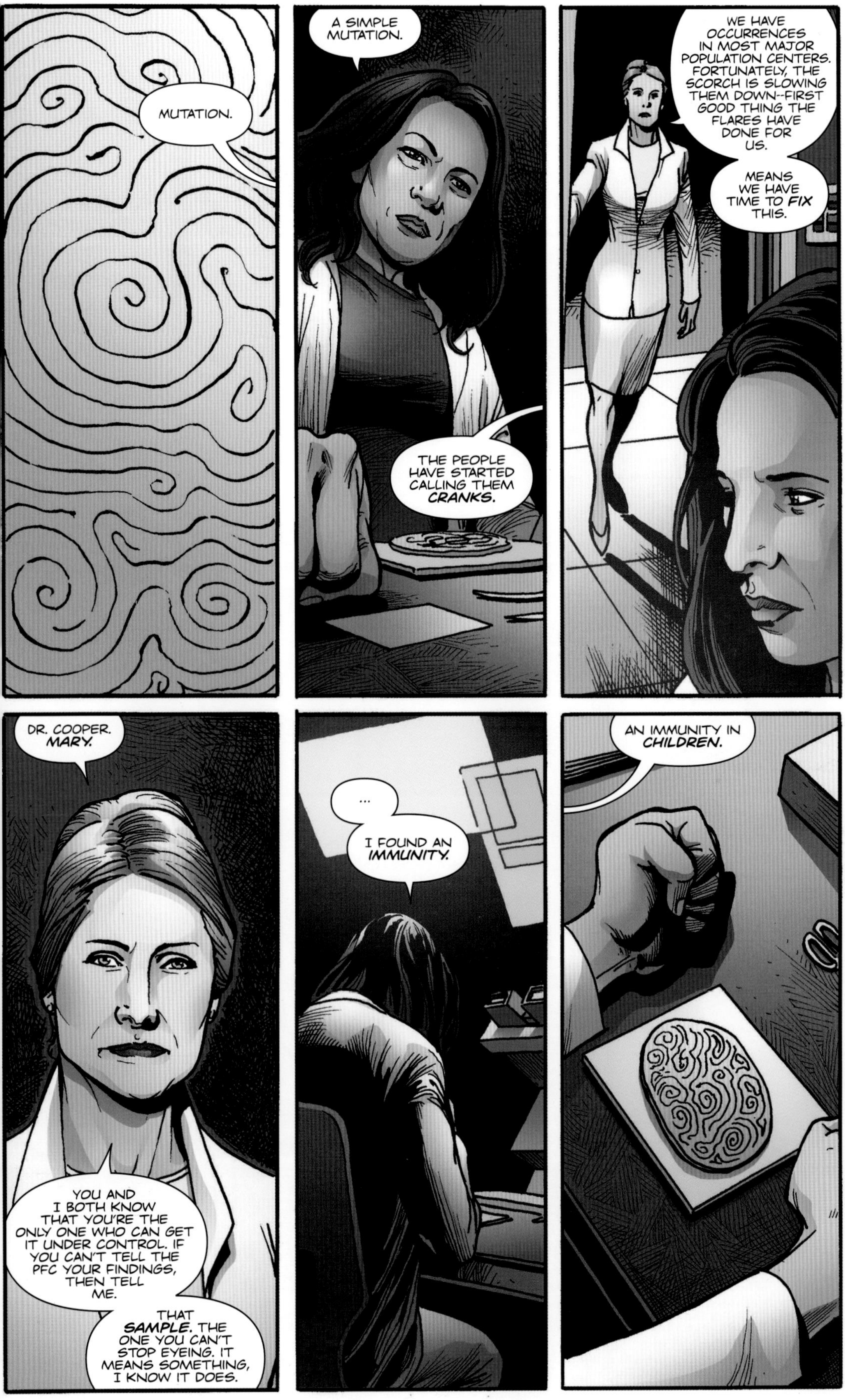
MUTATION.
A SIMPLE MUTATION.
THE PEOPLE HAVE STARTED CALLING THEM **CRANKS.**
WE HAVE OCCURRENCES IN MOST MAJOR POPULATION CENTERS. FORTUNATELY, THE SCORCH IS SLOWING THEM DOWN--FIRST GOOD THING THE FLARES HAVE DONE FOR US.
MEANS WE HAVE TIME TO **FIX** THIS.
DR. COOPER. **MARY.**
YOU AND I BOTH KNOW THAT YOU'RE THE ONLY ONE WHO CAN GET IT UNDER CONTROL. IF YOU CAN'T TELL THE PFC YOUR FINDINGS, THEN TELL ME.
THAT **SAMPLE.** THE ONE YOU CAN'T STOP EYEING. IT MEANS SOMETHING, I KNOW IT DOES.
...
I FOUND AN **IMMUNITY.**
AN IMMUNITY IN **CHILDREN.**

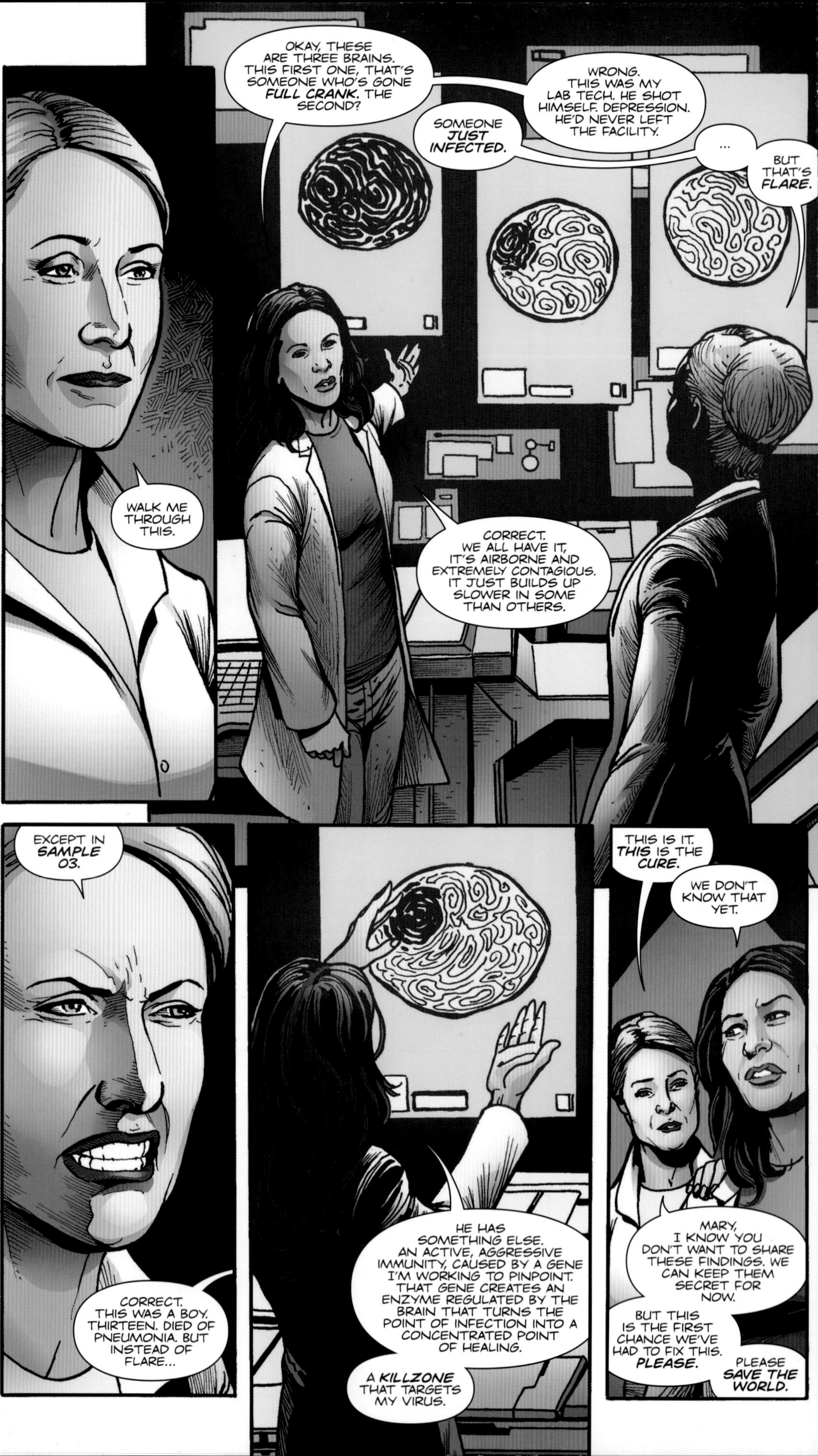
OKAY, THESE ARE THREE BRAINS. THIS FIRST ONE, THAT'S SOMEONE WHO'S GONE **FULL CRANK.** THE SECOND?
SOMEONE **JUST INFECTED.**
WRONG. THIS WAS MY LAB TECH. HE SHOT HIMSELF. DEPRESSION. HE'D NEVER LEFT THE FACILITY.
...
BUT THAT'S **FLARE.**
WALK ME THROUGH THIS.
CORRECT. WE ALL HAVE IT, IT'S AIRBORNE AND EXTREMELY CONTAGIOUS. IT JUST BUILDS UP SLOWER IN SOME THAN OTHERS.
EXCEPT IN **SAMPLE 03.**
CORRECT. THIS WAS A BOY. THIRTEEN. DIED OF PNEUMONIA. BUT INSTEAD OF FLARE...
HE HAS SOMETHING ELSE. AN ACTIVE, AGGRESSIVE IMMUNITY, CAUSED BY A GENE I'M WORKING TO PINPOINT. THAT GENE CREATES AN ENZYME REGULATED BY THE BRAIN THAT TURNS THE POINT OF INFECTION INTO A CONCENTRATED POINT OF HEALING.
A **KILLZONE** THAT TARGETS MY VIRUS.
THIS IS IT. **THIS** IS THE **CURE.**
WE DON'T KNOW THAT YET.
MARY, I KNOW YOU DON'T WANT TO SHARE THESE FINDINGS. WE CAN KEEP THEM SECRET FOR NOW.
BUT THIS IS THE FIRST CHANCE WE'VE HAD TO FIX THIS. **PLEASE.**
PLEASE **SAVE THE WORLD.**

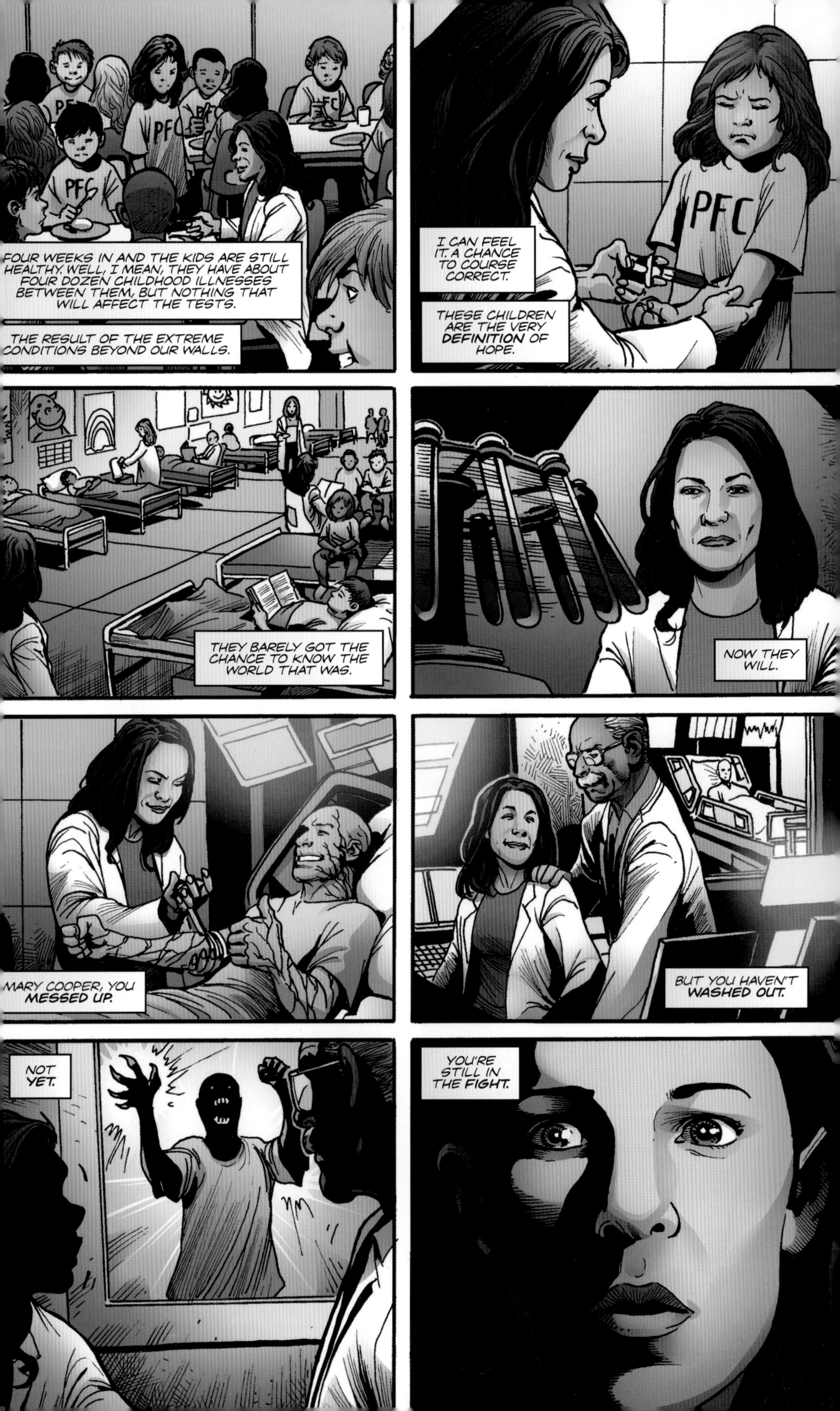
FOUR WEEKS IN AND THE KIDS ARE STILL HEALTHY. WELL, I MEAN, THEY HAVE ABOUT FOUR DOZEN CHILDHOOD ILLNESSES BETWEEN THEM, BUT NOTHING THAT WILL AFFECT THE TESTS.
THE RESULT OF THE EXTREME CONDITIONS BEYOND OUR WALLS.
PFC
I CAN FEEL IT. A CHANCE TO COURSE CORRECT.
THESE CHILDREN ARE THE VERY DEFINITION OF HOPE.
THEY BARELY GOT THE CHANCE TO KNOW THE WORLD THAT WAS.
NOW THEY WILL.
MARY COOPER, YOU MESSED UP.
BUT YOU HAVEN'T WASHED OUT.
NOT YET.
YOU'RE STILL IN THE FIGHT.

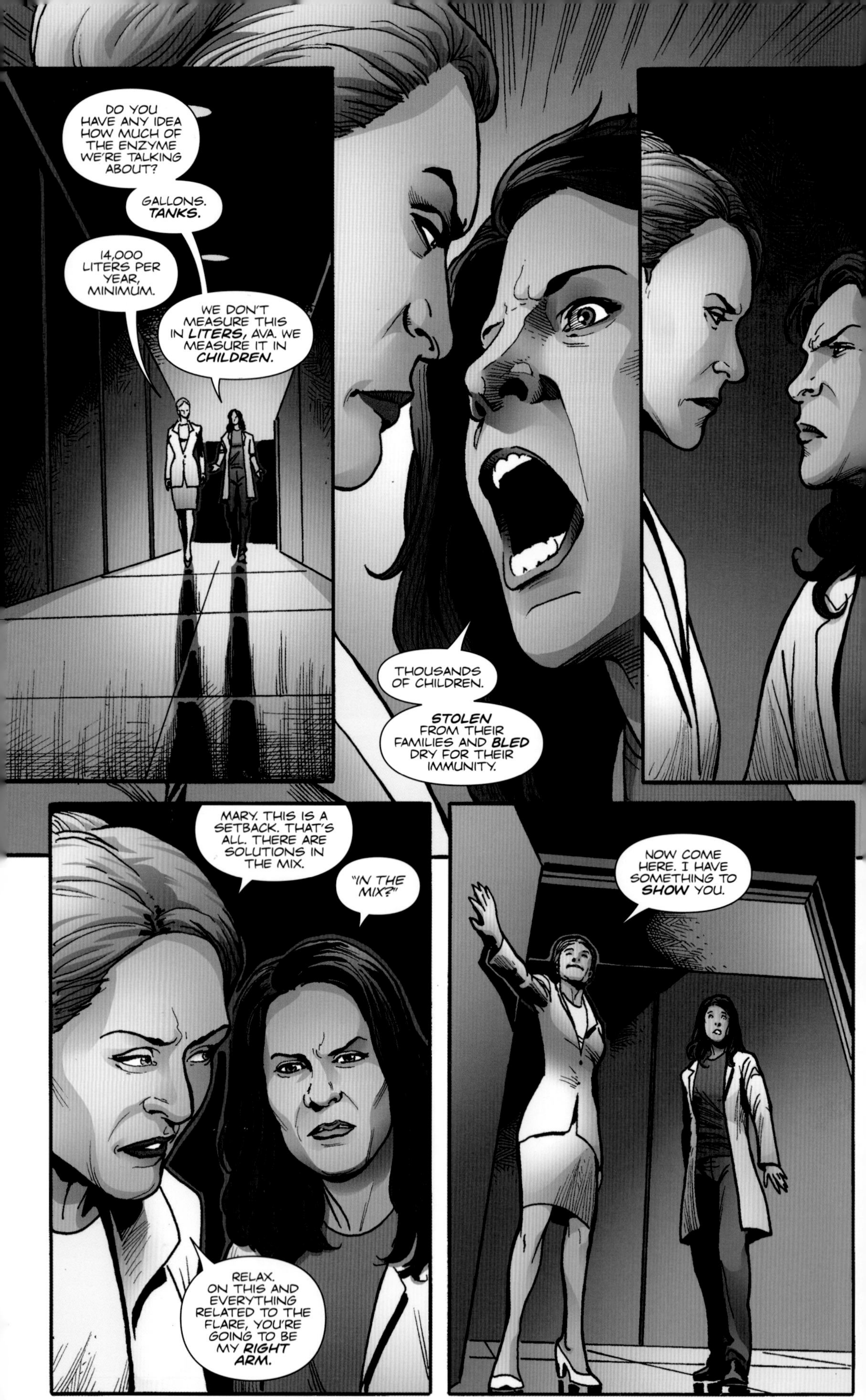
DO YOU HAVE ANY IDEA HOW MUCH OF THE ENZYME WE'RE TALKING ABOUT?
GALLONS. **TANKS.**
14,000 LITERS PER YEAR, MINIMUM.
WE DON'T MEASURE THIS IN **LITERS,** AVA. WE MEASURE IT IN **CHILDREN.**
THOUSANDS OF CHILDREN.
STOLEN FROM THEIR FAMILIES AND **BLED** DRY FOR THEIR IMMUNITY.
MARY. THIS IS A SETBACK. THAT'S ALL. THERE ARE SOLUTIONS IN THE MIX.
"IN THE MIX?"
RELAX. ON THIS AND EVERYTHING RELATED TO THE FLARE, YOU'RE GOING TO BE MY **RIGHT ARM.**
NOW COME HERE. I HAVE SOMETHING TO **SHOW** YOU.

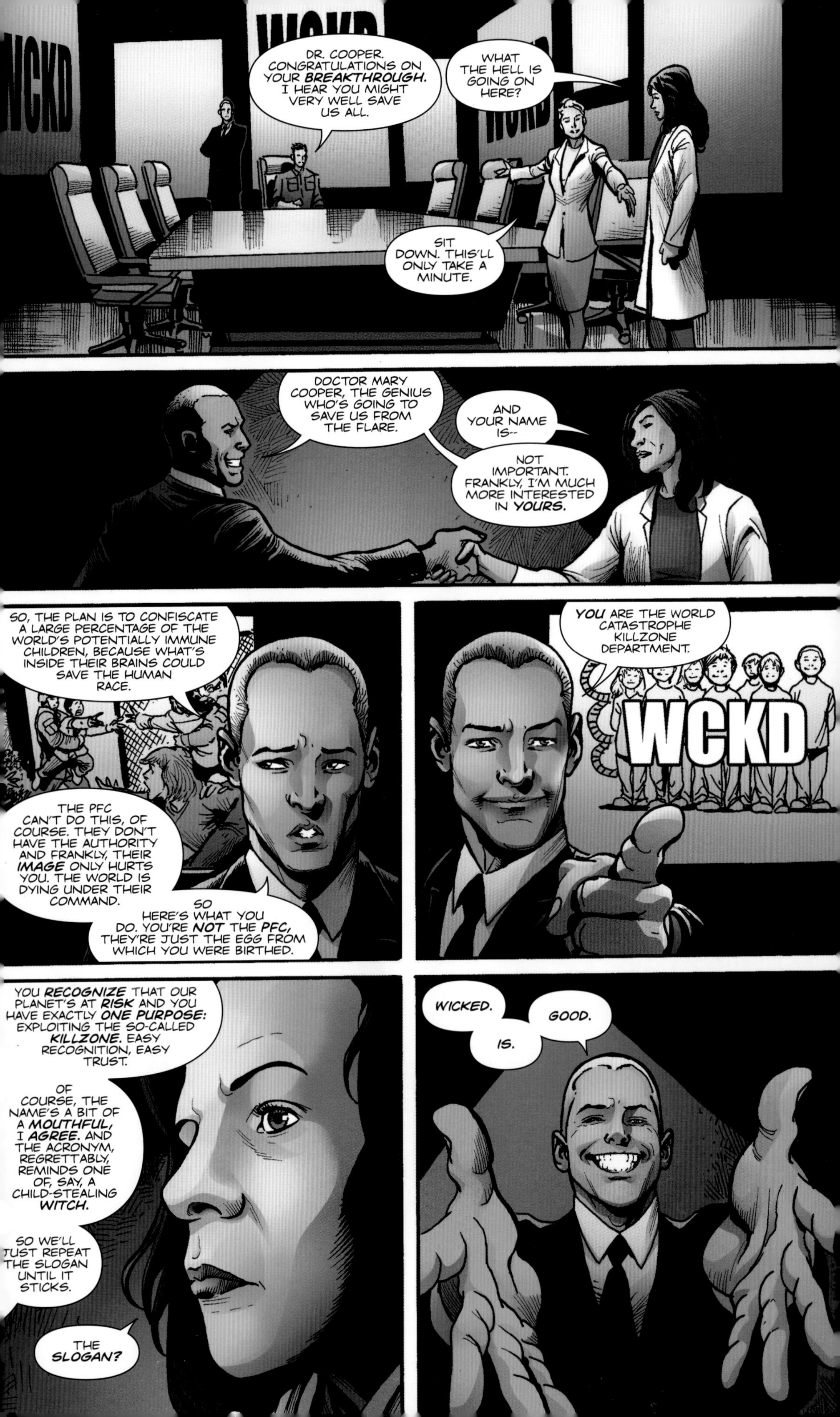
WCKD
DR. COOPER. CONGRATULATIONS ON YOUR BREAKTHROUGH. I HEAR YOU MIGHT VERY WELL SAVE US ALL.
WHAT THE HELL IS GOING ON HERE?
SIT DOWN. THIS'LL ONLY TAKE A MINUTE.
DOCTOR MARY COOPER, THE GENIUS WHO'S GOING TO SAVE US FROM THE FLARE.
AND YOUR NAME IS--
NOT IMPORTANT. FRANKLY, I'M MUCH MORE INTERESTED IN YOURS.
SO, THE PLAN IS TO CONFISCATE A LARGE PERCENTAGE OF THE WORLD'S POTENTIALLY IMMUNE CHILDREN, BECAUSE WHAT'S INSIDE THEIR BRAINS COULD SAVE THE HUMAN RACE.
THE PFC CAN'T DO THIS, OF COURSE. THEY DON'T HAVE THE AUTHORITY AND FRANKLY, THEIR IMAGE ONLY HURTS YOU. THE WORLD IS DYING UNDER THEIR COMMAND.
SO HERE'S WHAT YOU DO. YOU'RE NOT THE PFC, THEY'RE JUST THE EGG FROM WHICH YOU WERE BIRTHED.
YOU ARE THE WORLD CATASTROPHE KILLZONE DEPARTMENT.
WCKD
YOU RECOGNIZE THAT OUR PLANET'S AT RISK AND YOU HAVE EXACTLY ONE PURPOSE: EXPLOITING THE SO-CALLED KILLZONE. EASY RECOGNITION, EASY TRUST.
OF COURSE, THE NAME'S A BIT OF A MOUTHFUL, I AGREE. AND THE ACRONYM, REGRETTABLY, REMINDS ONE OF, SAY, A CHILD-STEALING WITCH.
SO WE'LL JUST REPEAT THE SLOGAN UNTIL IT STICKS.
THE SLOGAN?
WICKED.
IS.
GOOD.

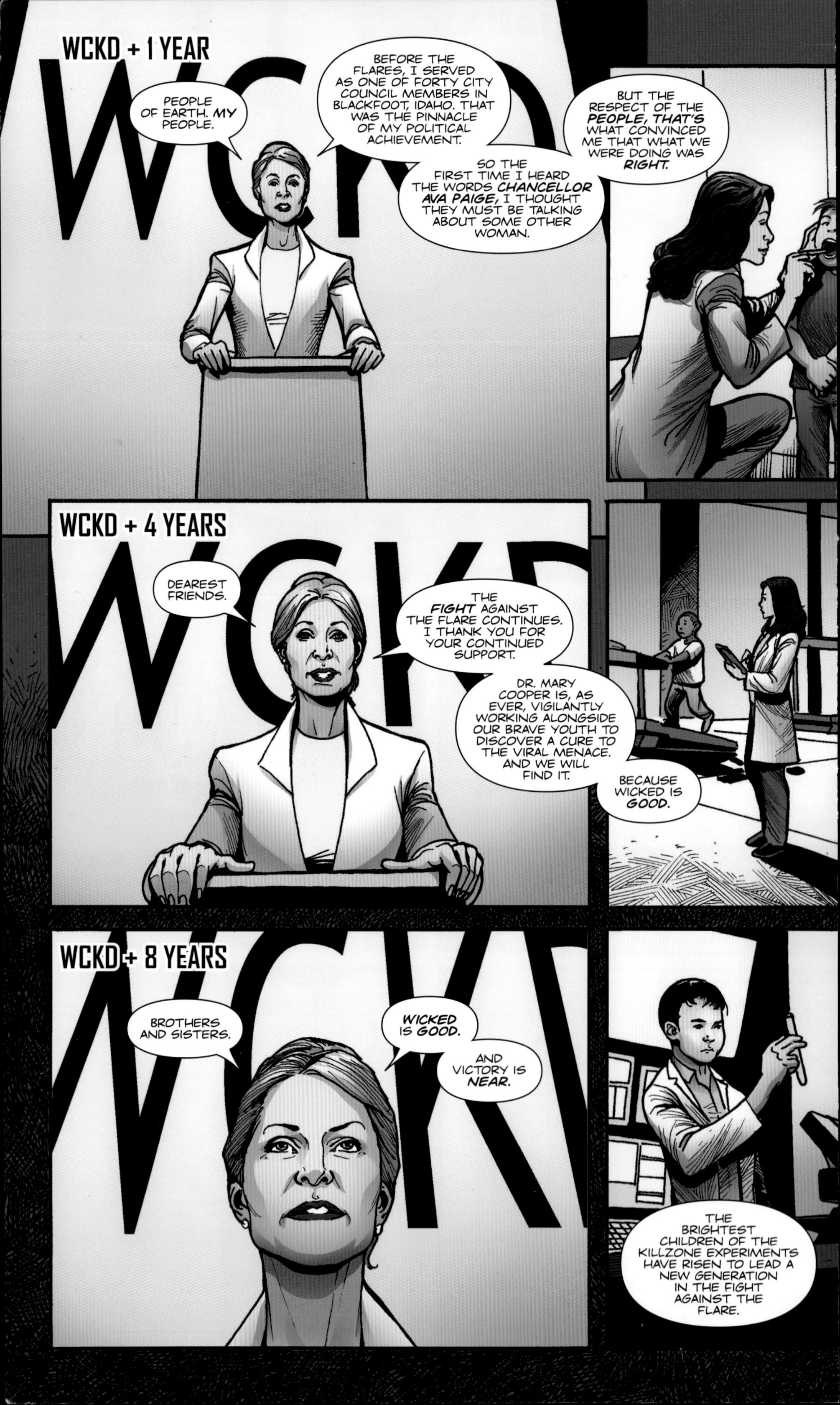

WCKD + 1 YEAR
PEOPLE OF EARTH. MY PEOPLE.
BEFORE THE FLARES, I SERVED AS ONE OF FORTY CITY COUNCIL MEMBERS IN BLACKFOOT, IDAHO. THAT WAS THE PINNACLE OF MY POLITICAL ACHIEVEMENT.
SO THE FIRST TIME I HEARD THE WORDS CHANCELLOR AVA PAIGE, I THOUGHT THEY MUST BE TALKING ABOUT SOME OTHER WOMAN.
BUT THE RESPECT OF THE PEOPLE, THAT'S WHAT CONVINCED ME THAT WHAT WE WERE DOING WAS RIGHT.
WCKD + 4 YEARS
DEAREST FRIENDS.
THE FIGHT AGAINST THE FLARE CONTINUES. I THANK YOU FOR YOUR CONTINUED SUPPORT.
DR. MARY COOPER IS, AS EVER, VIGILANTLY WORKING ALONGSIDE OUR BRAVE YOUTH TO DISCOVER A CURE TO THE VIRAL MENACE. AND WE WILL FIND IT.
BECAUSE WICKED IS GOOD.
WCKD + 8 YEARS
BROTHERS AND SISTERS.
WICKED IS GOOD.
AND VICTORY IS NEAR.
THE BRIGHTEST CHILDREN OF THE KILLZONE EXPERIMENTS HAVE RISEN TO LEAD A NEW GENERATION IN THE FIGHT AGAINST THE FLARE.

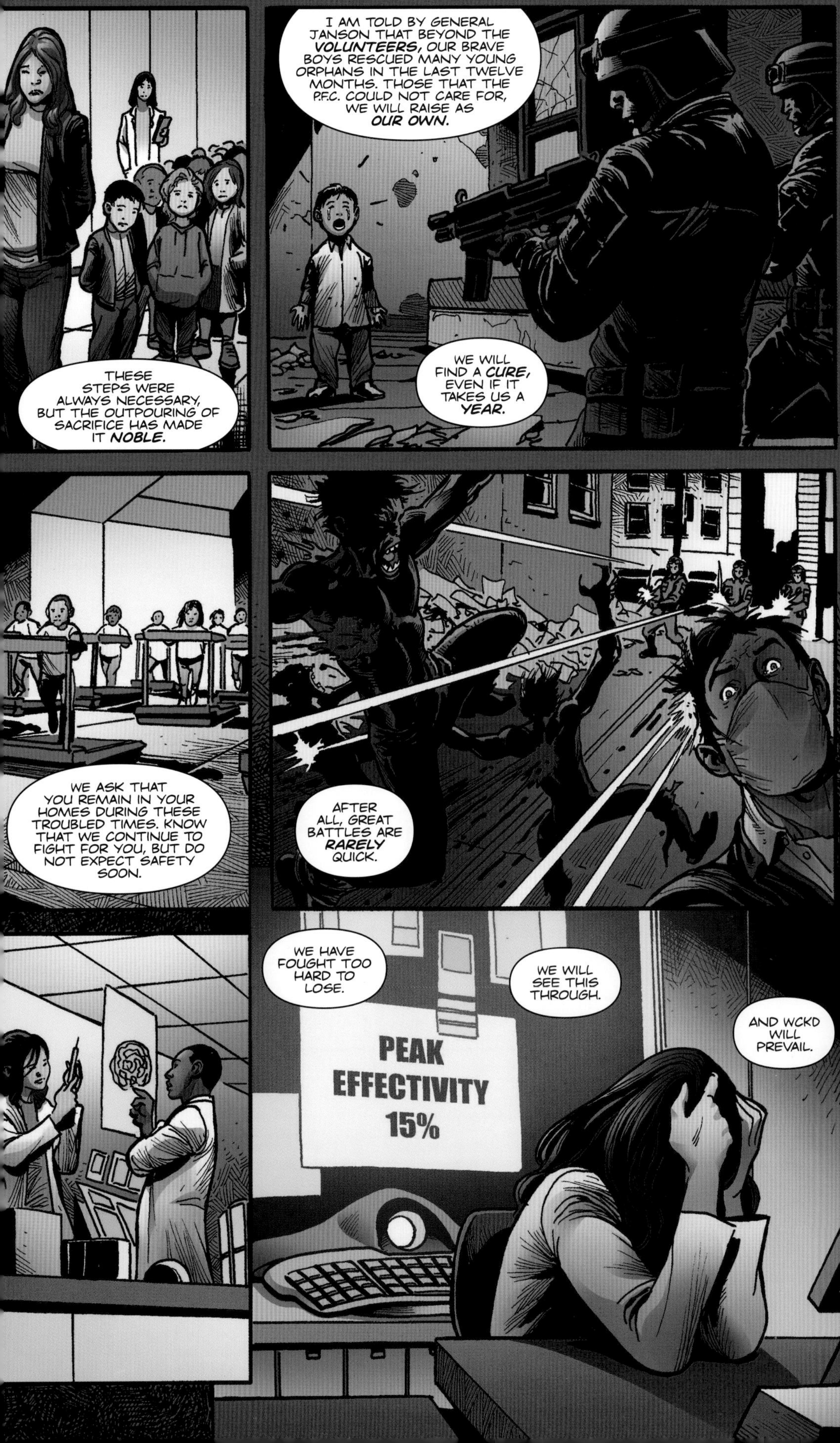
THESE STEPS WERE ALWAYS NECESSARY, BUT THE OUTPOURING OF SACRIFICE HAS MADE IT NOBLE.
I AM TOLD BY GENERAL JANSON THAT BEYOND THE VOLUNTEERS, OUR BRAVE BOYS RESCUED MANY YOUNG ORPHANS IN THE LAST TWELVE MONTHS. THOSE THAT THE P.F.C. COULD NOT CARE FOR, WE WILL RAISE AS OUR OWN.
WE WILL FIND A CURE, EVEN IF IT TAKES US A YEAR.
WE ASK THAT YOU REMAIN IN YOUR HOMES DURING THESE TROUBLED TIMES. KNOW THAT WE CONTINUE TO FIGHT FOR YOU, BUT DO NOT EXPECT SAFETY SOON.
AFTER ALL, GREAT BATTLES ARE RARELY QUICK.
WE HAVE FOUGHT TOO HARD TO LOSE.
WE WILL SEE THIS THROUGH.
AND WCKD WILL PREVAIL.
PEAK EFFECTIVITY 15%

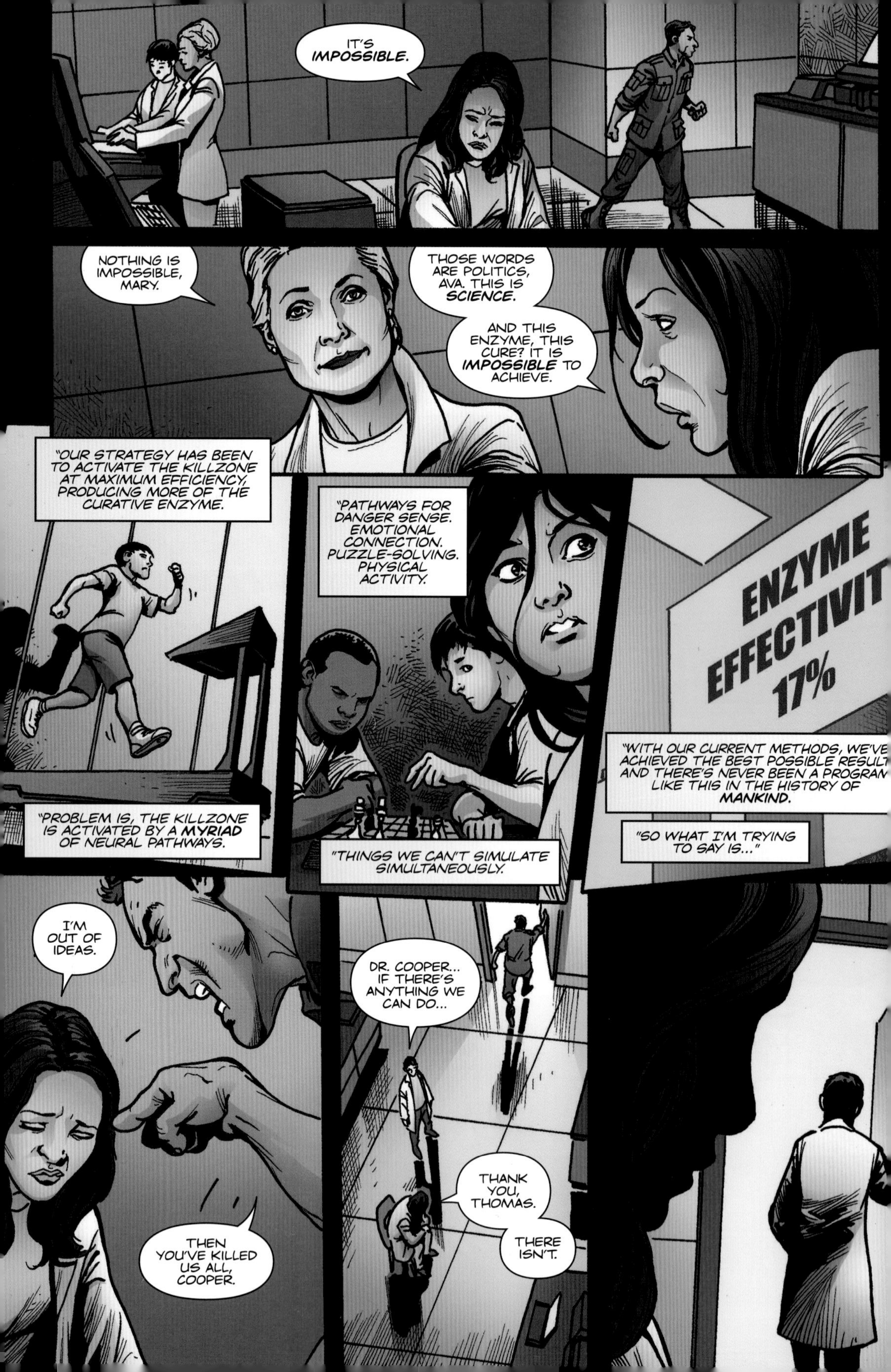
IT'S IMPOSSIBLE.
NOTHING IS IMPOSSIBLE, MARY.
THOSE WORDS ARE POLITICS, AVA. THIS IS SCIENCE.
AND THIS ENZYME, THIS CURE? IT IS IMPOSSIBLE TO ACHIEVE.
"OUR STRATEGY HAS BEEN TO ACTIVATE THE KILLZONE AT MAXIMUM EFFICIENCY, PRODUCING MORE OF THE CURATIVE ENZYME.
"PROBLEM IS, THE KILLZONE IS ACTIVATED BY A MYRIAD OF NEURAL PATHWAYS.
"PATHWAYS FOR DANGER SENSE. EMOTIONAL CONNECTION. PUZZLE-SOLVING. PHYSICAL ACTIVITY.
"THINGS WE CAN'T SIMULATE SIMULTANEOUSLY.
ENZYME EFFECTIVIT 17%
"WITH OUR CURRENT METHODS, WE'VE ACHIEVED THE BEST POSSIBLE RESULT AND THERE'S NEVER BEEN A PROGRAM LIKE THIS IN THE HISTORY OF MANKIND.
"SO WHAT I'M TRYING TO SAY IS..."
I'M OUT OF IDEAS.
THEN YOU'VE KILLED US ALL, COOPER.
DR. COOPER... IF THERE'S ANYTHING WE CAN DO...
THANK YOU, THOMAS.
THERE ISN'T.

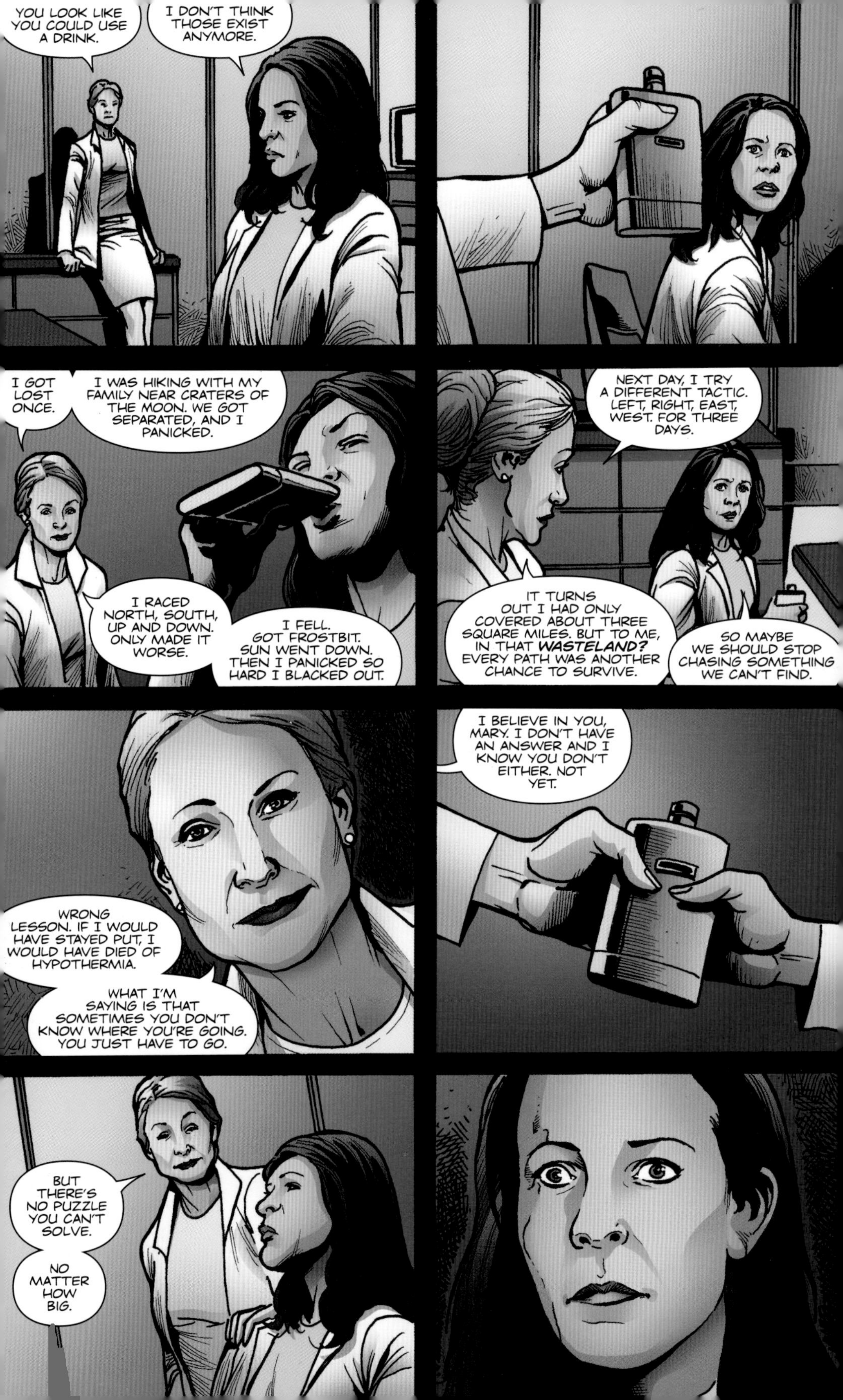
YOU LOOK LIKE YOU COULD USE A DRINK.
I DON'T THINK THOSE EXIST ANYMORE.
I GOT LOST ONCE.
I WAS HIKING WITH MY FAMILY NEAR CRATERS OF THE MOON. WE GOT SEPARATED, AND I PANICKED.
I RACED NORTH, SOUTH, UP AND DOWN. ONLY MADE IT WORSE.
I FELL. GOT FROSTBIT. SUN WENT DOWN. THEN I PANICKED SO HARD I BLACKED OUT.
NEXT DAY, I TRY A DIFFERENT TACTIC. LEFT, RIGHT, EAST, WEST. FOR THREE DAYS.
IT TURNS OUT I HAD ONLY COVERED ABOUT THREE SQUARE MILES. BUT TO ME, IN THAT WASTELAND? EVERY PATH WAS ANOTHER CHANCE TO SURVIVE.
SO MAYBE WE SHOULD STOP CHASING SOMETHING WE CAN'T FIND.
WRONG LESSON. IF I WOULD HAVE STAYED PUT, I WOULD HAVE DIED OF HYPOTHERMIA.
WHAT I'M SAYING IS THAT SOMETIMES YOU DON'T KNOW WHERE YOU'RE GOING. YOU JUST HAVE TO GO.
I BELIEVE IN YOU, MARY. I DON'T HAVE AN ANSWER AND I KNOW YOU DON'T EITHER. NOT YET.
BUT THERE'S NO PUZZLE YOU CAN'T SOLVE.
NO MATTER HOW BIG.

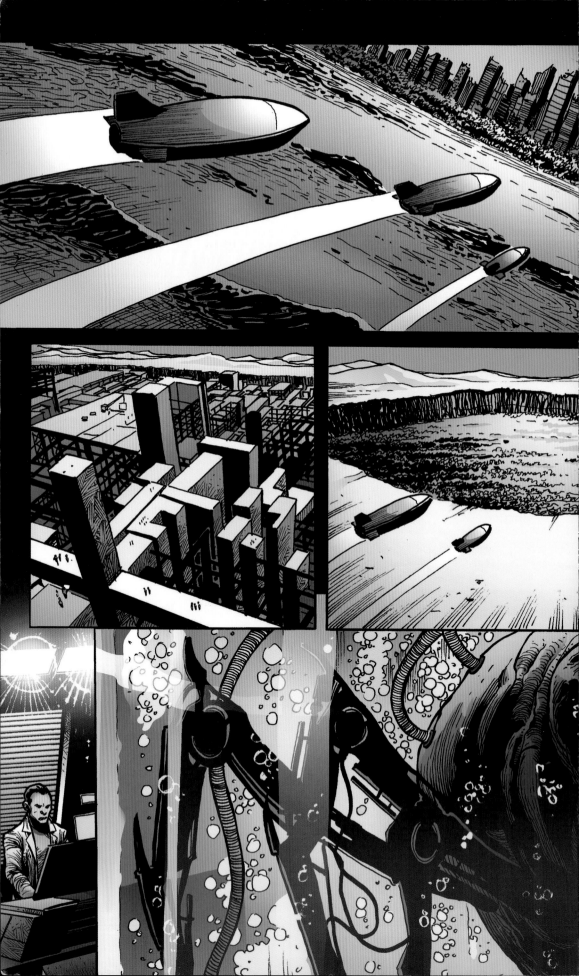

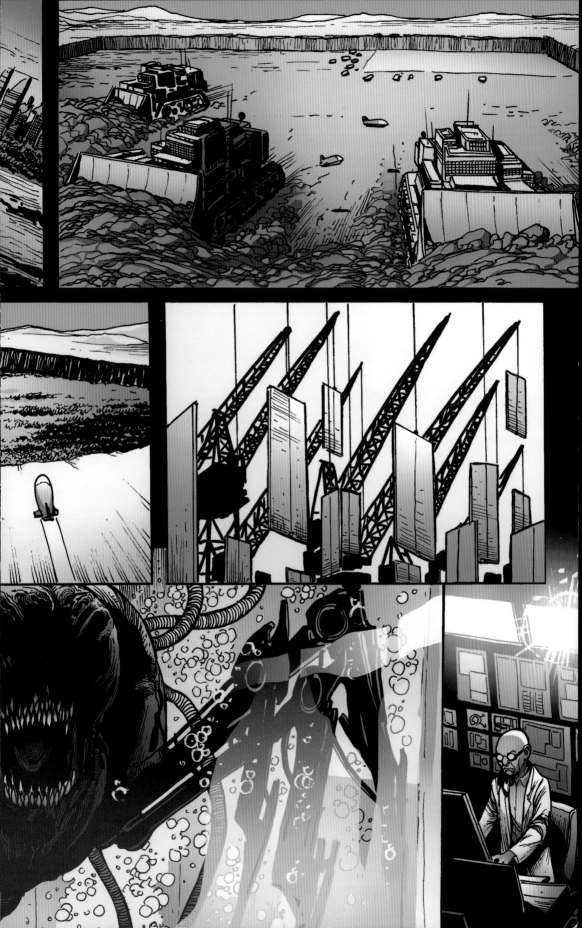

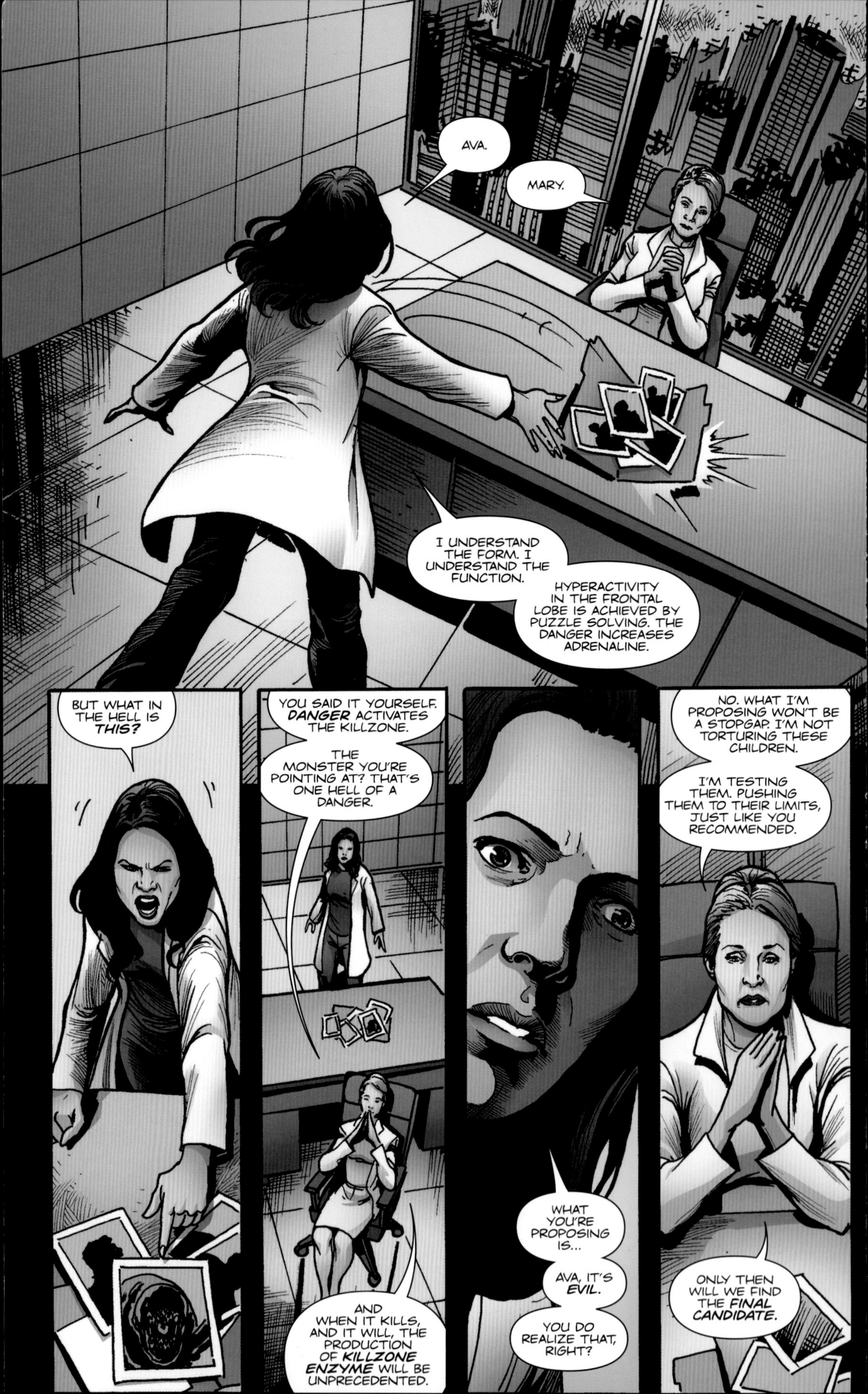
AVA.
MARY.
I UNDERSTAND THE FORM. I UNDERSTAND THE FUNCTION.
HYPERACTIVITY IN THE FRONTAL LOBE IS ACHIEVED BY PUZZLE SOLVING. THE DANGER INCREASES ADRENALINE.
BUT WHAT IN THE HELL IS *THIS?*
YOU SAID IT YOURSELF. *DANGER* ACTIVATES THE KILLZONE.
THE MONSTER YOU'RE POINTING AT? THAT'S ONE HELL OF A DANGER.
AND WHEN IT KILLS, AND IT WILL, THE PRODUCTION OF *KILLZONE ENZYME* WILL BE UNPRECEDENTED.
WHAT YOU'RE PROPOSING IS...
AVA, IT'S *EVIL.*
YOU DO REALIZE THAT, RIGHT?
NO. WHAT I'M PROPOSING WON'T BE A STOPGAP. I'M NOT TORTURING THESE CHILDREN.
I'M TESTING THEM. PUSHING THEM TO THEIR LIMITS, JUST LIKE YOU RECOMMENDED.
ONLY THEN WILL WE FIND THE *FINAL CANDIDATE.*

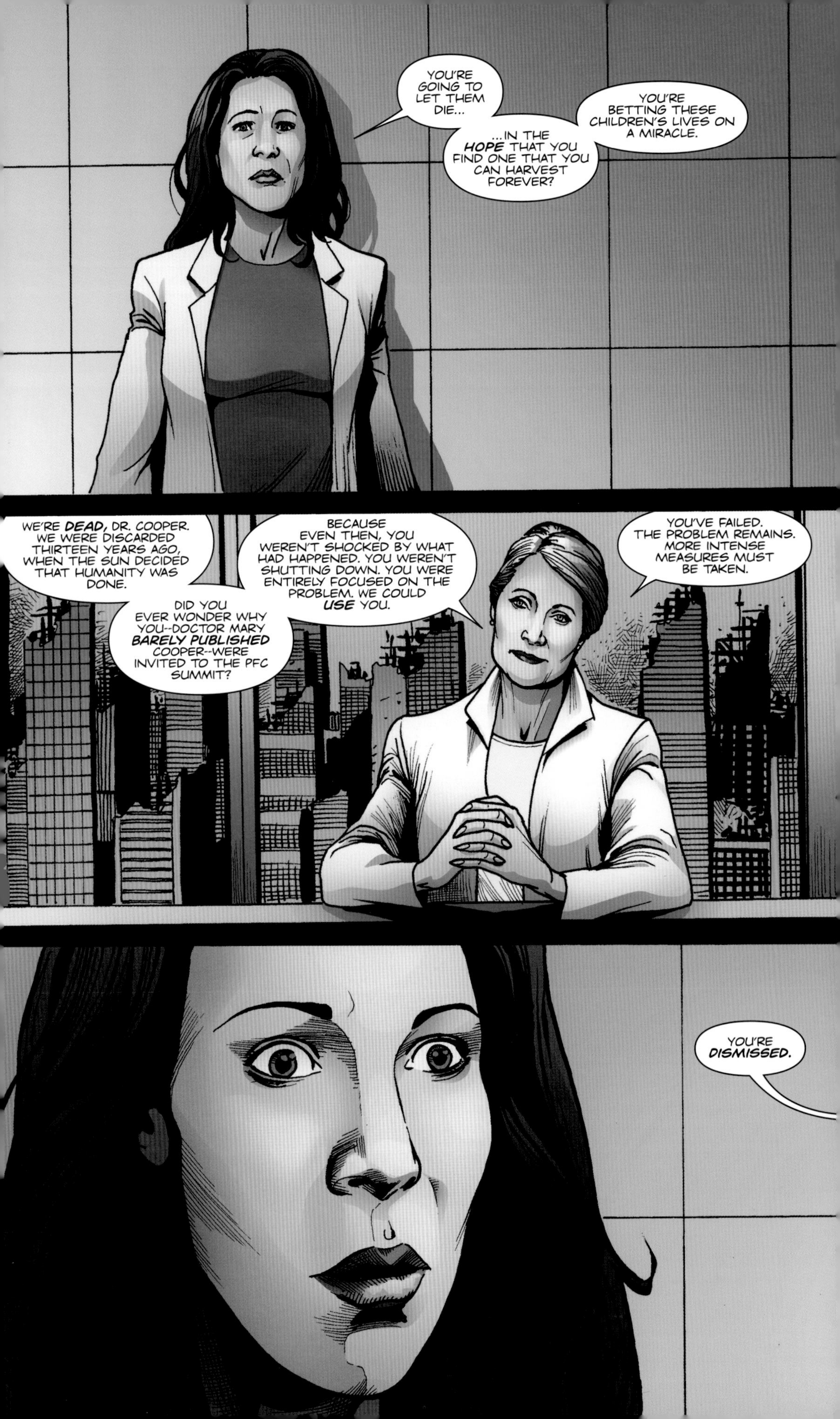
YOU'RE GOING TO LET THEM DIE...
...IN THE **HOPE** THAT YOU FIND ONE THAT YOU CAN HARVEST FOREVER?
YOU'RE BETTING THESE CHILDREN'S LIVES ON A MIRACLE.
WE'RE **DEAD,** DR. COOPER. WE WERE DISCARDED THIRTEEN YEARS AGO, WHEN THE SUN DECIDED THAT HUMANITY WAS DONE.
DID YOU EVER WONDER WHY YOU--DOCTOR MARY **BARELY PUBLISHED** COOPER--WERE INVITED TO THE PFC SUMMIT?
BECAUSE EVEN THEN, YOU WEREN'T SHOCKED BY WHAT HAD HAPPENED. YOU WEREN'T SHUTTING DOWN. YOU WERE ENTIRELY FOCUSED ON THE PROBLEM. WE COULD **USE** YOU.
YOU'VE FAILED. THE PROBLEM REMAINS. MORE INTENSE MEASURES MUST BE TAKEN.
YOU'RE **DISMISSED.**

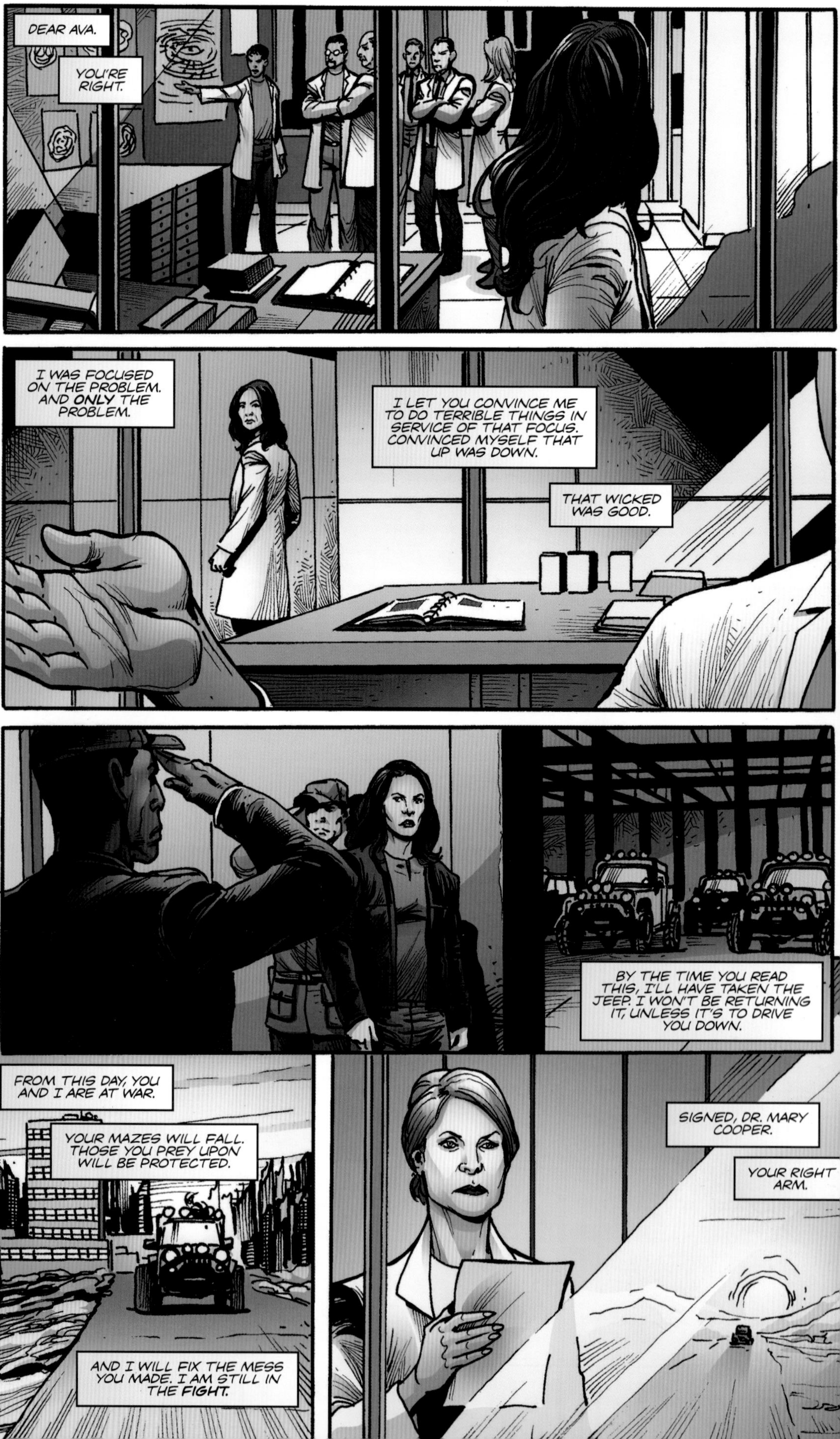
DEAR AVA.
YOU'RE RIGHT.
I WAS FOCUSED ON THE PROBLEM. AND **ONLY** THE PROBLEM.
I LET YOU CONVINCE ME TO DO TERRIBLE THINGS IN SERVICE OF THAT FOCUS. CONVINCED MYSELF THAT UP WAS DOWN.
THAT WICKED WAS GOOD.
BY THE TIME YOU READ THIS, I'LL HAVE TAKEN THE JEEP. I WON'T BE RETURNING IT, UNLESS IT'S TO DRIVE YOU DOWN.
FROM THIS DAY, YOU AND I ARE AT WAR.
YOUR MAZES WILL FALL. THOSE YOU PREY UPON WILL BE PROTECTED.
AND I WILL FIX THE MESS YOU MADE. I AM STILL IN THE **FIGHT**.
SIGNED, DR. MARY COOPER.
YOUR RIGHT ARM.

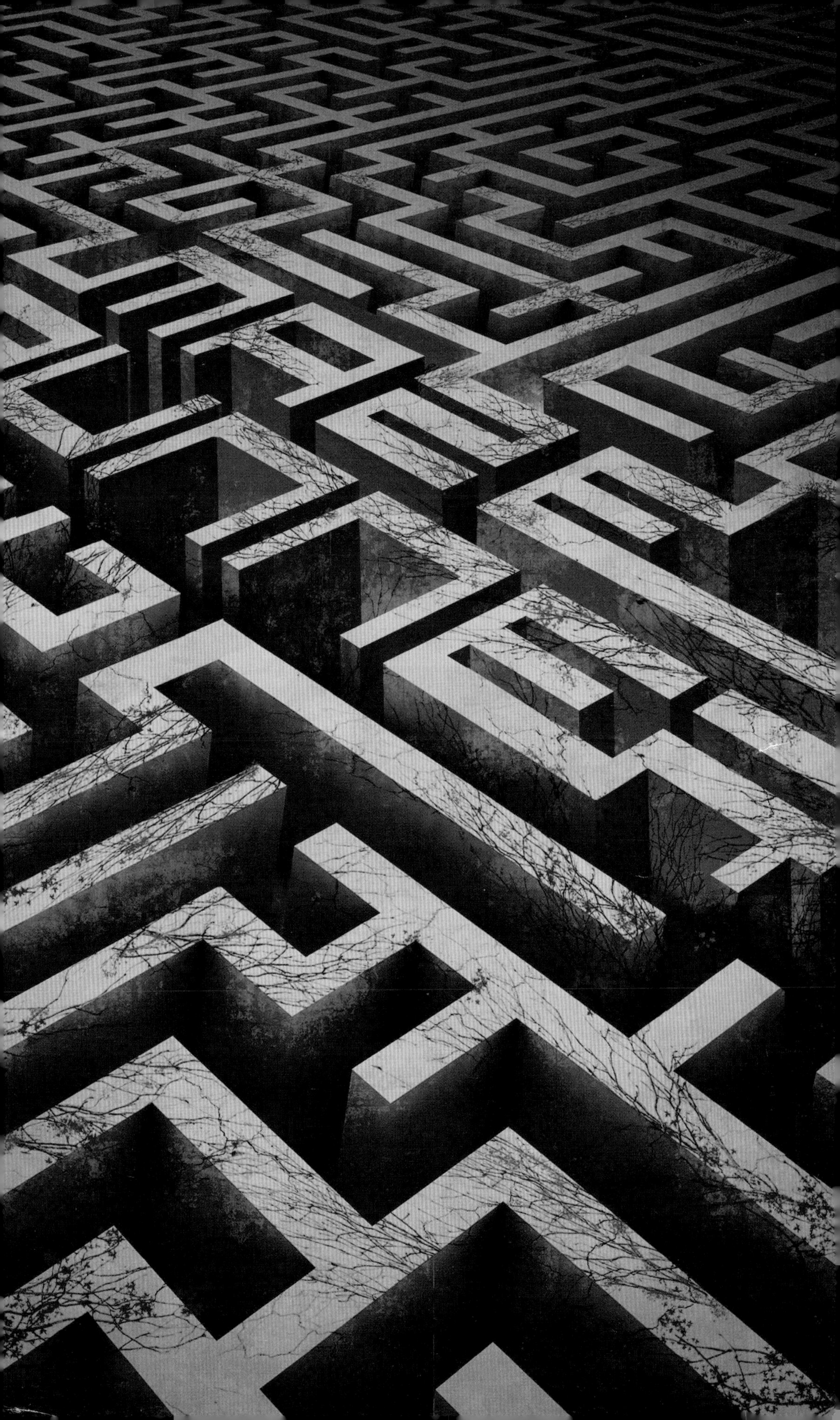

IF YOU LIKE *MAZE RUNNER* YOU'D LOVE...

THE WOODS

On October 16, 2013, 437 students, 52 teachers, and 24 additional staff from Bay Point Preparatory High School in suburban Milwaukee, WI vanished without a trace. Countless light years away, far outside the bounds of the charted universe, 513 people find themselves in the middle of an ancient, primordial wilderness. Where are they? Why are they there? The answers will prove stranger than anyone could possibly imagine.

As fans of James Tynion IV's work in the Batman universe *(Batman Eternal, Red Hood and the Outlaws)*, we were eager to publish his first original comic series. Plus, *The Woods* gives us that same eerie, small-town horror feel we get whenever we read a Stephen King novel. If you're fan of teen conspiracy comics like *Morning Glories, Sheltered,* and *Revival,* you'll immediately be sucked into *The Woods.*

THE WOODS
JAMES TYNION IV • MICHAEL DIALYNAS
VOL 1
THE ARROW

THE WOODS VOL. 1 TP
9781613983089

THE WOODS
JAMES TYNION IV • MICHAEL DIALYNAS • JOSAN GONZALEZ
VOL 2
THE SWARM

THE WOODS VOL. 2 TP
9781613983492

HEXED

Luci Jennifer Inacio Das Neves (most people just call her "Lucifer") is a supernatural thief for hire, stealing wondrous objects from the dark denizens of the netherworld for her mentor/mother figure, Val Brisendine. But when Lucifer accidentally unleashes a terrible evil from one of the paintings hanging in Val's art gallery, will any of the tricks up her sleeve be enough to stop it?

A mashup of Lara Croft and Buffy the Vampire Slayer, *Hexed Vol. 1* marks the ongoing series debut for newcomer Dan Mora, who brings a lyrical and unique take to the artwork, paired with the script from one of comics' leading horror writers, Michael Alan Nelson *(Day Men, 28 Days later, Dingo)*.

HEXED

HEXED TPB
9781613980996

MICHAEL ALAN NELSON
DAN MORA
GABRIEL CASSATA
HEXED

HEXED VOL. 1
9781613983898

SUICIDE RISK

Super-powered people are inexplicably rising from the streets and there's a big problem: Too many supervillains, not enough superheroes. Heroes are dying, and cops are dying twofold. Humanity is under-powered and good people are suffering untold tragedies trying to stem the flow. Beat cop Leo Winters is one of those struggling to make a difference. And the answer just might come in the form of two lowlifes with a dark secret.

The critically-acclaimed series by award-winning author Mike Carey *(X-Men, The Unwritten)* and fan-favorite artist Elena Casagrande *(Hulk, Hack/Slash)*. *Suicide Risk* is a high octane, mind-bending series created by one of the industry's greatest storytellers.

MIKE CAREY • ELENA CASAGRANDE
SUICIDE RISK

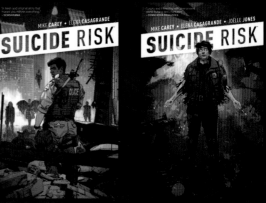

SUICIDE RISK VOL. 1 TP
9781613981863

MIKE CAREY • ELENA CASAGRANDE • JOËLLE JONES
SUICIDE RISK

SUICIDE RISK VOL. 2 TP
9781613982143

BOOM! STUDIOS PUSH **COMICS** FORWARD

10 TEN YEARS BOOM! STUDIOS

#COMICSFORWARD
WWW.BOOM-STUDIOS.COM